ARCANYM

J. M. Samland

Arcanym

Copyright © 2023 Jamie M. Samland

eBook ISBN: 979-8-9868949-3-5
Print ISBN: 979-8-9868949-2-8, 979-8-9868949-4-2

Cover art by MiblArt
Internal art by Ryan Allen

For Mom and Lori,
My biggest fans who keep me moving.
When you get to where Elvan wakes up from the nightmare,
just skip to the next chapter.

From the Author

Here we are, my fifth novel in two years. I debated heavily on what the genre is. "Is this a romance with an adventure/mystery subplot, or an adventure with a romance/mystery subplot?" Either way, it's my first time writing a sex scene, and my mother will read this.

Arcanym was actually the first book I planned, years before *Realms of Terswood*. The original full title was *Arcanym: The Art of Scamming Tweens for Cash*. The goal was to hit all the major tropes and hit them hard. I'm glad I waited for it. It starred Princess Miriam, who fell in love with a peasant boy. He, of course, dies, but she captures his ghost. Then they fall in love while he's a ghost, because… obviously. Quest to find a way to resurrect him, yada yada lich strikes a bargain, double crossing, etc. New York Times bestseller and two movie deals. My husband and I thought about it in depth while on long car rides, taking copious notes.

The problem was when I started down that road, that wasn't the story I wanted to tell. I wanted to write about a shy gay boy living in a queernorm fantasy world coming into his own. That's the story I would have loved to read growing up and dammit, that's what I wanted to write! So I did! That original idea with the ghost boyfriend will be my next book. I've already started on it.

A friend recently read The Chronicler's Awakening books and asked me where the characters came from. Lone has a lot of my better or idealized qualities. Daelin is an amalgamation of my father figures. Dehset is my shyer side. Aiden is the himbo I play in D&D. The friend's next question was, "Ooo, then who is Cazlandt based on?" No one; he's just a gross monster. Every character starts with a basic trope and grows as they interact with the story. I think the author's job is to pull the character far enough from that trope that they've created a believable person, but not so far that you can't distill the character to their core.

Enter Elvan Galmoth, "the innocent," the young noble with crippling impostor syndrome. He's riddled with moments of self-doubt that most can empathize with. When I made Cazlandt the star of *Necromancer of Urbus*, I put the deeply flawed character front and center. Except that Cazlandt will happily take the spotlight. He's a doer and will tell anyone about his successful exploits. Elvan is a very different person. I found it cathartic to drive him through this story and let him surprise me when he took over.

So, which character is easier to write? The shy homebody or the arrogant person of action? I wouldn't have been able to answer that before putting Elvan's story to the page. Now I have an answer to it. … Send me a message, ask, and I'll tell you.

As always, so many thanks go to friends and family, for without their support, this wouldn't be possible. Whenever I start to feel dark, they boost me back up and sit me back in the chair. Thank you, Rob for being my sounding board on this project. Thank you, Ben for guiding me through new paradigms of story planning. Thank you, Mary for empathizing with the woes of being a writer. Thank you, Aaron for, despite not helping at ALL during the draft one process, wanting to read my book all at once when I was done. Thank you, mom and Lori for your continuous support and endless love.

Prologue

SELAYNA TORE THE PAGE FROM the notebook, ripping away any excess, and folding it to a tight square. She shoved that deep into the bodice of her blue silk dress as the banging at the front door started. She dipped her quill again and smoothed out a fresh, full sheet.

"By order of His Majesty, King Pearce VI," came the strained and familiar voice, muffled through the heavy door. "Open immediately."

She wrote faster.

The thumping continued.

"Selayna? Are you going to answer that?"

She looked up at the man standing in the entryway to the dining room, wearing a disheveled gray suit, his hair a mess.

"Go out back to the gardens, Miles." Her eyes lingered on the crystal glass of amber drink in his fist and returned to her furious writing.

He walked past her while the banging and shouting continued.

"Miles, no!"

Selayna watched him walk through the library to the foyer, gripping her quill tighter with each step he took until he reached to unlock the front door. "Worthless gobshite," she whispered, leaning back in her velvet armchair as soldiers in red and gold shoved her paltry excuse for a husband out of the way, flooding the manor. They surrounded her, muskets cocked and raised, but she paid them no mind as she set her quill back in its inkwell among the neat stacks of manifests and invoices.

The click of a steel cane on the polished tile pierced her mind, regular with the limping gait of the one who wielded it. Selayna folded her hands on the desk in front of her as a man in voluminous black robes strode through her front door.

She pushed back her chair and stood, smoothing the creases of her silk dress.

"Inquisitor Nilranke." Selayna ran her tongue over her teeth, tasting the foulness of the man's name. She sniffed, curling her nose at the miasma of tobacco and herbal remedies surrounding the inquisitor when he stopped within arm's reach.

"Lady Galmoth," he said and reached to snatch the page from the desk beside her. His dark eyes scanned the words quickly and drifted back to meet hers, along with a predatory grin. "You maintain your lies, it would seem."

Selayna raised her chin to look down her nose at the inquisitor. "The princess—"

His hand flashed across her cheek, snapping her head to the side. She looked back at him slowly, the coppery blood taste of blood filling her mouth.

"You will keep the princess's name from your traitorous mouth," Nilranke said.

Selayna spat blood onto the man's face.

Nilranke didn't flinch. He tucked his steel cane into the crook of his elbow and held the single sheet of her missive, tearing it in half, before passing it to a soldier, who tossed it into the small fire in the hearth. He only then raised a gloved hand to wipe the blood and spit from his cheek, flicking it to the floor.

"Guards, leave us."

The men in red and gold exchanged hesitant glances but retreated from the study.

"It's not often, I hear, that a man finds a vocation that he truly enjoys performing." Nilranke pulled the leather glove from his right hand, one finger at a time, as he spoke. "Rarer that the vocation is one such as mine, with such a profound importance to the proper function of the crown."

"She won't succeed. Someone else will stop her."

"The king thanks you, Lady Galmoth, but your services will no longer be required." Inquisitor Nilranke shot out his right hand to touch her neck. Electricity arced through her, dropping her to her knees with a single cry. It only lasted a moment, then he was tugging on his glove, grinning.

"You're one of them!" She held a hand to her neck, falling backward against her chair.

He tapped his cane on the floor and grinned down at her. "One of what? Anything you say is just the ravings of a felon." He laughed, stepping back. "Guards, bring the irons."

1

SURROUNDED BY THE MUSTY SMELL of leather and parchment, Elvan Galmoth traced ink-stained fingers down a column of invoice numbers. The values didn't add up; not without considering at least two other books laid out in front of him. He brushed the feathery end of his quill across his lips and made yet another note of the discrepancies in the ledger directly in front of him. Elvan reached across the table and tugged another book from the middle of the stack, scattering those above it into a pile. He flicked through the pages to find one he'd earmarked and groaned at the number that matched nothing else in front of him.

"I've the post for you," said the small voice, breaking through Elvan's concentration.

Happy for any distraction, Elvan looked up from the ledgers to see Cenna enter and place a stack of papers beside him. "Thank you." Setting his quill back in the inkwell, he took the daily news on top of the pile and shook it open to scan over the headlines. "Another raid on an Artist family in Spheris. Barely a week goes by without one. I wonder how they find them all."

"They can only catch them in the act," Cenna said while straightening and stacking the papers and tomes enough to clear space to serve lunch. "Otherwise, they're no different from the rest of us."

"I hope they find all these people, eventually."

Cenna paused with a stack of loose parchment in her hands and gave Elvan a knowing look. "Really, Elvan? You, of all people, are cheering on the inquisitors?"

Elvan waved off the conversation and flipped through the other pages, pausing at the narrow sales ads; people selling furniture and clothing in bulk. *That'll be me soon enough*. He roughly folded the paper and tossed it onto the stacks of ledgers of data spanning decades before him. Picking up a thin stack of envelopes, he set aside the past-due bill and invoice notices until he held a single red square of folded parchment with his name written in a looping hand. He tore it open and flattened the letter, letting his eyes travel first to the delicate signature at the bottom.

"It's from Her Royal Majesty, the High Duchess." He blew out a loud breath and read the short missive, his heart and shoulders sinking with each sentence.

Cenna chuckled. "And how is your sister?" She set a bowl of cold soup and crusty bread at the head of the table.

"She's invited herself to visit."

"That'll be nice. I was visiting my mum the last time she was here. I think I've only seen her once since she moved out."

"If you say so." Elvan tossed the letter on top of the bills and pushed back his chair to move to the head of the table. His eyes grazed over the dusty trinkets on the fireplace mantle and the dingy tint of the curtains framing the floor-to-ceiling windows looking out at the overgrown garden. The dining table that only a few years ago had served a noble house now lay covered with a mess of thick tomes, the only place in the house large enough for Elvan to spread out his work.

"When is she coming?" Cenna asked.

"Next week. She's not bringing her husband, but I know she'll have a retinue of handmaidens trailing her. At least I doubt Princess Lorelai would come. I can't very well deny playing host, but…" He let the sentence hang with a sigh. Cenna knew as well as he the financial state of the Galmoths.

"You have more books out than I usually see you with," said Cenna. "You have to be making some progress."

Elvan snorted and paused with a hand on the chair's back. "My mother is a true master at maneuvering money. I wonder if I'll ever understand her method." He reached to pick up a smaller notebook, fanned his thumb across the edge quickly, and tossed it back on the pile. "Layers upon layers, so much more complicated than it should be. I still don't doubt her innocence, but how she deliberately obfuscated the finances would make a lesser man wonder." Sitting in front of the cold soup, he flourished a cloth napkin over his thigh.

"With your determination, I'm sure you'll find the truth in it all." She picked up a stack of papers, marginally neater than the others, and walked her fingers through the pages. "What are these? What's Magpie Aoith?"

"Is that how you pronounce that? They're invoices for a shop in Spheris. My mother spent a lot of steel there, but I can't trace the items she purchased."

"Why don't you go find out? Take a trip into town and look up this shop. A change of scenery might help."

Elvan's spoon paused halfway to his lips. "You're joking, right?"

Cenna took a step back and folded her hands before her. "You really should go. I haven't seen you leave the house in weeks."

Elvan looked down at his rumpled clothes. "I think it would be better to stay out of the public eye for a while longer. I'm still scarred from what happened with the Council of Houses. Besides, I can't scrape together the steel coin for a carriage. I barely find enough to pay your wages and all..." He waved at the stack of bills a few chairs away, "That."

Cenna pulled back another step, picking at the fraying fringe of her apron. "I have a bit stashed away that should be enough."

"What? Cenna, no. Don't be silly."

"I'll be fine, I..." She looked down to focus fully on the apron.

"I will not steal from the last person left to me in the world just to go..." He watched her fidget with the hem, not meeting his eyes. "What is it?"

Cenna took a deep breath, raising her chin, her eyes glimmering with unshed tears. "The Kae house has reached out to me. They need a governess."

"I see." Elvan set his spoon down and watched it reflect a distorted image of the ceiling's mural. "Better Kae than Serhane. Have you responded?"

"Yes." Her single word shot through him like a nail into a coffin lid. "I'll start there the first of next month. They wanted me sooner, but I couldn't leave on such short notice. I've been trying all this last week to find a time to tell you. I'm so sorry. I held out as long as I could."

"There's nothing to be sorry for; we both knew this would happen, eventually." Elvan looked up at the governess and maid who faithfully served him every day for almost two decades, had stuck with him through his family's darkest moments these last years. His mother hired her when Cenna was his age and she gave her best years serving a failed house. "If they want you sooner, you should start right away." He forced a smile even as his eyes burned.

"I couldn't, young master. I can't leave you alone, especially now with the Duchess coming."

"It's no longer your concern, Cenna. You've gone so far beyond your duties for years. I won't hold you back a single day more."

She focused on the apron's hem again. "Thank you. I'll send up a flare and get my steel."

Elvan knew the carriage would probably drain her of the last bit of steel in her private coffers, but Elvan's mother taught him to never refuse a gift. He stood and took her hand in one of his. "Thank you, Cenna. I will pay you back and more." He wanted to kiss her on the cheek, but she stepped away with a curtsy, never raising her eyes as she fled the room.

He watched her leave, her tan and blue uniform disappearing toward the servant's wing, and raised his eyes to the mural overhead depicting the Sovereign King in all his divine, abstract glory. Elvan muttered a curse to it, another to the stacks of ledgers spread over the dining table, and several more while he closed the binding on the book he used for his note taking. A long piece of leather attached to the back cover ended in an ornate silver key. Elvan wrapped the leather twice around the book, tucking the key between the strap and cover, securing the book closed before turning to the empty, dusty halls on the way back to his room.

Elvan turned right where the grand staircase split and paused at the top. He glanced behind him through the dim shafts of light to the double doors at the far end of the hall, to what was his parents' bedroom. He had every right to move into that room with the wide, south-facing windows overlooking the valley and river, but it somehow felt wrong. Like giving up on his parents ever returning to the house. Beside those doors, his sister's room was the second largest. Despite him being eldest, she got the larger room because, as their mother said, "girls need more space." Delphina would never return to live here.

He scratched at his head and strode to his childhood room. Even living for the last two years with only the dwindling manor staff, and soon to be completely alone, Elvan never spread out from here. Every object he acquired over the last nineteen years he kept in his relatively small space with narrow windows facing the north, to never feel the sun. He crossed to the wardrobe, pulled out the chest tucked into the bottom, and dug through it to find a set of plain gray and tan traveler's garb. Elvan held it against himself before the mirror and muttered a curse. It still fit. He wore roughly the same size now as when Ser Vazadon gifted him the clothes almost three years ago.

"I'll go to town, but not as Elvan Galmoth. Tomorrow I'll be," he paused, and a smile flickered at the edges of his lips. "I'll be Tristan Griffith, wandering scholar." He clutched the clothes closer and grinned. The story of Tristan's life blossomed in his mind; the persona he would adopt to go unnoticed in the city. Tristan wasn't a disgraced noble, shunned by his peers. Tristan's father, a local merchant of no particular fame, raised him. His mother died when he was young, but Father didn't like to talk about it. Tristan came to Spheris in search of a rare book dealer. No, Elvan shook his head. Rare book dealers were too, well, rare. Textiles. That's boring enough. Maybe this is Tristan's first time away from his small village home, but he's not a wandering scholar yet, just aspires to be one someday.

A knock at the door frame. Elvan yelped and dropped the clothes. Cenna stood at the threshold holding a small leather sack.

"I didn't mean to interrupt you. I saw the response flare from town," she said, while pulling at the strings of the bag. "The carriage will be here first thing in the morning, young master." She crossed the room to stand near him by the mirror. "Playing a bit of dress-up?"

Elvan's cheeks burned. "I think it might be easier to move through the city if no one recognizes me."

"You can't hide from the other Houses forever."

Elvan looked down at the dark pouch she pressed into his palm, feeling the weight of coins within it. His eyes burned again. "I don't know what to say, Cenna."

Empty-handed, she took a step back. "It's been an honor to serve you all these years. This isn't goodbye forever, just for a little while. I know you're close to understanding your mother's books. If not, maybe I could get the Kae's financier to help."

That would be the last possible thing he would want, for a rival family to understand his mother's embezzlement and money laundering.

She unclipped a ring of keys from her apron and handed those to him as well. "I... Goodbye, Elvan." She leaned forward to kiss his cheek and was gone a heartbeat later.

Elvan stood alone in his room with a maid's savings in one hand, the keys to his manor in the other, and a set of unassuming traveler's clothes at his feet.

2

T HE CLOP OF HORSE HOOVES on cobblestone announced the carriage's arrival. The coin in Elvan's hand felt like an anvil's weight, knowing he'd go to the city only to return to a house in total ruin. As he climbed into the carriage wearing long robes of gray and tan, the driver paid him little attention.

The hour and a half it took to get to Spheris gave Elvan plenty of time to think, but his mind was blank. He caught himself more than once staring, unblinking, at a piece of torn fabric near the ceiling of the carriage. With Cenna gone, he would be alone in the huge manor. Alone… with only a mountain of debt to keep him company. The idea of selling floated by him, but any family that could afford a fraction of what the manor and its grounds were worth would already have their own estate. Maybe a family from one of the outer provinces? Slenas to the south held a lot of wealth.

He shook the thought away. Selling the manor would absolutely be giving in to defeat and dismissing any chance of redeeming what the Galmoths lost when the inquisitors took his mother away in iron.

His mind drifted back to the ads in the newspaper and he began a mental inventory of what was left in the house. His mother's gowns and furs would fetch a decent price, as would his father's rifles and whiskey. He touched the invoices, folded and tucked into an inner pocket. *I'll find this shop, then maybe a broker to help sell things.*

The city's polluted choke penetrated Elvan's wandering reverie. Merchants hawking their wares, distant screams of delight, and discordant notes from a few dozen instruments surrounded him while the carriage slowed at the line before the main gates. He fished coins from his pouch to cover the fare and a meager tip before stepping from the carriage. The driver showed no interest in having ferried the head to one of the great Houses as he pocketed the steel and urged his horse from the line.

Elvan pulled up his cowl and wrapped the long robes a little tighter before adopting his most casual stroll and striding past the lines of carriages to enter the southern gates of Spheris.

Shops and apartments loomed four or five stories, framing the wide streets, drawing the eye upward to the high smokestacks of the industrial north district and the delicate spires of the palace further west. Elvan quickly turned his eyes down to the perpetually damp cobblestone.

Nothing to see here, I'm no one. Just Tristan Griffon looking for some interesting textiles. Griffon? Griffith? The persona unraveled in Elvan's mind with the misremembering of a fake name. *I don't need a name and backstory if I don't talk to anyone.*

As he walked, tents and vendors narrowed the road until barely a single horse could fit through. Color, sound, and energy assaulted Elvan from every angle, mixed with the scents of a dozen meat and sweet vendors, all trying their best to stir him into a better mood. He clutched the cloak closer and kept a firm grip on his light coin purse, pausing at the first major crossroads. Straight ahead, a throng of people clustered around a stage in the park usually reserved for plays and concerts. Massive painted signs announced there would soon be a presentation by the Leystrider Guild, the experimental development branch of House Frostspark. They skirted a fine line of legality with their products that certainly looked like magic, but they were committed to the statement that everything was purely based in science. No one could doubt their effectiveness, though. House Frostspark owned the gas manufactories that kept the lights on in Spheris, as well as the steam ferries that connected the manor houses and smaller villages to the east of the city, the Galmoth manor included.

The road to his right promised exotic foods and trinkets from across the continent and beyond, games of chance, and smaller tents hinting a peek at some mind-altering person, object, or act within. The Night Market, despite being open and crowded before noon. Every tent seemed in silent competition to have more distinct colors than any around them, but each displayed a gold banner with the symbol of the Sovereign King: a two-headed winged dragon clutching a book in one claw and a spear in the other.

A woman in a plum dress that swept the ground stepped from the curtains at stage right, to the enthusiastic applause of those gathered. Andrina Frostspark, lady of House Frostspark. Most of her words were lost to the distance and din of the crowd, but Andrina gestured toward the curtains, and her wife, Edna Frostspark, head of House Frostspark, entered wearing a matching dress. Three assistants followed her, pushing a contraption that looked like a large box with two stiff rods sticking out of the top at a slight angle.

All the other heads of Houses are like her. Suave, savvy,

powerful. Not me. I'm just Tristan the scholar.

Elvan looked over the crowd, all either holding their breath with anticipation or chattering excitedly with those around them.

Without a word, Edna activated some control on the device and with a droning hum, lightning sparked between the rods extending from its top. Elvan stood on his toes, but the density of the crowd between him and a good view was too much, and he didn't press forward.

Harnessing the elements now? What possible use will that be? And really, how is this not magic?

Whatever applications the Leystrider Guild might showcase would be covered in tomorrow's news and the last thing Elvan wanted was to get caught up in anything related to magic.

Elvan's stomach complained with a grumble when he turned away to the narrower path to his left. Local artists and vendors lined the street with bright awnings that choked around the regular entrances to shops. He pulled the invoices from his pocket and unfolded them just enough to remind himself of Magpie Aoith's street. Tucking it away, he, Tristan Griffson, kept his head down and set off in what he hoped was the correct direction.

He ignored the hawkers calling at him to see their wares. Every yell reminding him of the coin purse's lightness. His fists and jaw clenched while he imagined a dozen scenes with his sister. She would come to brag about the new seaside manor her husband, the prince, bought for her. Or she only gets the best tea served to her in the Green Palace and wants a reminder of the sludge she once endured and even convinced herself that she liked. He very briefly considered she was coming for an honest visit, but that thought didn't last long in his mind.

Elvan exhaled the breath he hadn't realized he was holding and noticed the din of the vendors was behind him. Glancing around, he stood alone in the narrow cobblestone street his feet had led him to. In the far distance behind him, a crowd cheered in unison. He looked up at the flaking sign reading "Magpie Aoith" over an oddity shop door. The window showcased stacks of books, strange things suspended in glass jars of murky fluid, bundles of dried herbs, and dusty mechanical devices with unknowable uses.

Frivolous occult rubbish, nothing but a waste of time and a quick ticket to jail.

Elvan pushed away his mother's words and wondered even more at what the honorable Selayna Galmoth might have purchased from such an odd shop. Purchased a lot of, based on the invoices in his pocket. His palm pushed on the rough wood of the door.

The hollow jingle of a bell greeted him, along with an assault by an array of incense and a stifling heat. He pulled back his cowl and pinched his robes to billow air against this chest as the door shut behind him, sealing off any last whisper of the city sounds, leaving him with a dull emptiness buzzing in his ears. Elvan ran a finger along the ridges of a lizard or rodent skull beside a stack of leather-bound books while craning his neck to the tall shelves arranged to block the view into the back of the narrow shop. They stretched to the ceiling with thick tomes and jars with peeling labels. Elvan bit back a grin, knowing this would be exactly the shop his alter ego, Tristan the book collector scholar, would adore. It was also exactly the type of shop his mother warned him against ever entering.

His grin soured as his memory cycled back to his mother and he again pressed her away.

He could only guess at the function of half the items in view. Barrels of long bones lashed with reeds, taxidermized birds and rodents, jars… so many jars. Elvan imagined this was the sort of shop Ser Vazadon might frequent after one of his grand adventures to unload the spoils looted from some distant monster cave.

The stacks of intricately bound journals brought back overwhelming thoughts of his mother's ledgers, and the dead-eyed stare of a chipped porcelain doll brought its partner: dread over his sister's coming visit. Even as a child, his younger sister had been insufferable, rude, and demanding. Getting betrothed at fourteen to a lesser prince and married less than a year later, mere months before their mother was arrested, only added to her condescension.

"Be right there," called a deep voice from somewhere in the twisted tangle of the shop.

Elvan's mind snapped back to the cramped space, and he spun to the exit behind him, momentarily dazed by the cloying incense.

"Can I help…" called the voice behind him as Elvan's loose robes caught the edge of the table, toppling a stack of books and sending the skull to crack on the stone floor.

"Sorry," Elvan muttered and dropped to sweep the fragments of bone into his palm.

"Don't worry about it," the shopkeeper chuckled. "I've been thinking we have too many skulls in here."

Elvan stood, cupping the bits of bone in front of him. He turned to the shopkeeper, a dark-skinned man about his age and half a head taller. Elvan tried to ignore how the tight white shirt under the man's apron clung to his chest and arms as the shopkeeper set down a stack of books.

"Sorry," Elvan repeated and set the skull fragments on the table.

"I said don't worry about it." The man waved and focused his amber gaze on Elvan with a crooked smile. "You're not here for a reading, are you?"

"No, I…" Elvan started, before letting the question sink in. "What do you mean, *reading*?" He forced his eyes to the shopkeeper's hair, twisted into short locs, rather than meet his mischievous stare.

"Most that come here want their fortune told."

"Are you Ao… A…" Elvan remembered the name over the door, but couldn't trust himself to remember how Cenna pronounced it. "Is this your shop?"

"No. Aoith's my Nana. Name's Drace." He wiped a hand over his apron and offered it.

Elvan stared at the hand for a breath, his own growing slick with sweat, before finally taking it in his own, feeling the warm, calloused strength in the firm grip. "Tristan. Tristan Griffith."

"Well, Tristan Griffith," Drace shoved both hands in the pockets of his apron. "Pleasure to meet you. I apologize it's so hot in here, I haven't been able to fix the regulator. If you're not in the market for a reading, what I can help you find?"

He didn't come to buy anything, but to ask about the invoices. *Why would a wandering scholar have the invoice?* Elvan silently cursed himself for not giving the fake identity much thought. The invoices included the purchased item's inventory number. Maybe he could find it based on that? Except… His eyes flitted over the haphazard stacks of oddities thrown around the mangle of shelves with no discernible order. He'd find nothing in here on purpose without Drace's help.

"Nothing in particular. I'm a wandering scholar." He turned to the table on this right and picked up the book closest to him. Bound in coarse leather, it was written in a language he'd never seen before. *Idiot, how can I bring up the invoices now? Think…*

"I'm sure you are." Drace stepped around the table and leaned over it, squinting and biting back a grin. "I shouldn't be giving away business, but it's been a slow day. How about a free reading, Tristan?"

Elvan glanced up, meeting Drace's impish smile. "What? Why? I don't know what that means."

Drace stood straight. "I only get old women and disguised politicians in here. Sometimes politicians disguised as old women. It'll be fun to do a reading for someone with some years left."

Elvan started to decline, but Drace shushed him while pushing down his hand holding the book. "It'll be fun, I promise. Free of charge." He slipped his fingers around Elvan's and tugged him toward the back of the store.

What in the hells is going on here?

Elvan stepped around the table and allowed Drace to guide him through a maze of high shelves and racks. He lost sight of the front door almost immediately. Drace let go and pushed his hands into his pockets as he led the way.

"Wandering scholar, huh? You must have some stories."

Memories flashed past Elvan. He sat between his younger siblings by the hearth while Ser Vazadon recounted scenes of his heroic past. Delphina twirled the hair of her doll while his little brother Bennoc chewed the end of his blanket, all in rapt attention. Slaying a daemon lord, befriending a half-dragon, reuniting a skeleton with her skeleton dog. Thrilling tales told to an audience hanging on to every word, but none appropriate for the life of a scholar.

"Not really," he finally said. "Just a lot of time looking through books, making notes."

"You might have more fun than you think. I just shuffle things around in here all day. Would you believe this place is organized compared to what it looked like a year ago?"

"Hard to believe." Elvan turned sideways to squeeze between two racks of scrolls and ducked under a tarp hanging low from a catwalk overhead. "You make old women go through all this?"

"They usually come in the back." Drace smiled back at him. "The thing in the park today with Leystrider is pulling a lot of business away, giving me time to really rip the place apart and clean it up."

Around another shelf, they reached a wall of deep purple fabric. Drace pulled it aside, revealing a small room with two wooden chairs on either side of a round table draped with red satin.

"Gods, it's hot in here," Drace moaned and stepped around the table.

Elvan let the thick curtain fall behind him and his eyes adjusted to the dark while Drace lit two tall candles on either side of a glass ball set on a thin pillow at the table's center. Elvan gasped for air in the oppressive, still heat of the small room and billowed more air down his chest.

"Have a seat, Tristan Griffith, the wandering scholar." Drace gestured to the only other chair, his grin flashing in the soft candlelight.

Elvan hesitated for a breath. *Nothing is free*, his mother would say, but he couldn't sense a drop of malice behind Drace's eyes. Despite the confounding walk through the sweltering heat and shop's maze, he was enjoying himself. He pulled out the chair and sat as Drace set the glass ball on the floor beside him.

"Let me see your hand," Drace said and spread his, palm up, on the table between the candles.

Elvan put his hands on top of Drace's and the shopkeeper ran rough fingers over the wrinkles in his palms and knuckles. Elvan fidgeted in his seat at the intimacy of the touch, but swallowed hard, remembering how easily Drace took his hand at the front of the shop. *It doesn't mean anything, he's just friendly and weirdly fine with touching.*

"I see the ink stained deep into your fingerprints," Drace said without looking up. "Calloused from holding a quill. A feather quill, traditional." He took Elvan's left hand in both of his and traced the faint blue veins on the wrist, following a nerve down to the fingerprint of each digit. "You've seen tragedy. Not death, but it may as well be, to someone close to you. Multiple."

Elvan bit his cheek to keep from speaking. How much of this was just the product of a careful eye? This surely wasn't an Artist's gift, but would he recognize it if it were?

Drace set down the left and took up Elvan's right hand in the same way, but rather than tracing the wrist, he pressed both his thumbs into the center of the palm.

"Your future is pocked and fractured," said Drace. "I see many paths that intertwine and cross, but converge to only two outcomes."

Drace pressed Elvan's fingers to his forehead. "I can feel your heart racing, Tristan. I don't mean your actual blood pumping heart, though that is too." Glancing up, his smirk faded into a serious guise. "Something is pushing you close to your breaking point at home."

"What are the two outcomes?" Elvan asked.

Drace set down Elvan's hand, and he quickly pulled them both back into his lap.

"If I could tell you that, I'd know enough to hire an assistant or five around here. When next you're faced with a big decision, you'll look back and remember how clever I am." Drace smirked and reached to the floor beside him. He slapped a single piece of parchment onto the table and a small leather pouch beside it. "There's one more thing I want to try. Can I have your hand again?"

Elvan wrung his hands together in his lap, still feeling the gentle but rough graze of Drace's fingers. He swallowed dry, shifted in his chair, and put his right hand on the one Drace held extended over the parchment.

"This won't hurt," said the shopkeeper, with a flash of silver too quick for Elvan to avoid. A heartbeat later, he cradled his hands in his lap again, pressing on the shallow nick at the tip of his middle finger.

"What in the hells are…" Elvan blinked at the parchment. Drace held the long, silver needle and drew a single rune in the center of the page. Symbols drawn in crimson appeared from that one point until they reached the edges of the parchment. Drace pulled the ties on the leather pouch, dumping glittering sand into his palm before carefully blowing it over the blood runes.

He picked it up from the edge, shook off the excess glitter, and offered it to Elvan. "A present for you."

Elvan shied from the page, pushing back in his chair. "Are you an Artist?"

"I'm legally obligated to deny that, but the savvy business person in me knows an air of mystery is good for the coffers."

"So this is…"

Drace sighed. "I prime the parchment in advance to do that little trick, nothing magic about it. Sorry, I…" He leaned back and rubbed at his cheek, tinted with stubble. "It's been slow in here. I got excited when I saw you. I—"

The bell chimed at the front of the store, somehow clearly audible through the heaps of goods and the thick drapes of their little private room.

Drace's shoulders slumped with a sigh. "Hold that thought, Tristan. I'll be right back." His fingers traced across Elvan's shoulder as he passed through the curtain.

Elvan turned his attention back to his hands in his lap, and specifically where Drace had touched him.

3

I'M BEING STUPID. EMOTIONAL FROM *Cenna quitting. Drace is just being nice.*

Elvan picked up the page covered in glittering runes, holding it to the light of the candles. The trick to fill a page from one drop of blood was ingenious, assuming the blood wasn't just a flare of showmanship. He moved the page nearer to the candle, tracing a finger along the clean lines of foreign script, if it even meant anything. Elvan yelped when the page caught in the candle's flame, flashing into blinding ash before it hit the tablecloth.

He noticed the heat again, stood, and pushed through the curtain. The shop was only dimly lit, but after minutes in the dark private fortune telling room, he had to blink away the sudden glare.

Muffled words with a heated tone came to him across the stuffy shop. Elvan weaved through the racks, moving toward the front, using the voices as a guide. There was something familiar about the cadence in one of them, something that made his skin crawl.

"The hells you can!" Drace shouted. "We're citizens! We have rights!"

"By order of His Majesty, King Pearce VI," called a familiar, gravelly voice, "this shop and all contents contained herein are property of the municipality of Spheris. All occupants are ordered to personal search and detainment."

Elvan froze and retreated a step. Of course he knew that voice. How could he forget the man who arrested his mother?

Drace grunted. "Get your hands off me! I know my rights!"

Elvan heard the clatter of glass vials, followed by the smashing of something much larger, then wracking coughs and a wave of heat. Drace rushed by him an instant later, grabbing his elbow, tugging him to the back of the shop.

"Tristan, we have to get out!" Drace hissed. Elvan tried to keep up, but couldn't match Drace's agility in the tight shop. Drace half dragged him back to the private fortune telling room without a word, tossing the table over and the rug beneath it. He grabbed an iron ring in the floor and yanked up a trap door, waving for Elvan to go first.

Elvan glanced back at the curtains, then down the ladder descending to darkness. *Let the inquisitors catch me or go with this mystery man with the nice arms and smile?* The crash of shelves somewhere in the shop snapped his attention back to the present, and he made his decision. He could barely see his hand in front of his face at the bottom of the ladder, but Drace followed a few seconds later, dropping the trapdoor into place, leaving them in complete darkness. He felt the shopkeeper crowd against him, smelling of the herbs and incense from above, and a single gas lamp came to life a breath later. Drace twisted a knob, igniting dim flames along a roughly hewn stone hallway.

"The shop will go up quickly. We have to move." He grabbed Elvan's hand again and tugged him to a curtain-covered doorway a few feet down the hall. Within, piles of old newspapers and magazines were neatly stacked on a simple wooden desk along with what he recognized from a distance as invoices and inventory ledgers.

A fellow businessman.

Drace grabbed a canvas rucksack and stuffed it with a handful of clothes and a framed portrait off the desk.

Elvan noticed the meticulously made cot against the far wall. "This is your bedroom?"

"No time, Tristan." He took an oil lamp from the wall and pushed Elvan out of the room.

A muffled explosion above caused dust to cascade from the ceiling.

The hall turned sharply right, ending abruptly at a steel-reinforced wood door with a complex locking mechanism that looked to drive deep into the stone. Drace pulled a ring of keys from his rucksack, selected a small, delicate brass one, and stuck it into the lock. With a dull *click*, cogs turned, and the deadbolts pulled back until the door freely swung inward.

The smell of rotten eggs immediately curled Elvan's nose. He coughed and gagged at the stench. Drace lit the oil lamp with a spark from a flint box and handed it to Elvan.

This is what I get for leaving the house.

Elvan followed Drace through the door, onto a narrow walkway beside the slow-moving sewer water.

At least it's cooler down here.

"The alchemist fire around the shop will do its job, but we need to make some distance." Drace jumped into the water that splashed to his knees, waving for Elvan to join him.

Elvan winced at another crash above.

"Tristan!" Drace grabbed his arm and tugged Elvan into the

wastewater.

Elvan allowed himself to be led as they trudged with the flow. His mind attempted to make sense of it, how he'd gotten to fleeing from the king's men through the sewers of Spheris. *A series of innocent misunderstandings, nothing worthy of a conviction.* He frowned, thinking of the stacks of ledgers in his mother's study. The king didn't need evidence to find someone guilty of a crime, whatever the crime might be.

Drace pulled them to a stop beside a tunnel blocked by vertical bars. Two were bent enough to allow a lithe person careful passage through. He gulped at the fetid air to catch his breath.

"I'm sorry I got you mixed up in this, Tristan. This tunnel will lead you to the east end of the Night Market. You can slip out unnoticed and carry on with things."

Elvan looked down the dark tunnel. "I recognized the voice of Inquisitor Nilranke in your shop. Were you getting raided? Are you an Artist?"

Drace shook his head and wiped at his brow with a sleeve.

"Why was Nilranke in your shop then?"

Drace took a deep breath, running his tongue over his teeth. "They were after my Nana. She's not really my Nana, but she raised me. She told me to do that to the shop if the king ever came." He choked on a single sob. "It's all gone." Drace leaned back against the wall, slid to a squat, and hugged the rucksack, not caring that sewer water wetted his seat.

Elvan glanced down the tunnel again and crouched beside Drace. "Where will you go?"

Drace sniffed and shrugged. "Maybe I can hitch a ride with one of the performing troops as they leave town. I could make a new life in Oxmoore."

Elvan met Drace's amber gaze for a long moment, watched a

single tear roll down the young shopkeeper's face. He could barely reconcile that look of anguish with the playful smirk of the man who just wanted to have some fun with him scarcely half an hour ago. "My house is outside of the city. It'll be a long walk, but you can borrow some fresh clothes and stay a few nights while you sort out what to do."

Drace's expression wavered between joy and confusion. "You'd do that for me?"

"I mean, it's not much to offer. I know what it's like to lose something to the king that's so… vital."

Drace put a gentle hand on Elvan's cheek. "Thank you, Tristan." He pushed to his feet.

Elvan remained stunned in the mucky water for a moment, touching where Drace's palm had been. "My name's…" He could barely hear his words over the soft gurgle of the sewer. "My name's not Tristan. It's Elvan."

"I know. Elvan Galmoth, eldest son of the shipping magnate." Drace offered a hand. "Head of House Galmoth."

Elvan took it and stood. "You knew who I was the whole time?"

Drace shrugged. "Not the whole time, but I put it together. I knew you looked familiar. I knew from the moment you first looked at me, holding a broken lizard skull like it was a baby bird, that you'd give a false name."

Elvan looked down at the nondescript traveler's robes, wondering what gave him away, before looking back at Drace with a flicker of suspicion. "Did you know who I was when you dragged me through the shop?" He chuckled to ease the unintended heat to his question.

"No, I figured it out during the reading. I'm sorry, Elvan, but we can't stay here. If you don't want me at your home, I understand. We can part ways here."

Elvan looked once more at the bars leading toward the Night Market. Had Drace really done him any harm? Would there be any risk in having him at the Galmoth estate for a few days? *Even if he just lies around reading Delphina's trashy books and eating what's left in the larder, it's better than being alone.* He rolled back his shoulders to stand a little taller, though still much shorter than Drace.

"Lead the way," said Elvan.

They reached another sewer grate set in the ceiling within moments. Drace didn't pause as he unhooked the simple locking mechanism and pushed the grate forward on rusty hinges. Elvan went through first, crawling up and into a dim alley, then watched Drace deftly reach through and relock the grate behind him.

Drace must have noticed Elvan's lingering eyes on the grate's lock. "What? I picked up a few things about moving around the city. Come on, market's this way." He led them down the alley and peeked around the corner. Elvan mimicked him, seeing into the tight press of the Night Market.

Despite being mid-afternoon, hundreds of small gas lamps and oil lanterns blazed in the scores of booths that sold anything a person might need, whether or not they knew it. Elvan smiled, remembering the many times Ser Vazadon accompanied him and his siblings through the Night Market. He always convinced the old knight to buy him something frivolous.

Drace ducked back, pulling Elvan with him. "Guards. Four of them. They don't look in a rush. Did anyone see you come in my shop?"

Elvan craned his neck to see back into the market, but couldn't make out any guards among the throngs of shoppers. "No. I was alone on the street."

"Good." Drace pulled off his apron and shoved it deep into a pile of refuse at the alley's edge. "Can I borrow your robe?"

Elvan nodded and pulled it off, leaving him in a light linen shirt and trousers, wet to the knees with sewer water.

"Maybe we should part here, Elvan," said Drace. "I'm basically a fugitive now. I don't want to risk someone at your house seeing me and causing issues."

A wry smile crept over Elvan's lips. "No one will see you."

"You sure?"

"I made an offer, and a Galmoth sees their offers through."

"Well… thank you." Drace squeezed Elvan's forearm and pulled up the robe's cowl before peeking back into the market. The rucksack tied in front of him, under the cloak, made him look fat, adding to the disguise. "Guards have moved. There's probably no point in trying to avoid them. It's the Night Market. There will always be a guard in sight."

Elvan squinted into the crowd and finally saw the hint of blue and silver marking the Serhane hired guards. As the Galmoths took care of all shipping and logistic needs for Spheris, the Serhane family managed security. Three of them stood around a stand selling silk scarves.

Drace pointed toward the opposite direction. "That road leads to the Market Gate. We go out there and your place would be a bit south-east."

"A bit? More like ten miles." Elvan frowned. "Are you worried about the guards? Do you think they would know to be looking for you?" He watched the three laughing at the scarf stand, two now holding streamers of silk against the last.

"It was the Royal Inquisitor and his men in the shop. These guys are just city guards. I doubt they'd know about me, but best to be safe and avoid them." Drace watched the crowd for another moment. "I'll meet you outside the gate. Just act casual."

Drace slipped into the market and Elvan immediately lost him in the press and flow of travelers and local shoppers. He took a deep breath and entered the crowd, bumping shoulders and elbows with muttered apologies while trying to maintain momentum in the gate's direction. He tried to rush without looking rushed, tried to look relaxed even as his nerves made his hands shake. Elvan paused to catch his breath while pretending to peruse a stall strung with strips of dried meat.

Why am I nervous? I've done nothing wrong. I was in a shop when a fire broke out and I escaped. Perfectly normal. I offered the now-homeless shopkeeper a place to stay while he gets affairs in order.

Elvan heard the cowardice in his thoughts and growled at the jerky in front of him. His mother granted him a shrewd mind for numbers and negotiation, but this was his father's thinking.

No spinning excuses. I'm helping Drace.

Elvan set his jaw with a firm nod and turned back toward the gate.

And slammed into a wall of blue and silver.

Elvan stumbled back a step and glanced up at the angry red face of the city guard.

"Oy! Watch where you're going!"

Elvan dashed away, pushing and shoving past shoppers with no attempt at apologies.

"Come back here!" he heard the guard shout. "Stop him! Tan shirt!"

The constant press of shoppers turned him around. Elvan wasn't sure which way to go. Rough hands gripped his collar, and the crowd suddenly thinned. People parted for the guard marching toward him, stopping only inches from Elvan and leering down a broken nose.

"Where you going in such a hurry?" He shoved his fist forward and Elvan recognized his money pouch — Cenna's money pouch — in his meaty grip.

"You startled me." Elvan tried to stand tall with the hand still holding his shoulder.

"You sure you didn't steal… wait…" The guard leaned closer, squinting into Elvan's eyes. "You're the Galmoth boy." He waved, and the hand released Elvan's collar.

Elvan tugged at the bottom hem of his shirt to straighten it, then at his collar. "You found my coin purse. Thank you, soldier." He held out his hand, and the guard pressed the leather bag into his palm.

"Sorry, I didn't think any from the Houses would wander the market at this time. Do you need an escort?" He sniffed, then again harder, before taking a step away from Elvan.

"No, thank you." Elvan willed himself to ignore the reek of sewer. "I'm just on my way out." He turned, nodded to the guard behind him, glanced around to get his bearings, and strode away with confidence.

Elvan kept his gait steady until the crowd closed around him. He still felt the eyes of the guards on his back, but when he looked around, he saw no sign of them. Wrapping his arms around his chest, he hastened toward the Market Gate looming over the end of the road.

He loitered at a stall selling paper lanterns until a large crowd passed and he slipped in amongst them. The sentries on either side of the archway and more on the far side of the short tunnel through the wall never called out. Elvan kept his head down and, after a few steps, ducked beside the trees lining the right side of the road.

Elvan breathed a sigh of relief while the logical part of his mind reminded him he was in no danger, that his excitement was purely manufactured.

"Well…" He blew a quick breath into the chilling evening air. "First adventure of Tristan Griffith wasn't a total letdown."

Something touched his wrist. Elvan yelped and jumped away, back into the road.

"It's me!" Drace tossed back his cowl and shushed Elvan with hands held out in front of him.

"You scared me to death!" Elvan tapped his chest as if trying to convince his heart to settle. He glanced back at the gate, but the sentries didn't seem interested. He stepped back behind the tree with Drace.

"We should go," said Drace. "It'll be almost an hour's walk to your manor."

"Closer to three."

"Three?" Drace chuckled. "Maybe if you take the roads. We'll cut through the woods and fields. We can get there before the sun sets."

"You know all the shortcuts, don't you?" Elvan gestured for Drace to lead the way. It struck him that a near-stranger was guiding him to his own house. After a few minutes, the walls of Spheris were lost to the bulk of trees and he realized the absolute faith of goodwill he was showing to the shopkeeper.

Cowardice and mistrust. He had every chance to see me dead, robbed, or arrested.

My mother wouldn't want to catch me dead in the forests surrounding the city. Neither would Tristan be here. Elvan hopped between stones fording a creek, frowning at the water that splashed onto his already ruined boots.

Brutal Axe, the seasoned woodsman and survivalist, wouldn't care about some water on his boots.

Elvan stomped into the next puddle, grinning and trying not to care about the mud that splashed up his trousers.

That's a stupid name. Aspen Birchson, master huntsman… No… Fox Quillrunner…

"You doing alright back there?" Drace called, interrupting the character creation process. Elvan had been too deep in thought to feel the stitch developing in his side.

"Yeah, just thinking."

Drace splashed across another shallow creek and paused in front of the ridge of stone and dirt somewhere close to six feet high running along the far shore. With a small hop, he scrambled up the rock and earth to offer a hand down.

Elvan looked up at the hand and the one that offered it. Those warm amber eyes, the lopsided smirk… *What am I getting myself caught up in? Snakewood Ironheart, grizzled lone hermit wouldn't invite some complete stranger into his house.*

With strength that left Elvan slightly out of breath, Drace heaved him up the lip of stone and mud. Elvan staggered, but Drace steadied him with a hand on his chest.

"What were you thinking about?" Drace asked.

How I want my robes back so I can see that tight shirt. "Just how impressed I am that you can navigate through these woods."

Drace shrugged and resumed their pace. "It's easy enough to track the sun. If we keep going in the same direction, we'll hit the river circling the city, cross it, and your manor will be easy enough to find from there."

Elvan looked up and could tell nothing of their heading by the small windows of deepening blue between the breaks in the canopy.

"I hope you're not upset I knew who you were," said Drace.

"No," Elvan frowned. "No, of course not. It wasn't like I spent months on a disguise that failed."

"No, you didn't." Drace flashed a smirk over his shoulder. "So, what does a head of one of the five Houses do all day, when not impersonating scholars?"

Elvan cringed. "Mostly combing through financial and legal documents. House Galmoth has hit a rough patch."

"I read some in the news, but I never know what to trust. I'm sorry about your mother."

Elvan slowed at the mention of his mother until Drace stopped and turned back.

"Sorry, am I not supposed to mention her?" Drace asked and stepped nearer. Elvan looked down at his hands, wringing nervously in front of him, then back to Drace.

My father would mumble gross comments about this man's intention to do me harm once we're far enough from the city. Yet... Elvan again met Drace's eyes, reading only empathy and warmth there.

"No, it's fine," Elvan said at last. "I might just have realized I haven't had anyone to talk to in a while."

Drace put a hand on Elvan's shoulder. "We need to get out of the woods before dark, but if you can talk and hike, go ahead."

Elvan glanced at Drace's hand and flashed him a weak smile. They resumed their travel, walking abreast rather than Drace leading by a half dozen paces. Elvan started by admitting the manor was empty. He worked backward with a brief overview of his investigation into his mother's dealings, to her exile, his sister's sudden marriage, and ended with a few quick anecdotes from Ser Vazadon.

When they reached the wide river with a steam ferry's plume of oily smoke in the distance, Elvan bit his lips, realizing the slurry of words that had poured from him, unfiltered, for a half hour through hilly forests and lumpy, plowed fields.

"I'm sorry, that was a lot."

"Thank you, Elvan. Thank you for feeling you could share it all with me."

"Still, it was a lot. I've never talked to anyone about my father running off."

"Sounds like you needed to tell someone. I've had the shop about two years and haven't talked about my Nana… About her leaving. Maybe we'll get a chance. Let's get to the road."

The "road" was less than a quarter mile down the river and was the same path Elvan traveled his whole life between the manor and city. They crossed at the high stone bridge as the aches settled into Elvan. Two years spent hunched over books had done him few favors, physically. They crunched onto the gravel path leading to the manor drive, Elvan grabbed Drace and pulled them both against the hedges lining the way.

Lit by a dozen gas lamps, five white carriages flying red and gold banners spread across the yard in front of the main doors. Four were pulled by a pair of horses, but the largest carriage had a team of four.

"This is bad," Elvan muttered and squinted into the fading light. A small swarm of women in fine dresses and gloves to their elbows milled around the front door. Elvan pulled Drace back further when he spotted the gray-haired knight in regal quilted armor with two swords on his left hip. "Ser Vazadon," he hissed.

"That doesn't look like the king's men."

"No. It's my sister."

4

"**S**HE WASN'T SUPPOSED TO COME for almost a week." Elvan's eyes swept across the scene while he imagined every entrance; door or window.

"Why is he wearing two swords?"

"He... I don't know; that's new. We can circle around to the stables. There's a door in the wall there and we cut through the repair yard to the servants' wing."

Drace's brow pinched with confusion. "Why? We could hide until she leaves or you could just walk up right now. It's your house, right?"

"Yes, of course, but..." Elvan watched Ser Vazadon enter the front door. "If Delphina's here so far off her schedule, I don't think she's up to anything good. I want to know what she's doing before she finds out I'm here."

Drace blinked hard. "Sure."

They ducked across the main gate and followed the stone wall for almost a hundred yards before it was broken by a mossy wooden gate. Elvan pushed it open carefully to keep it on its hinges and closed it behind them just as slowly. The stables that held twenty of the finest horses until only a few years ago now lay barren. Peeking around the edge gave a distant view of the front gate, but the manor blocked any sight of the carriages and main entrance. Elvan waved them through the mess of half repaired wagons to a plain wood door.

He pushed that open, and they entered the near darkness of the servants' waiting room. Rows of dusty bells glinted in the little light that passed through the narrow windows set high on the walls. A white cloth was thrown over the chairs stacked in the far corner and the long table pushed against the wall.

"You should stay here," said Elvan. "I'll go see what my sister's up to. How do I look?"

Drace ran his eyes over Elvan and grinned. "Like hell. I don't think you'd pass for much of a scholar now. At least stomping through the river washed off some of our stink."

Elvan grumbled and ascended the short set of stairs to the main level, coming out into the drawing room. *She'll be in her room or the study.* He cocked his head to listen, and Delphina's shrill yell was clear. Cutting across the back veranda, he crept into the dining room with the table covered in ledgers from his investigations. He edged near the door leading into his mother's study and peeked inside. One oil lamp sat on his mother's desk and another bobbed in a royal valet's hand.

"Bugger it all. We'll take the whole lot of it," Delphina spat.

"Will that be necessary, Your Grace? You need only the one document," asked the valet.

"So what? This is all my mother's, and she's gone, so it may as well be mine. Box it all up and I can get out of this stinking shithole."

Elvan glanced at the drink stand at his side. His father made sure to have one in every room. He quickly poured himself a glass of whiskey, messed up his hair even more, and stepped into the light of the oil lamp.

Enter Drunk Elvan, casual and flippant.

"Oh, dear sister," he flashed her a casual grin, swaying slightly. "I didn't know you were coming this evening. What a pleasant surprise."

Delphina spun toward him, twirling her petticoats against the desk and heaps of ledgers and scrolls at her feet. "There you are." She sniffed and adjusted the wide brim of her hat. "Dear brother," she added with as much sincerity as he. "We banged on the door for ages. It was giving me a migraine before Ser Vazadon remembered he still had a key."

"That's a shame. I'm glad our old knight came to your rescue."

"And where've you been? You look like shit. Smell like it too. Are you drunk?"

"I went for a run in the back garden."

She snorted. "Is it true, then? You've no servants left?"

Elvan smiled and took a sip of the whiskey, savoring the sharp bite. "It's just me and my thoughts. I finally have all the time to focus on my own projects."

"And what have those been? Judging by the state of this dump, you haven't been working too hard on rebuilding the business. Looks like you gave up."

Elvan chewed his lip to keep from saying anything that would only prolong the visit.

"You, valet." Delphina waved at the man holding the oil lamp. "Fetch us tea." The valet's shoulders slumped, and he left toward the dining room. "Why do you keep it so blasted dark in here, Elvan?"

"I've lived here my whole life. I don't need to see to get around the manor." He looked over the pile of discarded scrolls around the hems of her dress and another in her hands. "You said you were coming for dinner. Next week. What are you doing in mother's study?"

"What? I can't be in here?"

"I'd think the palace would have finer parchment for you to throw on the floor." Elvan waved at her mess. "What are you doing?"

"I wouldn't expect you to understand."

Elvan crossed his arms, leaning against the door frame, swirling his drink in its glass. "Try me."

Delphina rolled her eyes dramatically. "I'm looking for mother's writ of export. That's the official document signed by the king giving permission to mother to export—"

"I know what a writ of export is. Why are you looking for it?"

"That's official, royal business. Princess Lorelai would like to examine the document."

"Well, I can't deny the princess's wishes. They took some, but not much, of Mother's paperwork when they arrested her. I know I've seen that writ in the last couple months. I'll find it and get it to you when you're back for dinner, Duchess." Elvan extended his right leg forward for a deep bow and turned on a heel.

He was almost through the library when he heard her weakly calling his name, drawing out the vowels. After a few breaths of debating feigning deafness, he returned to the study.

She pouted a lip at him with wide eyes. "Do you know where the writ is? I'll get ink on my gloves if I have to keep going through these. I really need to find it."

"Just have the poor valet box up everything, then."

Her soft expression darkened. "Don't tempt me, Elvan."

Elvan muttered a curse. He crossed the study, to a rack of thick leather folios stacked high on individual shelves by the window, returning to the polished maple desk with one in hand. Spreading it open, Elvan leafed through the crisp parchment and pulled out a sheet signed with a silver wax seal.

"Why do you need this so bad? You realize this is now void?"

Delphina's pouting lip hardened, and she snatched the page from Elvan's fingers. He watched her eyes scan down the parchment, slowing at the list of signatures at the bottom.

"This is the original. Where's the updated one from a decade ago?" Delphina asked.

Elvan's fingers traced the other parchment in the folio and bent to pick up the scrolls his sister tossed to the floor. "I haven't been able to find it. I've combed through everything in this study for the last couple of years," he said without looking up. "They must have taken it with her. That or it's in Mother's records office downriver, but I doubt that."

She tossed the writ back onto the desk. "Tell me about any warehouses she might have kept off the records," Delphina demanded in a lower, slower tone than usual. "Or anything stored in the manor or on the grounds."

Elvan froze at the question. "I can't tell you about something that doesn't exist. Our mother ran a shipping company. Not storage."

"She must have had cases where the product came sooner than the buyer was prepared to receive."

"What is this about?"

"Everything well in here, Duchess?" asked a gruff, but friendly, voice by the door. Elvan turned to Ser Vazadon, wearing his perfectly fitted armor, but the royal red and gold baldric replaced the House Galmoth colors the knight once wore. "Elvan! I'm delighted to see you, young master." A grin creased the corners of his eyes.

"You too," Elvan said. He set the scrolls on the desk and crossed to take the man's hand.

Delphina was beside them immediately. "You know Mother was up to no good, Elvan. You know she was guilty of far worse crimes than the tax evasion lies they told the public. They only said that to save the Galmoth name from complete destruction. I'll find out what she did and bloody well make sure everyone knows the truth."

Elvan stared at his sister with his jaw slack. "Why? Why would you do more harm to us?"

Delphina's nose crinkled, and she snorted a laugh. "Everyone knows I was a Galmoth. Mother's a villain and father's a damn coward, a drunk." She looked down at the glass in her brother's hand and scoffed. "You should join me, Elvan. The manor is clearly in decline. Get out now and I could get you a job doing something easy at Marshall's winter estate."

Elvan chewed on his lip and silently counted to five. "Thank you for the offer, but I decline. I believe our mother—"

"Offer made, rejected, revoked. Bye, Elvan." Delphina patted him twice on the cheek and stormed from the study before he could raise his hand to bat her away. Elvan and Ser Vazadon watched her stomp into the foyer. The valet came from the other direction holding two saucers with cups of tea, offering one to her. She took one sniff and shoved it back at the man, splashing hot tea on his crisp uniform.

"Have you heard from your brother?" asked Vazadon without taking his eyes from Delphina.

"No, but I hear the monks' initiations can take a few years."

"What a shame."

After berating the valet, Delphina adjusted her gloves and

hurried through the front doors. Ser Vazadon realized his quarry was getting away and turned back. "Pleasure to see you, young master. Fare thee well." He took one of Elvan's hands in both of his, gave it a firm squeeze, and fled after the Duchess.

"I don't like your sister," Drace said from the dining room doorway after the front door closed.

"She takes some getting used to. Did you hear all that?"

"A man came bumbling in, cursing about making tea. I snuck around him before he saw me. The knight seemed nice."

Elvan smiled fondly and bit it back. "Ser Vazadon did more to raise me than my parents. That man has some wild stories about his past. I should tell you the one where he killed a daemon lord with a magic sword."

"A magic sword? How's he a knight if he carries around magic items?"

"He said he lost the sword, but never told me how. I always assumed it happened outside the continent. A man like that, I'm sure he's been west across the ocean."

Drace put his hand on Elvan's shoulder to pivot him back toward the study. "I'm pretty sure your sister is working against you, Elvan. If she exposes the truth of why your mother was exiled, that might put you in very immediate danger. Exiled for tax evasion? You know there has to be more than that."

"I... I know," Elvan said. "It's insulting how clear it is that there's a larger story here. Tax evasion doesn't get you exiled. They only took a few random handfuls of books when they arrested her. Just enough to make it look like they were taking away the needed evidence." He chewed his lip and returned to the desk with the open folio.

"What's so special about the paper she wanted?" Drace asked.

Elvan pulled the piece of parchment on the desk closer to the oil lamp. "A writ of export. It's a paper signed by the king saying the Galmoths are trusted agents. Anything in our wagons can leave the city without all the paperwork and slowdown of individual inspections."

Drace whistled and sat in the high-backed leather chair behind the desk. "That is a lot of power."

Elvan crossed to the sole window of the study, facing the manor's front yard. He watched the last carriage in his sister's caravan pass through the gates. "It saved a lot of paperwork."

"But it's all void now." Drace leaned over the desk, closer to the writ between them. "Why does she want it?"

"Well, sounds like she wanted…" Elvan returned to the desk and flipped through the leather folio. He pulled out two more documents that looked identical to the first, complete with silver wax seals, setting them beside each other in a line, tapping a finger on the last one. "This one. Updated almost a decade ago."

"You sneaky devil."

Elvan shrugged.

"What's different? Why are there three?"

Elvan pointed to the parchment on his far left. "This is the first one when my mother took over the business and proposed the writ, signed by King Pearce V and an array of financier and monetary guild members. This one," he indicated the middle document, "is a couple years later by King Pearce VI, with a few replacements in the retinue because, well, they died. The last has a few added or removed shipping lanes, but re-signed by mostly the same people."

"Signed by the king and his father? Wow." Drace gathered the parchment and held the signatures to the light, seeming in awe. "Pearce VI signed the first one, too."

"Yes, he's always been a big supporter of anything that leads to less paperwork."

"Something odd I've admired," said Drace, "is how people that sign their name all day get to be great at it always looking the same. That isn't the king's signature." Drace set the updated writ in front of Elvan and tapped the block of autographs.

"What?" Elvan snatched up the pages, comparing the looping swirls and slashed lines of Pearce VI's name. Thirty and twenty-five years ago, as prince or king, it was the same. The updated writ perhaps lacked polish, but Elvan barely noticed a difference, even staring at it, looking for one. "What would that mean, if that isn't the king's signature? Someone forged it?"

Drace raised his palms with an exaggerated shrug. "I hear the king's been going mad. Maybe that's it."

Elvan dropped the pages, leaning back against the door frame. He stared at the sheets of high-quality parchment, then at Drace, sitting in his mother's chair. *What about this man made me trust him to have this conversation hours after meeting him? I admit I was lonely, but...* "Say it's a forgery. Who would do that and why? Where does that lead us?"

Drace propped his elbows on the desk, dropping his chin in his palms. "I run... ran an oddity shop. You've studied the workings of a massive shipping industry for years. You tell me where that leads us. Your sister seems to think the differences in the updated writ are meaningful."

Elvan shoved forward, setting his glass on the desk, not caring about the whiskey splashing onto the carefully preserved documents. Snatching up the two newer writs, his eyes scanned the lists of shipping lanes, looking for what they added ten years ago, discounting the names he recognized until only one remained.

"Arca-Nult Holdings," Elvan said, lowering the page to stare at Drace, hoping to see some spark of recognition in the shopkeeper's eyes.

Drace shrugged. "Maybe the king sneezed and I'm wrong. But if you don't have any other leads, that sounds like a place to start."

Two years of pouring through finances, trying to piece together how his mother moved money between a score of lesser businesses, and the first solid lead to understanding what she was doing fell right in front of him. He strained to remember any line in a ledger with that name, Arca-Nult Holdings, but he was dead on his feet. Running from the fire felt so long ago. A grin traced across his lips with the memory of when Drace's hand was first in his own. All his stolen glances as they traveled through the woods, the ghost of stubble along Drace's jaw, the hint of his flat stomach as Drace pulled off his apron to put on Elvan's traveler's robes…

"You awake over there?" Drace was waving at him from behind the desk. "I said, let's pick this up tomorrow. You look exhausted, and I know I am."

"Right." Elvan cleared his throat, forced a grin, and spread his arms to encompass the room. "Welcome to the Galmoth Manor. This is the study. Formal dining, which I've been using as a workspace, is back that way with a splendid view of the gardens. Library is that way, main foyer with the stairs, ballroom, kitchen, larder, and servants' quarters, which we've been through, are to the north. Bedrooms are all upstairs."

"Great," Drace smiled back. "Where do you want me?"

Elvan licked his lips while he considered the options. This would have been his first night alone in the manor, with all its creaks, groans, and drafty whistles. He hadn't realized how he dreaded it until it was no longer about to happen. "My brother was about your size and left everything. Come on. You can get set up in there and I'll find us something to eat before bed."

Elvan led them up the stairs to the door beside his own. Pushing into his brother's room, Elvan couldn't remember when he last entered any of the other bedrooms. The servants stopped cleaning them years ago, leaving a layer of dust covered what few things Bennoc owned. Elvan crossed to the wardrobe and pulled out a rough linen tunic. He turned and held it against Drace's chest, careful to hover an inch from touching him.

"Looks like a decent enough fit. Help yourself to whatever."

"Your brother didn't have much, did he?" Drace's eye lingered on the plain bed with a stack of rough woven blankets folded neatly at the foot. He tossed his rucksack onto it and sat down.

"It was by his choice. Bennoc got deep into the ascetic lifestyle a few years before joining the monastery. I honestly don't know why or how he got wind of it all. We were never that close, but I was still sad to see him go." Elvan stared at the extremely plain bed. "We can search the servants' clothes later for more that would fit you. Maybe some of my father's stuff, if you don't mind the belly being stretched out. If you don't like Bennoc's bed, you can sleep in any other room you want. There are the two bedrooms in the front and Ser Vazadon's. We'd just have to find linens."

"Where's your room?"

Elvan froze. Drace's amber eyes danced in the light of the gas lamp, framing a mischievous smile. "It's the next over." He cleared his throat. "I'll be right back with some food."

"Elvan," Drace called just as he reached the doorway. He turned back to Drace holding a wad of clean, if dusty, linens. "Thank you, again."

Elvan nodded and left the room. He paused on the stairs, glancing back at the open door and Drace's shadow shifting beyond. His legs ached from the miles hiked from town. His eyes ached from being awake for too long. But for once in years, he felt a flicker of hope curling his lip into a smile.

5

"**Y**OU'RE UP EARLY," DRACE SAID, entering the dining room with a yawn. Elvan looked up from the books spread in front of him to see Drace in loose trousers and a dressing robe that hung open to contrast his dark skin against the light linen. A thin, silver chain around his neck suspended a cut ruby nestled in his chest hair, which lead to a trail down his trim stomach.

Elvan grabbed his mug of coffee and choked down another sip of the gritty sludge, wincing at the taste and texture, but glad for a reason to hide the blush on his cheeks. "I couldn't sleep. There's coffee in the kitchen. Well, what might pass for coffee."

Drace stepped beside Elvan and took the mug from his hand, sniffed, shuddered with a grin, and handed it back. "The plight of nobles. You decide the fate of the working class, yet can't make your own coffee." He leaned forward to scan the ledgers and documents on the table. "What's all this?"

Elvan felt Drace's open robe brush his shoulder, but kept his eyes forward. "This has been my work these last two years.

Behold, the deepest under-workings of Galmoth Logistics." He gestured a hand theatrically across the table. "I did some searching specifically for Arca-Nult Holdings. There are regular shipments labeled 'A.N.' from the city by wagon, a transfer to ferry, to a warehouse down the river. I glossed over these before, assuming they were for Arrie Norman, a watch broker who my mother did a lot of business with. The last one was just a month before her arrest."

"Sounds like you have a warehouse down river to visit." Drace walked around opposite the dining table from Elvan. He took a folded stack of parchment from the pocket of his robe and leaned forward with his palms on the table. "We should discuss this." He pushed the paper to rest between them.

Elvan knew the invoices before reaching for them, recognizing how he'd folded them to fit in his pocket just yesterday morning.

"Found that in the robes I borrowed. I'm guessing that's what brought you to my shop?"

"It was, yes," Elvan admitted. Unfolding the familiar invoices with Galmoth Logistics printed across the top, he picked up the one on the top of the stack. "It was as much an excuse to get out of the house. I found a half dozen invoices for the same part number, but I couldn't find what it was or who she was buying it for. It's a lot of steel invested in something I can't trace."

"AS-452b," said Drace, and pulled out a chair to sit. "Arcane steel."

Elvan glanced back at the invoice and up at Drace. "What is that? My mother spent a lot on it ten years ago." He rolled his eyes and shook his head. "Of course, about the same time as the updated writ."

"It's used in small quantities in alchemy. Arcane steel usually comes as a thin sheet of metal that's worked to block the detection of... items emitting certain energies."

"Meaning?"

"You can't detect magic through it."

Unsure of how to respond, Elvan watched Drace roll the ruby on his necklace between his fingers.

Drace sighed and leaned back. "Smugglers use it to line their crates so no one can detect they're carrying magic artefacts."

"Artefacts?" Elvan read the word every week in the papers, how the inquisitors would recover boxes of the magic-imbued items from the Artists they raided. He narrowed his eyes at the implication. "Why would your shop stock something with such an illegal use?"

"Just because something can be used as part of an illegal scheme doesn't make it illegal to sell. Selling pistol shot is legal, but killing someone with it isn't."

"That my mother bought this, but didn't seem to resell it, implies she used it herself." Elvan looked back at the invoice for a single item and the weight of it slowly set in. "Someone altered her writ ten years ago to give her access to move magical artefacts out of the city." He looked up, but by Drace's expression, Elvan could tell the shopkeeper had come to the same conclusion before coming downstairs. "There must be a legal reason for buying so much of the stuff, right?"

Drace shrugged. "Sure, but I don't know who or what else would use that much arcane steel."

"What if you had to guess?"

Drace scratched his ear. "Frostspark or Leystrider Guild, maybe? They say their stuff is all science, but have you seen their designs for an airship? Come on, that's magic."

"If she was moving artefacts, no matter who she might have been moving them for, it would have been wildly illegal."

"I'm sorry." Drace leaned forward again with a look of genuine pity.

Elvan sighed. "She bought some other odd items in bulk back then, like a ton of nitric acid. Vats of it. At least I can sort of trace that to House Daggar as fertilizer, but those numbers don't add up, either. A lot of it is unaccounted for."

Drace narrowed his eyes, but said nothing.

Elvan picked up the closest ledger and tossed it across the table. "Years wasted tracking her spider web finances, trying to prove she didn't actually have unpaid taxes, and it was right in front of me. My mother's a smuggler. The king found out and removed her. He didn't make a big fuss over it to save the Galmoth name, which I've now let languish in trying to prove her innocence."

"Well, if it makes you feel better, I think you succeeded a bit. She didn't evade taxes."

"Except now she's a smuggler, using a forged writ. Though, what was she smuggling? Any kind of magic is strictly illegal. Leystrider Guild has the greatest lawyers and public relations people in the world to not be in jail for how they skirt the law. Who would she have been smuggling from and to who?"

"There're hidden caches of magic in the city. There must be, with all the Artists the inquisitors keep finding," said Drace with a shrug. "So what now?"

"I…" Elvan tapped a finger on the notebook in front of him. "I could let it all go and rebuild the company."

"Really? You'd walk away? You said this was your passion for two years."

"I don't like it either, knowing I'm giving up on some larger conspiracy." Elvan drummed his fingers on the notebook. "But what else can I do? My mother bought a lot of arcane steel and was given a new shipping lane. That's not enough to go on."

"A shipping lane that ends in a warehouse." Drace grinned. "Again, sounds like we have a warehouse to visit."

"Well, the goods must continue on after the warehouse, but I can't find record of it— Wait, *we*? You don't have to come, Drace."

"I know, but I decided while still lying in bed. Nana sold your mother something that probably led to her arrest. At least somehow related. It's a loose connection, sure, but what else have I got going on right now?"

"What about your Nana? You should check on her and ensure the inquisitors have left her alone."

"Nana went south to stay with her sisters outside of Slenas." His gaze drifted for a heartbeat, but he took a deep breath and shook his head. "Thanks for the thought, Elvan, but I want to help. Besides," he winked and flashed the smile that Elvan was starting to look forward to seeing, "I like you. If you'll excuse me a moment, I'll try my hand at remaking the coffee."

Elvan stared at the parchment around him for a long moment, stunned and confused by the admission. Despite barely knowing the shopkeeper, that feeling was mutual.

Not to mention he's really easy on the eyes.

He blinked himself back to reality and closed the notebook, wrapping the long lead of leather around it twice, careful to secure it with the key at the end, laying it amongst the piles of books and ledgers.

He knew from one line of an invoice that my mother's an artefact smuggler.

A warring voice tried to convince him it might all be a lie, an elaborate grift. To what end? Elvan owned a house at the city's edge, but there was no money. The Galmoth name wasn't worth a fraction of what it was two years ago. He had nothing to give and very little to lose.

The earthy smell preceded him as Drace returned, with his robe still infuriatingly open, carrying two steaming mugs. He handed one to Elvan, who breathed it in deeply.

"What's next?" Drace asked and blew across the steam rising from his mug.

Elvan sighed and watched the bubbles in the foam of his coffee. "I need to go to my mother's records office. That'll get me the exact details of the warehouse and keys, if there are any."

Drace glanced across the mound of paperwork on the table and craned his neck into the office lined floor to ceiling with more. His eyebrow twitched up. "There's more than this?"

"A lot more. Galmoth Logistics has, in some capacity, been in operation for one-and-a-quarter centuries. All this," he chuckled and waved over the mess, "is just financial records for the last seven years and core documents."

"Where's this office?"

"It's just down the river, one ferry stop, in the east suburbs. Then the warehouse is a couple more."

Drace shoved his free hand in the robe's pocket. "I only have the steel that was on me when we fled the shop. I hope this isn't expensive."

Elvan drummed his fingers on the notebook beside him, thinking of Cenna's mostly empty pouch sitting on the table in his room.

"Wait, ferry's free on the weekend," said Drace.

Elvan gasped and snapped his fingers. "Of course! Thank you, House Kae! Let's get dressed and go."

Drace followed him up the stairs and to the left, running a hand over the dark floral wallpaper outside of Delphina's room. Elvan paused with a hand on the knob of his parents' bedroom door, quickly summoning the courage to enter.

Elvan twisted the knob, stepped into the room, and blinked at the sudden light from the south windows blazing in the morning sun. To his left, the fourposter bed, stripped years ago, looked sad now with its sagging mattress, as if it represented the state of House Galmoth. He took a sip of coffee and crossed to his father's narrow wardrobe beside the windows. Throwing the doors wide, he gave the garments within their first breath of fresh air in years.

"We should come up with an alias; a backstory," said Elvan, and pulled a dark wool suit to hold against Drace.

"How well did an alias work for you yesterday?" Drace hid a smirk behind his coffee mug. "What was your plan, Tristan Griffith? How were you going to bring up those invoices in casual conversation as a wandering scholar?"

Elvan licked his lips and shied back a step. "I'm… I'm not sure. I got carried away with the role."

"Why the role? What's so bad about being you?"

Elvan blew out a long breath, stalling for time to collect his thoughts. "I haven't been in the city in a while. I thought it would be easier if no one recognized me. Then I introduced myself to you as Tristan and immediately realized I had no plan." He forced a grin.

Drace snorted and chuckled. "You're cute. But I recognized you. Even looking as disheveled as you do right now," he ran a hand through Elvan's hair, curling around his ear, "you're still obviously a noble. I can tell by how you walk and hold yourself."

"It's that obvious?"

Drace nodded and hummed an affirmative. "Why haven't you been in the city? I thought the heads of the Houses all held a council."

Elvan raised a hand to touch the hair behind his ears, wishing

Drace would run his fingers through it again. "That's a whole other story. We need to get moving to the ferry dock."

Drace finally accepted the suit Elvan was offering and held it against his chest. "It's a bit loose, but it'll work."

"You didn't have time to pack much from your room yesterday. Take whatever you want from my brother's or father's wardrobes."

"Thank you. I only grabbed small clothes and a few mementos." He stepped to the bed and tossed Elvan's father's suit onto it.

"I'll get dressed and meet you in the hall in a few minutes." Elvan kept his eyes forward and sped toward the door as he saw by the shadows that Drace shrugged the robe from his shoulders.

"What's all that?" Drace asked, forcing Elvan to turn back to him.

Elvan held back a gasp and felt a shiver down his arms at seeing Drace shirtless, outlined by the bright sun from the windows. He caught his breath and followed Drace's muscled arm, pointing at the floor around his mother's armoire beside the door. Thankful to look away, Elvan stared at the floor, but saw nothing.

Drace approached and squatted low, tilting his head and squinting. "Semi-circular scratch marks on the floor like…" He trailed off and stepped next to the armoire. Over eight feet tall, the massive piece of furniture was tucked tight to the wall. Drace ran a hand along where it met the wallpaper, then peeked past Elvan, into the hall. "Any chance there's a secret room behind this thing?" He waggled his eyebrows.

Elvan laughed, but after a moment, searched Drace's face for a sign of jest, and found only excitement. "A secret room? Why would you think that?"

Drace stepped in front of the armoire and waved at the plank floor. "The doors are a few inches from the ground, yet there's a faint scratch pattern in the floor. It's as if the whole thing swings out."

Elvan scoffed. "The manor is over a hundred years old and who knows when the floors were last redone." As he spoke, his gaze drifted back to the hall. Delphina's door was seven feet away, but her room didn't extend back in this direction more than a foot. He imagined the view of the manor from the back and there was no weird indent, meaning that the space behind the floral wallpaper was filled with... something. *A chimney? No. Dead space? That's a waste.*

Elvan stepped in front of the heavy armoire doors and crossed his arms. "Say there was a secret room. How might one access it?" He ran his fingers along where the cabinet's solid wood met the wall, but it was a tight fit. Drace checked the other side and shook his head. Remembering one of Ser Vazadon's stories, Elvan tugged and twisted the gas lamp sconces nearest to the cabinet, checking them for levers or buttons, but found nothing.

Elvan grasped the delicate iron handles and pulled wide the doors. *This is a waste of time. Yet...* Elvan squeezed through his mother's fine gowns and furs, stepping around the shoes piled on the floor, and ran his hands over the cedar back. He smirked, feeling silly. As an adult and head of his House, he knew there would be nothing, but the kid in him thrilled with the adventure. He ran his hands over the armoire's back, blind behind the wall of clothes he'd soon have to sell to pay the gas bill. When he reached the bottom-right, he felt something against the flat cedar; a thin piece of wood that pivoted on a nail as he touched it. Elvan pressed his fingers into the space behind it and his breath caught in this throat.

A keyhole.

Elvan blinked back the sudden light when Drace parted the

clothes and he realized how he must look, sitting in the back of his mother's armoire, surrounded by her shoes. Drace, on the other hand, looked lithe and powerful with the bright morning light at his back.

"Find something?" Drace asked.

"There's a keyhole back here."

"Great!" Drace dropped to his knees beside Elvan. Despite the strong scent of the cedar surrounding them, Elvan caught a wisp of the lingering incense from Drace's shop as he crowded close. Drace ran his hand along Elvan's arm in the darkness to feel the keyhole at his fingertips. He looked up and bit his lip. "I bet a big house like this, you have lots of keys."

"Rings of them." Elvan swallowed the lump in his throat while not taking his eyes from Drace's that twinkled in the faint light.

"You want to grab them?"

"Yes… yes! The keys!" Elvan stumbled and tripped over his mother's shoes, falling out of the closet. He jumped to his feet with a nervous laugh and rushed to the hall. As he passed it, he glanced into his brother's room, where Drace had stayed the night. The bed was made and everything looked as it did a day ago, other than the canvas rucksack leaning against the foot of the bedframe.

In his own room, he stopped to catch his breath and wipe the sweat from his brow. "By the Six, he's easy on the eyes. And the ears. And the…" Elvan's fingers ran through his hair, blew out a breath, and grabbed the three thick iron rings of keys and one finer set from where they hung on the wall.

Drace lay sprawled on the floor of the armoire and sat up when Elvan returned. "This is fun." He winked.

This is just good-natured fun for him. He thinks nothing of — and means nothing by — being half naked on the floor. When he said he likes me, he just meant as a person. I'm likable, right?

Elvan stepped forward with the keys in hand, careful to not stare at Drace while trying not to make it look as though he was avoiding looking at him. He settled on focusing on Drace's hairline and didn't notice the piles of shoes until his heel came down on one. It might have been the same shoe that tripped him up on the way out of the wardrobe, but Elvan was falling forward again. He caught himself with his palms to either side of Drace's shoulders, his knees between Drace's thighs. The keys bounced away with a clatter.

"Sorry!" Elvan gulped. He looked away from the delicate ruby in Drace's chest hair, up to his face. He could see the wide shock of the other's eyes melt into an easy grin. *So close. He's so warm.*

"Don't be sorry."

Elvan felt Drace's hands gently touching him at his hips and quickly pushed back, jumped to his feet and nearly tripped a third time on the mischievous shoes. He snatched up the rings of keys and handed them down to Drace.

"So many. There must be doors all over this place," said Drace, looking past the iron to hold Elvan's gaze.

"Uh, no more than you'd expect."

"I'm just messing with you." Drace snatched the rings, rolled over, and crawled into the wardrobe.

Elvan picked up his coffee from where he'd placed it on a side table and faced the windows and the valley beyond. "We have to leave soon or we'll miss the ferry."

"Most of these are way too big," Drace mumbled around the soft clink of keys.

Elvan stepped nearer to the glass and squinted into the distance. A dark smudge marked the ferry far up the river.

"Well," Drace flopped onto his back with his arms spread to the edges of the armoire's cedar lining. "Unless you find more keys, this is a dead end for the moment."

"Can you pick it?"

Drace sat up and raised an eyebrow. "Excuse me?"

"Ser Vazadon had a few stories about traveling with a fellow that could pick any lock with special tools."

"That's odd. I must have missed where you handed me special lock picking tools. I only saw keys."

Elvan offered a hand down to Drace and the shopkeeper slapped the rings of keys into it before rolling to his front and pushing to his feet on his own.

"I guess we go to the warehouse?" Drace brushed his hands together, then on his trousers. "You said it's just down the river?"

Elvan nodded. "The record's office first, then we catch the next ferry to the warehouse. I'll… I'll go get changed."

Elvan fled back to his room and latched the door behind him. "Asking if he can pick a lock. Really?"

Elvan stripped and threw on fresh trousers, one of his few remaining pressed shirts, and a dark waistcoat. He scoured the bottom of the trunk in his wardrobe and came away with a cap to pull over his mop of hair hanging low to his eyes. He winced at the tightness — hats never seemed to fit well — but welcomed anything that might leave him unnoticed.

Elvan opened his bedroom door as Drace stepped out of his parents' room wearing a sharp pair of slacks, a stiff cream shirt, and a fine embroidered waistcoat. Everything sagged in the middle, but the length looked about right.

"How do I look?" Drace raised his arms and spun on a heel.

"Better than my father ever did. I know what will complete the look." Elvan opened the roll-top desk at the top of the stairs and dug to the back, pulling out a cloth pouch monogrammed with a stylized "M." He dumped a gold pocket watch into his palm and offered it to Drace.

The shopkeeper picked it up by the chain, watching it swing as a grin spread slowly across his lips. "Offering me a watch after only knowing me a day? How forward of you, Elvan Galmoth."

"What? No, it's…" Elvan stammered, not sure of the custom he was refuting. "My father's watch is broken, anyway."

"It's your father's watch? Scandalous."

"The ferry comes at noon and that's…" He consulted the silver watch in his waist pocket. "We have to run. Literally."

6

BEING A FREE DAY, A larger than average crowd filled the ferry dock when they arrived. No one gave the pair a second glance as they ran up, gasping and sweating. Elvan was happy to settle into the edge of the group of twenty waiting while the ferry puttered down the river toward them, belching a steady puff of black smoke behind it. Guided on stout metal cables that ran the length of the river, the operators' only jobs were to keep the fire in the engine steady and to ensure the boat paused long enough at each stop.

They waited for a few passengers to disembark before following the mass onto the flat deck of the ferry, plainly named Frostspark XI. Most dispersed to the second level, but Elvan guided Drace to an empty space near the noisy engine in the back while the ferry started again down the river, washing a cloud of burning oil over them.

"I'll be the affluent merchant and you're my ward," said Drace with a grin.

"What?"

Drace rolled his eyes. "You said you wanted to roleplay."

Elvan laughed. "What are my duties as your ward?"

Drace's eyes rolled up with thought, and he shook his head. "No, aren't wards like your children?"

"There can be adult wards. It's just a person you care for."

"I don't want to be taking care of you in this. How about you're my business partner? I'm the financier and you're…" He ran his eyes down Elvan and focused on the untucked shirt hem. "You're my disheveled husband."

Elvan jammed his shirt into his pants, careful to keep his eyes down. "H-husband? What? No, we only just met." His cheeks and ears burned. *Why would anyone that looks like him want someone like me?* He coughed and looked up when he realized his unfocused stare was at Drace's belt line.

"It's just a bit of play acting. And why not?" Drace crossed his arms with a pout. "No one will look twice at a young married couple."

"You aren't going to let that go, are you? About my disguise?"

"Not if I don't have to. I'm sorry that I find it cute. What's so wrong about just being yourself?"

"It's just easier… I don't know, easier to be someone else sometimes. Someone with different worries."

Drace ran his knuckle across Elvan's jaw. "I might be able to understand that."

"Maybe we just don't get noticed." Elvan raised his hand to trace where Drace touched him.

Drace put his hands on Elvan's shoulders. "Slouch a little, keep your head down, and you'll blend in. I'll do my best to look more interesting than you and no one'll look twice." He winked.

"I should have asked earlier," said Elvan, "but how are you doing? You lost a lot yesterday."

"I'm still processing it." Drace sidled closer where they leaned against the railing and lowered his voice to barely be heard over the engine beside them. "The shop's just stuff. A lot of stuff and all the stuff I ever had, but just stuff. No one was hurt. At least I assume the inquisitors all made it out. The fire was between me and them." His eyes stared at the distant shoreline without focus.

"Why did you do it?" Elvan asked. "What would they have found if you didn't burn it all?"

"That's what my Nana said to do," Drace said quietly, without taking his eyes from the shore.

Elvan cleared his throat, sensing that conversation was over, at least for now. "I hope my accommodations were sufficient. How did you sleep last night?"

Drace shook his head and looked at Elvan with a grin. "Sometimes on my back, sometimes on my side, but always alone."

Elvan chuckled and scratched at his head through his cap. "I've never met anyone quite like you, Drace."

"I'll take that as a compliment. Hey, to remain serious here a moment…" He turned fully to Elvan and leaned his hip against the railing. "It's awkward to bring up at all, but I want us both thinking about it, even if we can't answer it just yet."

Elvan turned to Drace and saw the grave look in the shopkeeper's amber eyes. "What is it?"

"Your mother. I never met her; she did business with Nana while I wasn't doing anything more than unloading boxes in back. Despite any evidence we've run across, she may be innocent. Why was she exiled and not, you know, something harsher?"

Elvan bit his lip, considering where to start. "For a while, I thought the king meant her exile as a harsh warning to the other families; a punishment that grossly outweighed the crime. After I couldn't prove unpaid taxes, I suspected a cover up and tax evasion was the lie told to the public. But if she's a smuggler, I don't know why they wouldn't have exposed that, other than to save the Galmoth image."

Elvan scratched at his cheek and continued. "The king can do whatever he wants, but he can't start executing heads of the families. He may run the country, but we run the city. Serhane and Daggar are struggling under the added load of the contracts I sold to them. We're all needed with our own roles. Exiling my mother got them in line and working hard, but had he killed her, the other families would have risen against the king."

The engine whined beside them, marking the first stop.

"Let's go," said Elvan. "We have forty-five minutes until the next boat." He looked down at Drace's hand on the railing and hesitated. *Do it.* He reached to grab it in his own, tugging the shopkeeper to motion behind him.

Few were departing the ferry and Elvan had to carve a path through the crowd of weekend passengers before the boat left with them still on board.

"I knew the ferry was free on weekends, but never knew why. Where's everyone going, dressed up so nice?" Drace asked once they had the wood dock under their feet and the ferry belched its line of smog down the river again.

"House Kae sponsors the ferries. They host plays and parties on most weekends. People come from all over to see them. Their estate isn't that far down the river."

"Kae, that's where your governess went?"

"Yes." *Only yesterday, but it feels like a week at the same time.* Elvan cleared his throat and nodded his chin to a squat stone building nestled among a handful of shops, offices, and apartments. Gravel crunching under their boots, Elvan dug into the leather satchel at his hip, pulling out a ring of keys before reaching the door labeled "Galmoth Logistics, East Office" in stenciled crimson paint.

"It's unlocked," he said, pushing the solid wood door open. He reached for the brass knob to bring up the lights, but they were already shining around the perimeter of the room. "Someone's here." An iron catwalk lined the outer walls that were covered floor to ceiling with tiny drawers, each with a delicate brass handle. A staircase to their left descended to a similar level below, and then three more beyond that.

"Who would be here?" Drace said.

"I don't know."

Drace leaned over the railing and blew out a loud breath; the sound deadened despite the openness of the space. "How do you find anything in here?"

"I know where to look." Elvan pulled a notecard from the leather bag. He paused at the stairs, a hand on the railing, and sniffed at the air. "Do you smell that?"

Drace stepped near and took a deep, loud inhale. "Yeah, we need a bath."

"No, I mean… Well yes, we do. There's…" He breathed deeply. The usual smell of musty parchment had something lingering over it. "Is that tobacco?"

Drace sniffed again, and his eyes widened. "Yeah, and I recognize it."

Elvan did at the same time. That distinct blend of smoke was seared into his memory for the last two years, since Inquisitor Nilranke took his mother away, leaving a cloud of his stink in the foyer.

Elvan jumped back from the stairs, snapping his arm to push Drace flat against the wall. "Is he below?" he whispered.

"I didn't see him."

"The levels below the next have branching halls. He might be down one of those." Elvan glanced down his arm, seeing it still pressed against Drace's chest, and let it drop.

"How big is this place?"

"Big."

"And it's just for your family's business?"

"Don't worry about that! We should come back."

"Your name's on the door," hissed Drace.

"I don't want him catching us."

"I might not mind that as much." Drace cracked his knuckles.

"He's horrible, but he's still an agent of the law, Drace."

"An agent that made me burn down my Nana's shop."

"We just need to get down one level." Elvan leaned forward, peeking over the edge of the walk way. "Stay here."

Elvan turned back to the stairs and swore the stink of tobacco grew to a sickening swell. He pulled off his boots and handed them back to Drace before taking the stairs one at a time. Halfway to the second level, he heard distant murmurs below him. He froze, fighting the urge to flee. *This is the only lead I've had on her in years. I'm only a few steps away.*

He reached the second level and glanced up at Drace, staring down at him with worry plain in his eyes. Turning back, Elvan walked his fingers over the drawers of documents, counting them down to the number matching what he'd copied from his mother's cryptic notes. He found it in the far corner and slowly pulled out the drawer, praying to the Six that nothing would squeak.

"The Duchess's information is flawed," a voice cut through his panic from below, deep and strained. Nilranke. "She's wasting my time here."

Sweat broke across Elvan's brow while his fingers flicked

through the documents. He almost flipped past it before his eye could register "Arca-Nult Holdings" written across the top in his mother's familiar script. Below it, she'd written "Storage 61," but the page was otherwise blank. A ring of four keys was tucked beside the papers, and he added them to his satchel.

The parchment in hand, he turned to retreat, but stopped and reached into his bag. Taking out a pen, he scratched over his mother's number, changing it to 87. *Hopefully that exists.*

Below, steel clicked against the metal flooring.

Nilranke's cane.

Elvan put the document back in place and pushed the drawer closed before padding back to the stairs as quickly as he dared. Drace met him at the top and they fled to the gravel outside before he ventured a breath.

"He's down there. I heard him say he's there on my sister's information."

"Your sister is working with Nilranke?" Drace cringed away.

"I knew she was terrible. I didn't expect she'd be *that* terrible." Elvan pulled on his boots and stood. "If they're looking for what I was, I might have delayed them. Let's get back to the ferry."

"Really? You just let that go?"

"Let what go?"

"Your sister. You hear she's feeding information to Nilranke and you act like you'd expect no less from her."

Elvan scoffed. "You don't know the girl I grew up with."

"Hmm. Did you at least find where the artefacts are going after the warehouse?"

Elvan glanced back at the door and cursed. "I'd have to dig deeper to figure that out. Let's get out of here. We can come back after seeing the warehouse, once Nilranke's gone."

As they arrived, a boat departed, mostly empty, puttering

upriver. A few couples loitered on the dock, wearing their best suits and dresses, craning their necks down the river for a hint of the next ferry to take them to the festivities. Elvan and Drace stayed in the shadows of the unoccupied ticket station at the crowd's edge. They tensed with every new person who approached wearing dark clothing, expecting them to be the inquisitors.

"I was thinking," said Elvan to break his tension. "My mother wasn't the one physically putting magic artefacts into crates."

Drace looked down at him and blinked. "Yes, back to that. Good point. Go on."

"Someone — forged king's signature or not — gave her permission to use a shipping lane and someone was collecting the goods on the other end. There are others involved in this. Exiling my mother might have been to keep her quiet before she could expose someone with more power."

"That's good." Drace squeezed Elvan's wrist. "Until we know more, the guesses are just guesses. But I like the positivity."

The ferry appeared around the bend and a few travelers cheered and raised their flasks. Some couldn't wait to get to the party, it seemed.

Elvan watched the passengers crowd into the boat and debated suggesting they wait for the next. That would give Nilranke's men almost another hour to finish whatever they were doing. They couldn't delay.

Drace took Elvan by the hand, tugging them into the stream onboarding, through the throng, and to almost the same place by the railing and less desirable space beside the engine. Elvan tugged his cap lower across his eyes and turned to face out to the water. Drace leaned against the rail beside him, trying to look unnoteworthy as well. The ferry jerked into motion.

We could just stay on this until we get to the Kae Estate. I could see Cenna. We'd take in a play while we sit in the grass together, drinking wine.

Elvan looked up at Drace beside him. The shopkeeper — former shopkeeper — looked lost in thought with his amber eyes staring unfocused across the water. He knew something of the loss Drace must have been trying to process; he'd experienced the same, but his had taken years, rather than instantly in a blaze of alchemist fire.

The engine grumbled as it slowed to a stop and yet more crowded on, pressing Elvan and Drace to the railing.

"Miserable on a weekend," complained a woman behind them. "They pack them in like beans in a can in here. Did you hear about the raid yesterday?"

"I thought I might have heard something about that," said a second woman. "The more senile the king gets, the more Artists they find hiding in Spheris. I swear there are more every week."

"Well, there was a fight, and an Artist injured a Royal Inquisitor."

"Goodness, no! Will they ever get control of those beasts? I don't feel safe in the city with all the raids. What happened?"

"The Artist threw around some wild magic and burned a shop down. An inquisitor is still in hospital with burns, but they assume the Artist went up with his shop. They had the place surrounded. You there, boy."

Elvan felt a tap on his shoulder. He swallowed hard and turned just enough to see the woman in her heavy petticoats, platinum blond wig, and wide sun hat. She snapped open a paper fan to cool her painted face.

"Be a good lad and let me by the railing." She waved her fan, indicating the direction she wanted him to move.

Elvan kept his head down and shoulders in his ears as he shoved through the press of passengers to the far side of the ferry near the bottom of the steps to the second level. Drace joined him a breath later.

"I think I owe your father a new pair of slacks." Drace chuckled wryly.

"Do you think those old women actually know what they're talking about? Do they think you died in the shop?"

"I don't think most old people know what they're talking about. But no, not unless they find some bones. Though, there were enough bones in the shop that they'd have a hard time telling which might be mine. Does it matter? I know I can't go back there."

"I suppose not."

"I'm not sad to hear an inquisitor was hurt in the fire," Drace grumbled. "Shame it wasn't Nilranke."

Other passengers pressed near to them, ending any conversation. A few minutes later, the engine groaned, and the ferry slowed by the cluster of abandoned buildings by the dock.

7

THE NEXT DOCK WAS BARREN of party goers to add to the ferry. Elvan and Drace waited beside a hitching post until the boat's belch of black smoke was far down the river before turning to their business. A few abandoned-looking stone buildings sat across a packed dirt road, creating narrow roads between them.

"Which way is the warehouse?" Drace asked.

Elvan pointed between the first and second building. They walked down the alley, marking off wide doors painted white with a number. They stopped in front of 61, the one with wide double doors secured by a heavy chain visible even from a distance.

"I hope we have more luck with the lock than we did this morning," Drace said as they neared.

Elvan took the iron ring from the leather bag at his hip as they approached, eyeing the lock securing the door. He handed the keys to Drace, hefting the steel padlock in both hands, straining to lift the weight.

"That's not suspicious at all," said Drace. "Having a massive lock on a warehouse in the middle of nowhere."

"This is where you need the most security." Elvan let go of the lock, taking the keys from Drace. "No one's going to break into a warehouse in the middle of the city without being seen. Out here," he waved to the lonely ferry dock behind them, "you could do anything all day and all night without being seen. The only security is a clever lock. Even if there's nothing of value, you don't want anyone squatting in here."

The lock fell open with the second key he tried.

"Here we go." Elvan shoved the keyring into his pouch then lifted the padlock in both hands, pulling it off the chain to drop at his feet with a thunk. He unwound the chain from the handles, taking one to pull the heavy door open. Drace stopped him with a hand on top of his.

"What do you expect to find in there, Elvan?"

He shrugged. "Proof of what my mother was doing."

"Say the place is stacked to the rafters with illegal magic artefacts in crates with your family seal, what then?"

Elvan shrugged again.

"What if it's completely empty?"

Elvan pulled his hand from under Drace's as his shoulders slumped.

Drace sighed. "I just think it's a good idea to go in not just with expectations of what we'll find, but also be ready for the total opposite. Basically, whatever you're expecting, don't."

Elvan looked down at his hand, then up at Drace. "The Arca-Nult Holdings contract is the only lead I've had in years. No matter what we find in here, we next find which family took that contract and find out why the king hasn't exiled them yet."

"So much finding to do." Drace put a palm on Elvan's cheek, then squeezed his shoulder before yanking the warehouse door open with a grunt.

Elvan entered first, slipping between the doors. The storage space was thrice as deep as it was wide. To his left, more than a dozen wooden crates lined the side under the leaded glass windows set high on the twenty-foot walls. In a far corner was a mess of wood planks, as though a stack of crates had collapsed, but the center of the warehouse lay mostly empty. On his right were two hand dollies and a pile of stained, white canvas.

Drace stepped beside him, coughing. "No one's been in here in years." He gestured to the undisturbed layer of dust across the floor, took a crowbar leaning against the wall, and paced toward the crates.

Elvan watched the shopkeeper's smooth gait and licked his dry lips. *I have to know.* He coughed to clear his throat. "What did you mean when you said you like me?"

Drace spun, keeping his pace, walking backward with his hands in his pockets, the crowbar looped over his wrist. "How do you think I meant it?"

Elvan starting moving forward. "I'm asking because I wasn't sure."

"Of all the ways I might have meant it, do you hope I meant it any way more than any other?" An impish grin twitched the corners of Drace's mouth as he stopped in place.

"I don't know. We only just met, but..." Elvan closed the gap between them, forcing a grin up at the twinkle in the shopkeeper's eye. "Do you fancy me?"

Drace stepped forward, halving the distance between them. "Is that what you hope I meant?"

Elvan couldn't hold Drace's gaze, looking down at his hands. They stood close enough that he could smell the incense from the oddity shop still clinging to the other man. He fought his reaction to retreat a single step, attempting to focus on stopping his hands from shaking.

Drace moved closer, touching Elvan's jawline with two fingers, but didn't apply any pressure to force his gaze upward.

Like a dam bursting, Elvan felt a rush of absolute loneliness, remembering each family member and staff leaving him these last years. Each abandoning him to be alone in a dusty, hollow house. He choked back a single sob, tilting his eyes upward. Any trace of Drace's devilish grin was missing from his wide, somber eyes.

"Yes."

Drace brushed his thumb across Elvan's lips and his smile returned, genuine and whole. "That is how I meant it, but as you said, we only just met." He dropped his hand, letting it graze Elvan's neck and chest in passing.

Elvan stood frozen while Drace turned, continuing toward the crates. Heat burned in his cheeks, lips, and neck. Reflexively, he traced where Drace had touched him. He counted five deep breaths before hurrying to catch up.

They reached the first wooden crates, and Elvan was happy for the distraction. He pointed to the red stamp resembling a four-winged insect on the torn paper seal glued over the lid. It was always an ordeal to explain that the seal of Galmoth Logistics was a bird's-eye view of one of the earlier sailing ships, not a bug. Drace flourished the crowbar and jammed it into the edge of the wood, popping the top with ease. They peered inside to a lining of hay and a few broken clay pots.

"Are those magic artefacts?" Elvan asked.

"No," Drace shook his head and moved to the next crate. "Artefacts don't break so easily." He opened another crate with similar contents.

"It's all junk," said Elvan.

"Calm down. Two crates out of fifteen doesn't mean it's all junk."

"And finding nothing doesn't mean there wasn't anything to be found. It just means they already moved it from here."

"Exactly." Drace opened another two crates of broken pottery.

Elvan looked across the other crates. "All their seals are broken. Someone's already gone through these. How will we know an artefact when we see one? If we see one?"

Drace jammed the crowbar into the next crate, but stopped, turning to Elvan. "What do you think an artefact is?"

"Why do you sound like one of my tutors all of a sudden? Responding to my questions with questions?"

"Why do you think I'm doing that?"

"Stop, please."

Drace laughed and tugged the crowbar from the crate, dropping it on the top. "Artists channel their power, their magic, at a given rate. It's like a resource that refills regularly, like a water canteen that you fill up in the morning. As they cast spells or something else that uses magic, they're taking sips from the canteen. Got it?"

"So far."

"An Artist can't get a bigger canteen. Whatever they don't drink at day's end, they dump out in order to refill. That's not exactly right, but close enough."

"Makes sense, sure."

"Someone clever a long time ago figured out that an Artist can pour some of their water, their magic, into another canteen. They can focus their magic into an item, storing it there, creating an artefact. Maybe it's a statue, a plate, scroll, piece of jewelry, but generally the harder the material, the better. There's a lot lost in the transfer and it takes a long time, but they would waste the magic anyway, so what's the harm."

"That sounds dangerous, being able to store up endless supplies of magic."

Drace sighed, leaning against the crate. "It's not like that. Artists are just storing a resource that would otherwise go to waste. They weren't and aren't creating stockpiles of war implements."

"You sure know a lot on the topic."

"I was raised by an Artist."

"Right, sorry."

Drace opened the last crate and reached in, digging through more broken junk.

Elvan growled his frustration and kicked the edge of the wooden box. He immediately regretted it by how his toe throbbed. "What a waste of a day!" He leaned against a crate and rubbed his foot through his boot.

Drace rested the crowbar over his shoulder and watched Elvan for a moment. "This was one outcome you thought might happen. You were ready for this."

Elvan pushed up to sit on the crate and leaned forward with his elbows on his knees. "I know, I know. After suspecting my mother of smuggling, I almost wanted to find proof. I don't want to think this way about her just based on circumstantial evidence."

"Got it. So we should be really sure there's nothing tucked away in here, right?"

Elvan glanced around the warehouse, empty other than the few recently opened crates. He pointed to the shattered mess in the corner. "I'm sure that's just more broken jugs and splinters." Elvan leaned forward, pressing his palms into his eyes. The pristine image he had held of his mother his whole life now had a giant stain splashed across it. Even if he learned she never dealt in magic artefacts, he believed it so easily, and that stung.

He jerked up at the first loud clang to see Drace heaving broken parts of boxes out of the corner. Elvan jumped down to run and help until they exposed one more crate, mostly intact in the corner. The edge had been smashed in, but otherwise it looked like all the others they'd opened. Drace retrieved the crowbar, dragging it along the Galmoth seal, tearing it. The damaged lid took more force to pry open, but with another heave, it fell back against the wall behind it with a thump. Within was another square crate, almost two feet on a side, bearing a golden seal with stenciled black text.

Grunting, Drace reached in to heave the smaller crate up to rest on the edge of the larger one. "That's fine. I got it." Elvan rushed to help, but was already too late to do anything. "It's not heavy, just awkward." Drace ran his fingers along the golden seal, reading it out loud. "Arcanym Vault, Row 84, Bin 12."

"Arcanym. Arca-Nult. This is what she was moving." Elvan looked up as Drace stepped away. The shopkeeper's face had gone slack and his eyes wide. "What is it?"

"Arcanym. This is from when the Sovereign King put down the last of the great Artists."

Elvan twitched away from the crate as if it might suddenly bite him. Or explode. "The king's? My mother wasn't just smuggling random artefacts from across the city, but plundering the king's vaults?"

Drace nodded slowly. "The power stored in those artefacts is said to be enough to decide the fate of nations. I mean, it almost did. The Sovereign King died fighting the last of the great Artists."

"We should get out of here." Elvan glanced at the door, half expecting his sister to walk in.

Drace returned to the edge of the crate. "No. We can't leave this here." Crowbar in hand, he was already slicing the golden seal, carefully wedging it into the lid. The wood cracked, making Elvan wince as the top fell away. A thin sheet of silver metal lined the inside of the crate's lid. Elvan swallowed, peering in, seeing the metal lined the rest of the interior.

"Arcane steel," Drace muttered, running his fingers along the etched interior. He sniffed and reached into the packing hay, pulling out a crude statue of an owl carved in what looked like pearl, small enough to fit in his fist. "It's an artefact."

Elvan backed away again. "Is that safe?"

Drace glanced slowly over one shoulder, then the other. "I don't see any powerful, ancient Artists in here. Just us." He winked.

"I mean, are they safe to touch?"

"Completely." Drace turned to let Elvan better inspect the statuette.

"That's it?" Elvan asked, leaning closer.

Drace peeked into the box, ran his free hand along the bottom, and nodded. He pushed the smaller crate back into the larger one with a thud. "This isn't enough?" He ran a finger along the sharp edges of the statuette. "Think about it, Elvan. Some long-dead Artist poured their soul, literally, into this while they chiseled away. This isn't just some little trinket, but something lovingly crafted over months. Artefacts are cherished objects, fragments of history, not something to be locked away under the palace."

Drace wiped at his nose as his misty gaze focused on the crudely carved bit of gemstone. Elvan bit his tongue, wanting to compare it against any of the great pieces of sculpture he'd seen in museums as a child. This looked like something he could have made, nothing of cultural importance or interest.

Elvan cleared his throat. "You said arcane steel blocks the detection of magic, meaning someone would be able to sense that, now that it's out of the crate?"

Drace nodded, pushing the heel of his free hand against his eye.

"This doesn't answer the invoices," Elvan said, tracing a finger along the sharp edge of the owl's wing. The pearl felt slightly warm to his touch.

"How so? We found the arcane steel."

"This crate is from the Arcanym, meaning it was packed decades ago, or more. Not by my mother. Where did she use all the material she bought from your Nana?"

A boot scraped on gravel outside and they both ducked to a crouch. Elvan heard the distinct mummer of conversation.

"We have to get out of here!" he hissed in Drace's ear.

"Maybe it's just a passerby."

A shadow passed the door, too quick for Elvan to make out any detail.

Drace tensed. "Red and gold. Royal soldiers."

"Where do we go? There's just the one door."

Drace stepped carefully into the crate, around the smaller one inside. "Trust me. Don't make a sound." Elvan couldn't react before Drace wrapped a powerful arm around his waist and pulled him into the crate. Drace held him close across the chest, pressing the owl statue against Elvan's shoulder. Mumbled phrases tickled Elvan's ear as his vision clouded then distorted just as the warehouse doors were yanked wide open.

The afternoon light framed the silhouette of a man in billowing robes and a tall hat. A soldier stepped to either side of him as he strode into the warehouse, leaning heavily on a cane that rang with a metallic tap with every step.

Elvan squirmed, wanting to duck into the crate, but Drace only held him tighter, crushing their hips together, whispering nothings across Elvan's ear. His shoulder burned where the statue pressed into it.

"Fan out," said the robed man in a voice Elvan recognized from an hour ago. "They may still be hiding in here." His eyes swept across the room, never hesitating as they passed over Elvan and Drace in the corner.

Three more soldiers entered, joining the other two in tossing through the crates Drace had just opened. They moved closer to the corner, eyes never focusing on the two men standing in a crate there.

Elvan gasped to breathe around Drace's grip. He grabbed at the arm across his chest, hoping to pry away any pressure. His fingers tingled, losing any strength where they touched the linen of Drace's shirt.

A soldier came within arm's reach, looking directly at the two. He blinked with an unfocused gaze, shook his head, and turned to the robed inquisitor. "There's nothing here, sir." Other soldiers shouted likewise.

"Tiresome." Inquisitor Nilranke's robes kicked up a swirl of dust as he turned to the door. "Burn it." His steel cane tapped with his uneven gait.

The soldiers followed the inquisitor out, with the last pausing by the crate closest to the door. He took materials from a pouch on his belt to strike a fire in the packing hay. The soldier watched it a moment before calmly leaving after the others.

Drace released Elvan with a gasp, slumping against the back edge of the crate. Elvan toppled forward, gasping in quick, shallow breaths, rubbing at his aching chest while his vision swam. He blinked down at his hand, unable to focus on it. His mind felt slow and fogged as he wheeled on Drace.

"You're one of them! You're an Artist!"

"Elvan, breathe," Drace panted. "Anyone can use arte—"

"You lied to me."

"No, I didn't. Elvan, the place is on fire. We have to go."

Elvan stumbled back, falling out of the crate, landing hard on his back. He pushed to his feet without taking his eyes off Drace. The glazed stares of the soldiers and inquisitor as they all looked at the two of them without seeing flashed in his mind. "What did you do?"

Drace held the owl in one hand, with the other raised defensively as he stepped from the crate. "I made them not see us. Elvan, come on."

Elvan retreated, tripping over loose planks. He looked up at Drace and it took a moment to realize he'd fallen again.

"Elvan, you're hyperventilating. Slow down. Take my hand."

"No! Get away from me!" Elvan shrieked, slapping at Drace's arm.

"Quiet! Nilranke couldn't have gotten far."

"I don't care!"

Elvan got his feet under him, turned, and ran, using the steady light from the open doors to guide him. In the street, he fell to his hands and knees, gasping in the cool air. Falling to his side, he saw Drace coming toward him as black smoke licked around the edges of the wide doors. He rolled to his front, trying to push up.

Strong hands at his ribs pulled him forward, away from the burning warehouse. Elvan elbowed them away, looking up at hearing a familiar mechanical groan. The ferry was ready to leave the dock. He ran for it, holding his chest and his aching shoulder. He waved an arm, shouting for them to stop. A man with brass buttons down his vest and a captain's hat waved from the ship's edge as it jerked to motion. Elvan's boots slapped against the sun-bleached wood of the dock while the ferry slipped farther into the river. He reached the end and jumped, falling against the captain.

"Something wrong with your pocket watch, young man?" the captain chuckled, easing Elvan to sit on the steps before he went on to other duties.

Elvan squeezed his eyes closed and forced his breath to slow, counting to ten. He opened them to see Drace standing at the edge of the dock. Their eyes met for a heartbeat before Drace turned to walk toward the road.

8

PASSENGERS AT THE NEXT STOP muttered curses as they stepped around Elvan at the bottom of the stairs. He paid them no mind, not looking up from his hands resting across his knees until the boat jerked to a stop again. His boots scraped the dirt and loose rocks in the road with every step until he looked up at the ornately carved front door of his manor, remembering little of the trip... only Drace's look of betrayal and disappointment; how his shoulders sagged as he turned away.

Elvan pulled the keys from his leather bag but paused, leaning forward against the door, thumping his head against the polished grain.

"Idiot."

Upstairs, he stripped off his vest and shirt in front of the mirror to trace fingers across his chest and shoulder, wincing at the touch. *That'll bruise.* He touched his waist, thinking of how intimate Drace's embrace would have been, if not for the harrowing situation. *What would Nilranke have done had he found us, if Drace hadn't used magic? The warehouse was full of my family's goods, I had every right to be there.* He stared at his reflection in the full-length mirror, finding he couldn't answer himself with any certainty. Nilranke surely didn't leave the palace with orders to burn the warehouse. Right? He was at the records office on Delphina's information, but what if she commanded the inquisitors in some capacity? He would have needed nothing more than a wave of his hand for a loyal soldier to crack the two of them over the head and leave them to perish in the fire. Who would miss either of them should they disappear?

His mind moved backward through the events of the warehouse, slowing every time Drace smirked or winked. He again ran a finger over his lip, remembering how casually Drace ran his thumb over it. Those thoughts circled back to Drace's deep sadness on the edge of the dock.

Elvan focused on his shirtless reflection in the mirror. Short, skinny, pale. Alone.

Unloved.

His hands balled into fists, his breath quickening, hating what he saw, hating what he'd let himself become. Two years of his life, wasted. Not just two. What had he accomplished in nineteen? He reached back, screaming, slamming a fist into the silvered mirror, wanting nothing but to smash his reflection to nothing.

Except the mirror was undamaged. His hand was not.

He yelled all the curses he knew while cradling his throbbing knuckles.

Elvan pulled on a clean shirt and counted how many remained folded neatly in his dresser, calculating how long it would be before he absolutely had to learn to do the laundry. Eight days. More if he stayed out of anywhere dusty. Not that it mattered. With the stack of bills due, he would have to spend the rest of Cenna's steel on retaining a trader to manage the sale of his mother's furs, the dinnerware, and his father's better whiskey. Even then, it was only delaying the inevitable.

Chewing on old bread with a mug of Drace's morning coffee in hand, he sat at the dining table littered with heaps of ledgers and parchment. Sighing, he stood and started the task of carefully piling up the remnants of his investigation into organized stacks to later put back in their proper slots in the study. Elvan reached for the notebook in front of him, the one he'd used to compile his notes for two years. Two years of wasted time while Galmoth Logistics took on no additional work and he sold off contracts at a fraction of their value just to keep the lights on. He traced a finger along the stitched edge of the front cover, across the etched image of a tree, and down the fine silver key that held the leather strap in place.

He stared at the key.

Elvan snatched the notebook, raced around the stairs, and up to his parents' room. Tossing the armoire doors wide, he tripped on the edge, falling to his knees. He barely felt it while he unraveled the key from the attached strap, shoving it into the keyhole at the bottom right of the cabinet's back. Elvan twisted it with a loud click, followed by the slow grind of gears. Remembering Drace's mention of scratches on the floor, he jumped from the closet to pull at the side of it. The armoire shifted slightly. He pushed with his back against the wall, straining and grunting through gritted teeth. When he'd managed a few feet of space, Elvan saw the dark outline of a doorway that might have been to a closet or dressing room for an earlier generation of Galmoths.

Elvan wiped his brow, squinting into the room, hoping someone had left a candle behind. Seeing none, he ran to his room and returned with a lantern he lit with a spark of flint.

Elvan transferred the lantern from this aching hand he'd used to punch a solid mirror before squeezing behind the wardrobe. He stepped into the small room, counting seven crates in all. One stack, three high, loomed over his head. Stark in the harsh light, Elvan recognized them, each almost two feet on a side, sealed with a strip of gold paper, stenciled text signifying where in the Arcanym they belonged; where they had been taken from.

Elvan didn't have a crowbar. There might be one in the workshop or the stables, but he had no desire to see inside the crates. *Just more evidence against her.*

They're not open. Maybe she didn't know what was inside them. Maybe she just stashed a few here as an insurance policy.

He brushed a hand across the arcane steel lining the walls and floors. Even the ceiling and the back of the armoire reflected a dull luster. The same as how the crate in the warehouse was lined.

No, of course she knew what was in these crates. Knew enough to make the investment that would obscure the contents. How much steel did she spend creating this room?

That number was easy enough to look up, summing the invoices made out to Drace's shop.

Elvan stepped around the crates, finding a knee-high wood case in the back corner with nine sealed glass jars, each large enough to hold a half-gallon. Letters and numbers were charred into the side of the case, which might match a shipping manifest, but nothing he recognized on sight. He picked up the jar in the center, darker than the others. Lifting it to the light, metal shavings like iron filings filled it halfway and shifted with the jar's motion. Elvan set that down and picked up one of the other unlabeled jars, holding it in front of the lantern to look through the clear liquid. He gripped the cork stopper on its top and pulled it out with a twist. After one quick sniff of the acrid odor, he shoved the cork back in place, and carefully returned it to the case, far from the lantern.

"Nitric acid. What in all the hells were you up to, Mother?"

Elvan set the lantern on the floor, dropping wearily down on a crate beside the stack of three.

She wasn't personally raiding a secret vault of the most powerful artefacts. Someone of power allowed this, orchestrated it.

He sagged, holding his head just above his knees, squeezing his eyes tightly, trying to think.

Delphina was acting weird. Weirder than normal. She might have known something about this and mentioned being on royal business for the princess to sound more important. Though, maybe she wasn't just blowing smoke.

His eyes peeked open, noticing a square of parchment on the floor bearing a broken silver wax seal. *Drace would have seen that immediately.* Elvan hopped off the crate to pick it up, turning over the paper without an addressee. Unfolding it, he caught another slip of loose parchment that fell out, but his eyes went first to the letter, penned in plain letters.

"S, the proposed route is enclosed. -L"

There was no date, but the other slip read "A.N." across the top in the same nondescript hand, along with a list of numbers and named routes. Elvan recognized it from his research into Arca-Nult Holdings.

"L proposed the route. They set my mother up with a regular transfer of items from the Arcanym." Elvan set the letter on the stack of crates in front him, smoothing out the parchment, tracing the signature. "L. Princess Lorelai."

He chuckled softly. "This is too easy. Years with nothing. Now everything falls together at once."

What if Drace is involved in all this and— He stopped the thought with a shake of his head.

Lorelai... Why? She is the heir, and the king is getting on in years. She'll have the throne before long. Is she really smuggling dangerous magical artefacts out of the palace? Why? Why risk something so dangerous? What would happen if the contents of just one of these crates got into the wrong hands? How many did they move that Mother was able to steal seven? They were doing this for eight years, how much magical power did they redistribute?

Who else might know more?

Delphina.

No, definitely not going to her. Can't trust her.

After the inquisitor took his mother away and the king declared her exile, he also revoked nearly all royal contracts held by the Galmoths. Most private dealings fell away quickly as people and businesses did not want to be associated with a person guilty of something worthy of exile. A grieving Elvan couldn't scale back the company quickly enough. It collapsed under its own weight. The king's administrators reassigned those royal contracts to the Daggar or Serhane families, whose usual business was in security and agriculture, respectively, forcing them almost overnight to acquire the assets and knowledge to move goods across the continent. One of them may have taken over for Arca-Nult Holdings.

Elvan drummed his fingers on his lips, imagining himself in the Daggar family drawing room, sipping exotic tea and offering his services. *They'd be daft to not let me look over their books with the experience I carry. Two years with my mother's book is ten for any sane accountant.*

He smirked at his plan. It was so simple, it couldn't fail. *I find evidence of them carrying on the princess's smuggling plot and exchange it for mother's freedom.*

Except, what if the Serhane family is doing the smuggling and I go to Daggar first and waste six months tracing through their books? What if they obscure it through their own businesses, which I'm not at all familiar with?

What if no one took over the contract? What if mother finished the work, so they exiled her to keep her quiet?

Who can I show evidence to? Who isn't in on this? If this goes up to the king, there's no one higher. Who can stand against the crown?

Elvan ran his tongue over his teeth, sucking in the air still tainted by the brief release of acid, and glanced up at the tall stack of crates beside him. Pivoting to kneel on the crate he'd been sitting on, he raised himself up to look on the top of the tall stack. He let out a loud groan at seeing a stack of a half dozen pieces of parchment and scraps of notes lying there. He grabbed them, sitting down again with the lantern beside him.

Elvan recognized his mother's hand on the top page outlining an informal but confidential contract between Galmoth Logistics and Princess Lorelai Pearce, dated almost eleven years ago. The language that followed lacked any detail of what work would be done, but included a proposed payment schedule.

Stupid for the princess to let her name be plain on a contract, but Mother would have insisted. I wonder how these numbers would help the ledgers downstairs.

He leafed through the other pages. They were invoices and manifests of differing sizes, but he set them aside to examine the last sheet. Elvan stared down at another handwritten note from his mother, torn on the edge as if ripped from a notebook and dated close to three years ago.

I have been working closely with the princess these last seven years. I believe in her cause to rid Spheris of an unprecedented threat and we have met nothing but success, yet I begin to grow concerned about her hidden agendas. I have begun my own inquiry into her motives, but I sincerely hope to find nothing so I might later laugh at my paranoia.

"And how did that work out for you, Mother?"

His eyes lingered on the words "unprecedented threat," assuming that meant the Arcanym and the power stored there. Or perhaps Artists as a people.

He ran a finger down the jagged edge of the page. *Did she have a personal journal?* Elvan's mind went to imagining loose floor boards hiding a dusty leather notebook full of all his mother's most damning secrets.

Crates of artefacts, dated notes hinting at intrigue, jars of acid.

Was it illegal if she was smuggling for the princess? Is that even smuggling, or just doing a job? Did the king know? Mother must have found something that threatened the princess's position.

This is too much.

Elvan left the notes on the crates. With the lantern lamp in hand, he closed and locked the secret door before returning to the hall. He paused at his brother's open doorway on the way to his room, lingering a moment before stepping in. Other than a little less dust, no one would guess the room had not been used in years. He stepped nearer the bed with the thin sheet folded neatly at the foot, exactly as his brother did.

Drace's canvas rucksack peeked from where it sat on the floor, leaning against the foot of the bed. "You stay right there. Drace will be back, and be angry if he knows I went through the only stuff he has left in the world."

Will he be back? It's just small clothes and a portrait of his

Nana. Not worth having to deal with me again.

His eyes burned with a wave of guilt and shame. Even if Drace was an Artist, so what? He behaved no differently from anyone and far better than most. The king waged his fight against Artists while Elvan was raised with newspapers full of stories demonizing them, but was there a single story in his lifetime of one harming anyone? All the reports of injuries happened during raids, like yesterday when Drace was only defending himself. The news only acted to keep public fear and distrust high. Elvan wiped his eye with his sore hand and blinked back the tears. He caught the stray scent of incense from the oddity shop, causing the weight of his combined failures to wash over him. He sagged to his knees, allowing himself to be overwhelmed.

9

ELVAN WOKE, STIFF AND SORE, in his brother's bed with a tear stained pillow held tightly to his chest. He pushed himself up, twisting his back and neck, and moved to the narrow window showing the early hints of dawn. Elvan squinted into the north orchards, knowing the warehouse lay someone far in that direction, but still hoped to see Drace approaching the manor through the rows of fruit trees.

His plan to infiltrate the Daggar family flowed back to him, feeling silly and flawed in the first light of a new day.

If they took over the smuggling, they'll know my mother was doing it previously. They'll see right through me.

Elvan looked down at his mostly clean, but now rumpled, clothes and groaned. He would have to learn to iron, as well.

Maybe I should just give it all up and get a job as a valet for the Kae family. I can work with Cenna. I'll serve wine to the play-watchers.

He went to the kitchen to make coffee which, by pure accident, turned out to be an improvement over his previous attempt. He chewed on the last bit of bread while carrying stacks of parchment work into his mother's study, carefully organizing each ledger, folio, and scroll. The simple task of putting everything back in its place left his mind blissfully blank for an hour until only the leather notebook with a silver key remained on the dining table. He dropped that into the desk drawer he'd found it in and went to his father's nearest curio. Elvan raised the decanter to pour himself a drink, heedless of the early hour, but paused, watching the amber liquor slosh against the delicate crystal. Instead, he took the full bottle to the back patio overlooking the gardens.

The arborists were some of Elvan's first cuts and almost two years without a trim left the gardens wild. Manicured hedges were now shapeless blobs. A flowerless and fruitless leafy vine was choking out the rose trestles. Shrubs crowded the paths leading deeper into the garden. Despite looking a mess, Elvan took a deep breath, enjoying the fresh, peaty smell. *It must have rained a little last night.*

Elvan's mind spun over the same ideas of what he might do next. Go to the Daggar family. Talk to the king. Talk to Inquisitor Nilranke. Go to the princess and join her scheme. Sell the manor and move somewhere with warmer winters. The level in the whiskey decanter went down as the sun came up. Elvan pushed into the musty, deep cushions, playing a little game with himself. If he thought about anything sad or pointless, he drank. He never considered how to win or lose the game, but it was over quickly.

Elvan woke with a start as the empty crystal decanter shattered against the tile beneath him. Someone moved behind the glass windows. He tried to focus, pushing himself upright, but his vision swam, his hand slipping on the chair's armrest.

"Drace?" he called out, managing to get his feet under him to standing, though leaning heavily on the chair back.

She entered in a twirl of pleated petticoats.

"Delphina." Elvan hiccupped and his chest ached where Drace held it during the spell.

"By the Six, Elvan, it's barely noon." She snapped open a paper fan, waving it lazily by her neck. "Did you sleep out here?"

"Twice in as many days. What an honor. Why are you here?"

"I am a Duchess. I can go wherever I bloody well want."

"Go away." The garden tilted, and Elvan gripped the chair back with both hands.

"Your hair looks like a rat's nest. Still." Delphina stepped onto the patio, circling Elvan but keeping her distance. "I see you cleaned up your mess on the dining table. Expecting company?"

Elvan didn't trust the whiskey to stay down if he opened his mouth to respond.

Delphina stopped pacing with a loud, drawn-out sigh. "I'm here to warn you, Elvan. Princess Lorelai needs something our mother hid in the house. She will seize the manor and everything in it if you don't give her what she needs." She closed her fan and stepped nearer. "Please, Elvan. Give her what she needs and she won't hold you in contempt, or obstruction, or whatever the jargon is."

Elvan watched his sister for all her usual tricks; one of her feigned niceties to get what she wanted. He was sure this was no different from any other time with her, but his bleary, drunken eyes couldn't clearly see it.

"What does she need?" He hiccupped painfully again.

"I don't know, but if you say you'll help her, you can ask her yourself. We can go to the palace right now. You can even ride with Ser Vazadon. I'm sure you'd love to hear one of his stories."

"The Duchess herself came all the way out here just to fetch me? What a sweet little sister."

"Are you coming, or are you going to make this difficult?"

Elvan had a dozen reasons to refuse, but none so succinct as, "I don't want to." *Maybe if I go, I'll learn something to use against her.* He snorted to himself, wondering if he could outsmart anyone after so much whiskey.

"What's so funny?"

Elvan shook his head. "Nothing. Fine."

"Good boy." She patted his cheek twice and left in a twirl before he could push her hand away. "Don't bother getting changed. They'll clean you up at the palace."

"I'm selling the manor," he called after her.

She stepped back around the glass doors, into view. "Say that again?"

"There's nothing left here. You were right to marry Prince Marshall and get out."

She took a single step forward, brushing her auburn hair behind her left ear. "As much as I love hearing you say I'm right, it only shows your ignorance. I didn't marry Marshall at fifteen to get out of the family. Mum set it up to bring our ties closer to the crown. Then she got herself thrown out almost immediately, leaving me to improvise. Of course I had to distance myself from this House and the shitshow you've let it become. I sacrificed everything for a House you've left for the rats. You're a failure, Elvan."

Elvan opened his mouth, but any decent response eluded him. He just stood with his jaw slack.

Delphina rolled her eyes, scoffing. "Whatever. Let's go."

Elvan followed her through the house, out the front door, and into the waiting carriage she pointed him toward. He slumped against the window with his head on the cool glass. The wagon rocked a moment later as Ser Vazadon entered to sit across from him on the plush velvet seat, leaning his sheathed swords against the wall. Elvan recognized the hilt of the blade he'd always seen the knight carry his whole life, but the other was a thing of beauty, inlaid with silver and pearl. He thought to ask Vazadon about it, but the answer was never a simple "I purchased it" with the knight. An animated story was the last thing Elvan wanted at the moment.

"Young master," the old knight grinned with genuine delight. "What a pleasure it is to spend this time with you after so long apart. Your sister tells me you wished to hear a story, but now that I see you, I am less sure."

Elvan pushed away from the window to sit straighter. "Did she tell you why she came here?"

Ser Vazadon leaned forward to straighten Elvan's collar and smooth the shoulders of his shirt. "The Duchess tells me very little, which is her privilege."

"I wish you'd stayed with us."

"Your sister needed a protector."

"Her lesser prince husband couldn't provide one?"

The driver in the lead called out as the carriage smoothly accelerated.

"What has she been doing since moving to the palace?" Elvan asked.

"She spends much of her time reading in Prince Marshall's library. She takes tea with Princess Lorelai at least twice a week."

"What do they discuss?"

"I would not know. I escort her between appointments, but never overhear. It is a skill I have developed, my selective hearing."

"You walk her around, but have no dealings with her personally?"

"Correct."

Elvan scoffed. "You're wasted there."

Vazadon shrugged. "Biscuit?" He offered Elvan a round tin

from the seat beside him.

Elvan pulled off the lid and shoved a slightly stale piece of shortbread in his mouth, glad for something to soak up some of the whiskey. "What about your book? Have you finished it?"

Vazadon touched his breast pocket and shook his head. "Duty keeps me on my feet all day."

"If you stayed here, you'd have that and a dozen more done by now." Elvan turned to face out the window. The slow rock of the carriage and motion of the passing fields churned his stomach, forcing him to look away after a moment.

"How are you, young master? It cannot be easy, being alone in the manor."

Elvan sniffed. "The place is full of ghosts and bad memories. But no, last night was my first alone in it and I don't even remember falling asleep."

Vazadon narrowed his eyes. "I thought Cenna quit two days ago?"

Elvan cursed under his breath, which Vazadon clearly heard by how his eyebrows raised. He watched the expectant interest in the knight's eyes, knew that if he trusted anyone within a thousand miles of Spheris, it was this man.

"I met someone in town while following up on an invoice. A shopkeeper. A boy."

The right corner of Vazadon's lip curled upward. "Go on."

"A man, not a boy." Elvan cleared his throat. "He's a few years older than me. While I was in his shop, something happened and there was a fire. I offered him a place to stay until he could get back on his feet."

Vazadon leaned forward. "I might have heard about this. Is this the most recent incident of the inquisitors raiding an Artist shop?"

"Yes." Elvan sucked his lower lip. "But Drace isn't an Artist. I mean, he used magic in front of me, but he was holding an artefact and I think he was saying you don't have to be an Artist to use one, but I had a fit and ran."

"Is that so?" The knight leaned back and scratched at his white beard. "I sense a fair amount of detail missing, but we have two hours ahead of us. I find it useful to start with the broad details when first deciding a story's structure. Where is Drace now?"

"I don't know." Elvan leaned forward and focused on his hands between his knees.

"You met this man and, because of the circumstances, invited him to your home. You must have taken a quick liking to him. Are you sad not knowing where he is now?"

"I mean, we only just met, but…"

"But?"

"We seemed to get along well, but I messed it up so badly. He said he liked me." Elvan chuckled and choked back a sob.

"I have always thought you most likable, young master."

Elvan rolled his eyes. "Not just liked me, he said he… I asked if he fancies me and he said yes. He made me jump through hoops to get the words out, but it was charming."

"Do you feel the same toward him?"

"I mean, we only just met."

Ser Vazadon raised his bushy eyebrows.

"I do, yes," Elvan said after a moment.

"These things can happen quite suddenly. There is nothing that forces the heart to wait some requisite period."

"There was never a love interest in any of the stories you told me."

Vazadon sank forward, mirroring Elvan's posture, reaching to squeeze both of Elvan's hands in one firm grip. "I must have told you and your siblings about fifty of my adventures from my younger days. Staying up late by the hearth while your parents were away… Those are some of my happiest memories from the last twenty years, but I was always careful to edit the details. There were questions I did not want the three of you asking."

Elvan looked up with a smirk. "I'm sure you exaggerated a lot of details, Ser Vazadon."

The knight leaned back against the seat. "Hardly. I was an adventurer of the highest degree. Me and Elruthon."

"Who?"

"That is exactly the question I could not stand to be asked then. Elruthon Spearguard was my partner in every way; in our adventures and in life. He and I crossed the wide oceans together, trekking across the lands, taking on jobs for steel or gold or polished shells, whatever the local currency was. We only needed enough to pay for a bed to share and the next day's meal. We adventured for the sake of adventure, not fame or wealth."

Elvan bit back a chuckle. "I always thought of you as, I don't know… chaste."

"Most children think and hope that about the adults in their lives."

"What happened?"

"We killed a daemon lord — I believe I told you that story with the magic sword — and barely escaped the lair with our lives. Elruthon wanted to give up adventuring and settle by the sea, but I refused and walked away. Your mother hired me within a few months. I realized later I was afraid of settling down. Elruthon and I only knew a life of action and I thought our relationship would fail if our situation changed so drastically."

"That's so sad… You didn't give it a chance."

"It is my greatest regret, and that is why I told you. You are so young, too young for the regrets of what could have been. I hope you find Drace and give each other a proper chance."

"And what if he wants nothing to do with me now?"

Vazadon raised his hands with a shrug. "Would you rather not know?"

"Fair. Where is Elruthon now?"

"He has a place on the cliffs overlooking the sea in Glenmany. I visited him recently, but our opportunity for a relationship has passed."

"I'm sorry... Is Elruthon with someone else now?"

"No." The knight brushed a thumb under his left eye and Elvan felt that added finality of the single word response. *Elruthon's place by the cliffs isn't a cute cottage.*

"I'm sorry..."

Vazadon turned to look out the window. "Thank you."

Elvan chanced watching the scenery, but the movement was still too much. He bit into another biscuit.

The old knight turned back and cleared his throat. "Enough of times past. Tell me everything about Drace. What was the first thing you noticed about him?"

Elvan chuckled and bit his thumb. "He's tall and his shirt was tight."

Vazadon leaned forward, steepling his fingers against his lower lip, his face impassive. "Go on."

It took Elvan a half hour to not preface every sentence with "I know we just met, but..." Two hours passed in a blur with him admitting to every stolen glance and how Drace's sarcastic grin made his knees a little weak. He even confessed to the less pure thoughts, like how good Drace looked sprawled on the floor of his mother's armoire in just those loose trousers or the other ideas that went through his mind as Drace held him so close in the warehouse.

"The effective radius of illusion magic can be fickle," said Ser Vazadon, showing no surprise at hearing how Drace made them invisible.

"You really have dealt with magic before, haven't you?"

"I am sorry you thought my life's events were a fiction. Unregulated magic may be illegal on this continent, but there is a lot more world out there."

"I mean, you told us about an invisible castle and a ring that controlled the weather," Elvan smirked. "We all thought they were ridiculous fantasies."

Ser Vazadon hummed thoughtfully. "I censored my stories for the minds of children and may have overemphasized sections for dramatic purpose, but the core details were truthful."

Elvan thought through the many long nights around the hearth and still couldn't believe those wild stories might have any basis in reality.

"We are nearly at the palace," Ser Vazadon said, leaning against the window. "What is your plan, young master?"

"I don't know. I don't know what Lorelai wants. I'm pretty sure she set my mother up with the trade route that led to her exile, so I'm not feeling the friendliest at the moment. And still a little drunk."

Ser Vazadon sighed as the carriage rocked to a gentle stop. "Remain calm. I do not know Princess Lorelai for allowing a lengthy discourse. Do not give her a reason to act brashly against you."

"It sounds like you don't particularly trust the princess."

"Though I am a knight of the kingdom, with fealty to the crown, I make no false claims of any personal love for the princess. She has added undue stress during her father's failing health, turning the people against Artists. My duty is to protect your sister and it is that which keeps me here."

A footman jerked the carriage door open, placing a set of stairs.

The old knight put a hand on Elvan's shoulder as the younger man stood to leave. "My skill for selective hearing is not flawless. Tell them nothing more than you must, young master. Tell them even less, if you can." He nodded his chin toward the open door.

Dark clouds gathered overhead, casting a shroud behind the soaring, gilded columns of the palace.

10

THE PALACE'S SPIRALING TOWERS TWISTED up toward the gathering clouds as banners flapped in the rising wind, signaling which of the royal family was at home. Delphina's retinue poured from the carriages, filling the yard before they could file through the tall, polished doors at the front of the palace.

Thunder rumbled in the distance.

"Let us get inside before the downpour," said Ser Vazadon. "It was a pleasure, young master." He struck a fist to his chest and bowed at the waist. As much as Elvan wanted to return the gesture, he could sense the judging eyes of a hundred valets, maids, footmen, grooms, gardeners, and butlers upon him. Vazadon was still a servant, and he was a noble. Elvan inclined his head and started to turn, but froze in place.

This man was more a parent to me than my actual parents. He's more a friend than anyone else I have.

Elvan fell forward to wrap his arms around the old knight, not caring what all the king's servants might whisper after their shifts. Vazadon laughed gently and put his arms around Elvan for a tight embrace.

"Go on, boy. You do not wish to keep the princess waiting." Ser Vazadon pushed Elvan to arm's length and gave his shoulders one last squeeze before turning him toward the door. "Remain strong."

Delphina, flanked by a retinue of soldiers and ladies-in-waiting, strode through the main double doors with her chin high and without a glance to her brother. A valet with his red hair slicked back and wearing a crisp white shirt under a dark vest took Elvan by the elbow to guide him to a side entrance, followed by two royal soldiers. Elvan shook his arm to free himself, but the man's grip was iron.

"The princess wants you cleaned up," the valet said unnecessarily while they passed through the narrow back passages of the palace. They arrived in a humid room no larger than his bedroom at home. A porcelain tub took up the majority of the center and a fresh suit draped across the chaise beside it.

Elvan peeked into the steaming tub, sniffing at the rosewood scent drifting from the milky water. "Looks like you expected me."

"I will return in twenty minutes to take you to Her Majesty. I will not be kept waiting." The valet tugged the door closed behind him.

Lightning flashed outside the narrow window followed by a boom of thunder rattling the tile under his feet a second later.

Fitting.

Elvan stripped, leaving his rumpled clothes in a wad on the floor, and slid into water that was almost uncomfortably hot. He sank to his ears to blow bubbles across the surface and piece together what brought him to this moment. His slow investigation into his mother's case only escalated when he stepped into Drace's shop. That lead to thoughts of Drace's breath across his ear while casting the spell, which lead to the memory of Drace standing at the end of the dock.

He shook away the thought and focused instead on what to expect from Princess Lorelai. He'd met her on a few occasions, but never for any extended conversation. Closer to his parents' age, the king's only child from his first of three wives largely kept her political leanings to herself and filled her days catering to foreign dignitaries. Elvan's opinions of the princess mostly came second hand, and predominantly from the skewed perspective of his younger sister. After her betrothal to one of the princess's much younger half-brothers, Delphina made a point to bring up all the grand travel opportunities she would have when the princess became queen.

If the princess acted against my mother, what can I do about it? What evidence would I have to provide for her to meet some justice for what she's done? Maybe nothing... Maybe I just have to mitigate what else the princess can do against my family name.

As Elvan worked fingers through his mess of hair, he caught the whiff of smoke even over the scented and oiled bath water, but he escaped from two fires in as many days. With no way to tell time and a feeling the valet was dead serious about his job, he scrubbed quickly. He dried off using the softest towel he ever felt and was just pulling on the tan cotton trousers when the door burst open. The valet with red hair sighed and stormed in.

Thunder rumbled and rain pelted the window as the valet tugged and yanked with practiced efficiency, forcing Elvan into a starched white shirt and a dark high-cut coat. He pulled at Elvan's hair while muttering dark things. Finally, he held out a pair of white gloves as Elvan stood from putting on the obviously fashionable and immediately uncomfortable slippers.

"I don't wear gloves," said Elvan.

"You will wear gloves when presented to Her Majesty." It was the first discernible thing the man said since barging into the room.

Elvan snatched them from the valet's hand. "Then I'll wait until I see her coming to put them on."

The valet stepped back to consider his work and shook his head with a drawn-out sigh. "I do my best with the time provided, but I'm no miracle worker. Follow me and keep up."

The soldiers snapped into formation behind while they moved through more of the narrow halls and finally entered a grand reception room lined with painted columns and three delicate crystal chandeliers. The valet ignored the grandeur and continued to the far end, where a circle of couches was nestled into a recessed pit. A table set in the center of the pit held a glass bowl filled with colorful spheres of different sizes. The valet stepped aside and Elvan descended the two short steps. He glanced up at the domed glass roof that flowed into the floor-to-ceiling windows overlooking a garden ten feet below. Rain slammed against the glass in sharp waves that perfectly matched Elvan's accelerated breath and blurred the view of the vibrant green gardens beyond.

Elvan waved the tails of his coat out of the way to sit.

"Gloves," barked the valet.

Elvan groaned and stood straight to tug them on. "Stupid hand socks."

"Mr. Galmoth, the charges against you are quite serious. I recommend you treat them with appropriate respect."

"Treat the gloves with respect? Wait… Charges?"

The valet's expression remained impassive.

Lightning flashed with an immediate boom of thunder that rattled the glass.

"Follow." The valet spun and made for the single door opposite where they entered the reception room. He rapped once on the inlaid wood of deep floral carvings and pushed it silently inward.

Elvan expected to be taken to some quiet meeting room to speak with Princess Lorelai, not the throne room. He'd been in here plenty of times, though not in the last four years, and never through this side door. Soldiers flanked the six wide steps leading to where she sat upon the gilded throne high on a dais. A bejeweled silver tiara sparkled in her hair, as dark as a moonless night and fashionably streaked with gray. Her flawless bronze skin made her age impossible to guess as she stared down at Elvan with disinterest in her amber eyes, the same hue as Drace's.

"Your Majesty, Elvan Galmoth, Head of House Galmoth," announced the valet. He gave a stiff bow and left through the side door. The soldiers who escorted him since the bath pressured Elvan to approach the dais.

Cue Courtly Elvan.

He stopped at the first step and bowed with all the practice of his upbringing. "Princess Lorelai, I thought we may speak somewhere more private. The matters I wish to discuss are sensitive."

The princess shifted in her father's throne. The chamberlain on the step below her cleared his throat and consulted the notebook tucked in his elbow. "Elvan Galmoth, you are charged with obstruction of justice and arson. How do you plead?"

"Charges? Arson?" Elvan raised his arms in a shrug. "What?"

"How do you plead?"

Delphina entered from a door behind the princess and swept the layers of her gown aside to take a seat beside the throne. Elvan waited for Ser Vazadon to enter as well, to have one friendly face in the room, but the door remained closed.

"Not guilty on all counts." Elvan crossed his arms, but immediately felt the aggression of that stance. He folded his hands behind his back and rolled back his shoulders instead, trying to retain the courtly decorum Cenna had instilled in him.

"You told me, Elvan," Delphina said calmly with her hands in her lap, "while I was on official business for the princess, that mother had no warehouses. Then Inquisitor Nilranke finds a storehouse full of crates stamped with the red ship and is forced to flee as it's set ablaze."

Elvan's fists tightened behind his back. "I didn't start any fires."

"So, you don't deny withholding information about the warehouse from me? From the princess?" Delphina raised her eyebrows.

"I already denied that. Maybe you didn't hear me over the starched ruffling of your dress."

"Mr. Galmoth," warned the chamberlain.

"I shouldn't say more until I have legal counsel," said Elvan. "I came, thinking this would be a discussion, not to have charges thrown against me."

The chamberlain looked back at the princess, whose expression never wavered.

"You should be aware, Mr. Galmoth," said the chamberlain, "that innocence is self-evident. Asking for legal advice is as good as an admission of guilt."

"Is this how your father treated my mother?" Elvan brought his fists to his sides as the heat rose in his cheeks.

"Watch it, Elvan," Delphina said.

"I know it was you, Princess, who smuggled artefacts from the city and the Arcanym. I don't know to who, but probably some foreign power. You're the traitor here!" Elvan's breath caught in his throat, immediately regretting the words that would end him.

Delphina and the chamberlain gasped. Princess Lorelai remained as stoic as the line of soldiers.

"A bold claim," said the princess in her rich, husky voice.

The chamberlain gaped and turned back to her. Clearing his throat again, he snapped back to Elvan. "Mr. Galmoth, have you any means to support such a statement?"

Elvan blew out a long, shaky breath, thinking of the single letter in his mother's secret room and her journal entry suspecting the princess in… something. It was barely enough to spark interest in an avid conspiracy theorist, let alone actual evidence. He licked his lips and squared his shoulders. There was no going back now. "Yes, I do."

Princess Lorelai leaned back and drummed her nails on the throne's armrest. "And what are those means?"

"Correspondence between you and my mother outlining the deal to steal artefacts from the Arcanym. Artefacts stolen by the Sovereign King a century and a half ago."

Lorelai scoffed.

"Have you told anyone else of this alleged evidence?" asked the chamberlain.

"Yes."

The chamberlain looked back at the princess, who pivoted her gaze to her right, to Delphina, who shook her head twice. Lorelai looked back to the chamberlain with disinterest in her eyes and twirled a single finger.

The man cleared his throat. "Slander against the crown constitutes no less than sedition and treason. Do you wish to revise your statement, Elvan Galmoth?"

Elvan stumbled back a step with weak knees. His wide eyes stared up at his sister, who seemed similarly surprised.

Barely five seconds passed before the chamberlain cleared his throat again. "Elvan Galmoth, for your high crimes made evident to all present on this day, we sentence you to death. All remaining assets held by the Galmoth family are now the property of the crown." He glanced at the notepad in his elbow. "At sunrise tomorrow, you will be hanged by the neck until dead."

"A moment," said Lorelai, drawing Elvan's eyes upward. Delphina leaned across her armrest, whispering to the princess. Lorelai nodded and Delphina drew back to her own chair. "Chamberlain, no matter the crimes, the crown cannot take a noble's head, especially for one so young and untempered. In my benevolence, I reduce the sentence to five years exile. Perhaps that will be a sufficient time that he sees his error."

Words of anger bubbled to the front of Elvan's mind but could find no purchase to be said in his confusion.

The princess waved a finger toward the door through which Elvan entered the throne room. "Put him in a private suite until everything is prepared."

Soldiers grabbed his elbows, pulling him toward the side of the room and tearing Elvan's eyes from his sister, who looked everywhere but at him.

They pulled him a few steps away when the main doors of the throne room burst inward. Inquisitor Nilranke strode forward confidently, clacking his steel cane with each step and leaving a trail of rainwater on the polished tile in his passing. Behind him, two guards dragged a hooded figure wearing a fine suit.

"Inquisitor Nilranke," snapped the chamberlain, "this is most irregular!"

Nilranke froze at the foot of the dais and offered a crisp salute and bow. "My deepest apologies, Your Majesty. We have captured the Artist of interest."

"You bring an Artist before the princess?" The chamberlain descended the steps to stand before the inquisitor, as if he alone could defend her from a magic user.

"He is quite subdued after our interrogations." Nilranke ripped the burlap hood from the prone figure.

"Drace!" Elvan lurched forward, slipping from the soldiers' grip, but they immediately latched onto him again. He was close enough to see Drace's left eye was swollen shut and blood soaked his shirt from a split lip.

Nilranke grabbed a handful of Drace's hair and yanked his head back. "Not surprising that a Galmoth would know an Artist criminal. Your Majesty, I caught him trying to sneak back into what remains of his shop. This was all he had on his person." Nilranke waved and the soldier who dragged Drace in stepped forward to offer a small wooden box to the chamberlain, who peeked inside and climbed the steps to offer the box to Lorelai. Delphina snatched her hand into the box, pulling out the gold pocket watch.

"This is my father's! Thief!" She turned the watch over in her hands and looked down at Elvan. "Wait, you said this man's name in your drunken stupor this morning. It's true. You're working with Artists."

Lorelai turned the owl statue artefact in her hands, but with no recognition that Elvan could discern at his distance.

"Let him go!" Elvan jerked against the arms holding him, to no use. "Let him go and I'll tell you everything I know, turn over every document, swear myself to secrecy. Whatever you want of me."

"You must realize the one-sidedness of such an offer," said Princess Lorelai. "Very well, Elvan Galmoth, may you never say I am cruel. You obviously care for the wellbeing of this man, so rather than the usual course given to Artist filth, he can join you in exile. Though the term is now life." She stood and took a deep breath. "Inquisitor Nilranke, you have tracked a mess through my throne room. I expect everything to be spotless when I return from lunch. Put them both in the dungeon for now." The princess spun and left through the back door with Delphina close behind.

Nilranke bowed to the princess's back and left through the main door. Soldiers picked up Drace and pushed Elvan after him, down a long colonnade, and into the stinging rain. He tried to gather any thoughts, but his mind only focused on Drace's limp form a few paces ahead of him. Down six flights of six steps each, Elvan stumbled across the palace's interior courtyard. Nilranke waved them to a door with a heavy padlock and left in the opposite direction through the shallow puddles in the tiled ground. A soldier unlocked and opened the door before they arrived, revealing a small landing with a desk and chair and beyond, steep stone stairs winding into darkness. The fashionable slippers were never intended for such terrain and were immediately soaked with rainwater. Elvan would have slipped on every step if not for the soldiers holding him.

Lit by a single gas lamp, the path straightened to a short hall lined with stout iron bars. Rusty hinges screamed as a soldier pulled open a door and others shoved Drace into the cell. He fell in a heap on his face, pushed up with a hand to roll to his side, and lay still.

"Shove 'em in together and let's get back to the game," one guard muttered. They jabbed Elvan, and he stumbled to his knees beside Drace. The door ground closed with a loud clank of the lock and the soldiers filed up the stairs.

Elvan fell over Drace, holding his face toward the dim light, but couldn't tell the extent of the wounds. He ripped off his gloves, wetted them in the water streaming down the wall, and dabbed the soft cotton gently against Drace's brow.

"I'm sorry. I don't understand how, but this is my fault you're in this, I'm sure."

Drace groaned.

Elvan rolled Drace to his back on the slick, damp stone floor and scooted around to elevate the shopkeeper's head, resting it on his thigh. He ran the glove through the cool water again, dabbing at Drace's forehead.

"I shouldn't have run from the warehouse. That was stupid. I was stupid. I can give all the excuses I can think of, but I'm just… I was scared."

Drace flopped an arm over his head, fumbling for Elvan's other hand. He found it and pulled it back to rest on his chest with a lethargic squeeze.

"Seeing your face as the ferry pulled away was the worst I've ever felt," Elvan said and bit his lip. "Even worse than when they took my mother away. I knew it was my fault, my doing. Now exile… I'm so sorry."

Drace's lips parted with a gasp and a wince. "We'll have… plenty of time for all that." He winced.

Elvan forced a grin in response. "Try to rest."

He hummed the tune Cenna often sang to him after tucking him in at night. The song must have had a name, but never one he knew. After a few minutes, Elvan set aside the glove and felt Drace's deepening respite. His own mind finally felt free of the cluttered confusion from the throne room, floating into an odd emotionless clarity. He saw no means of thwarting their fate and settled into thoughts of what would happen next.

What are the conditions like on the ship that will take us to where people are exiled?

How long will the voyage take?

Will Mother be there?

The crown made few announcements of exile as a punishment,

that was usually reserved for political prisoners. They threw criminals, including Artists, into prisons outside of Spheris, with execution still being an option, though rare. The more he thought back through years of newspapers remarking on the crimes and punishments within the kingdom, he remembered fewer than ten exiles, and none that returned from it.

Elvan dozed, catching himself twice before he tipped forward.

He woke himself with a sudden rasping snore and pushed his head from Drace's stomach, sitting up and lacing his fingers through Drace's hand across his chest, feeling the steady rise and fall. His breath caught in his throat, noticing the figure silhouetted against the gas lamp. Wearing a wide hat and wider dress, he guessed at who stood before him.

"Why are you here?" he groaned.

"I saved your life. The least you can do is thank me."

Elvan sighed and looked down at Drace. "Thank you."

Delphina stepped closer to the bars. "Were you telling the truth? Do you have evidence against the princess?"

"Does it matter anymore?"

"Tell me where it is, Elvan. I might be able to act in your stead. If I can prove the princess is behind the smuggling, maybe I can bring her to justice."

"So you know about the smuggling." It wasn't a question.

"Of course. She's been at it for a decade, moving artefacts from the vault under the palace."

Elvan looked up at her. "The Arcanym. To what end?"

"To overthrow her father."

"How?"

Delphina sighed, her expression muted in shadow. "I don't think the how matters as much as the why."

"Then why? She gets the throne when the king dies. No one is contesting her ascendancy. Why spend a decade working to overthrow him just to get something a few years sooner?"

"I'm close to figuring that out."

"Why are you telling me all this now? We could have worked together if you'd been honest with me days ago."

"I was hoping to protect you. The less you knew, the better. Please, where is the evidence linking to the princess?"

Elvan touched his palm to Drace's brow.

What's the harm?

"It's not concrete, but enough for me to put it together. There are notes from the princess detailing the route used to smuggle the artefacts. It leads to the warehouse I'm accused of setting afire. That's where we found that owl statue."

Elvan couldn't tell his sister's expression with her back to the light, but her body language remained steady.

"The owl statue the princess took from the box? That's an artefact?" she asked.

Part of Elvan screamed to shut up, that Delphina would somehow use all the information for her own gain, no matter how it hurt him and Drace. Another part just felt good pretending to trust her and tell his story.

"Yes. Drace used it to hide us from Nilranke in the warehouse. He's not an Artist, but I think anyone can use an artefact with training."

"Hmm," Delphina hummed. "Where in the house is all this evidence?"

Elvan opened his mouth, ready to describe the secret room lined with arcane steel behind their mother's armoire, but he blew out a long breath instead. If Drace was right, those crates might hold artefacts with enough power to, in the right hands, bring Spheris to its knees. He considered her shadow stretching through the prison bars for a moment before deciding what he already knew: he couldn't entrust his sister with the truth. "I hid the note in mother's study, in one of the folios on the left wall as you enter."

"That narrows it down, but not by much. Thank you, Elvan. I may never see you again, but know you did your kingdom a great service. Even if I'm too late to save the king from Lorelai's plans, I might temper the future by holding this information."

Elvan snapped to full attention. "Holding the... Extortion? You're going to use this to control the princess?"

"It's none of your concern now, dear brother." She turned to leave, but paused. Elvan saw the glint in her eye from the gas lamp as her lip twisted to a grin.

"Why are you like this?" he nearly shouted.

Delphina hesitated and turned back toward the cell.

"You're always the victim," said Elvan. "Everyone is always acting against you. You've always been like that, even as a child. What is the point of all this, Delphina?"

Delphina adjusted the silk glove on her left forearm. "Ambition, dear brother. Something you wouldn't understand, by how you've run the family business into the shitter these last years."

"You married a prince, but you're no closer to the crown. What do you hope to get from controlling the princess? Assuming she doesn't immediately poison you and claim it an accident, what would ever make you happy?"

Delphina sniffed and turned into the light so Elvan could see her sneer. "Like you're one to give life advice." She strode toward the stairs. "Say hello to Mum."

11

HOURS PASSED; OR PERHAPS ONLY a few very long moments. Elvan stared at the gentle flicker of the gaslight, considering what machinations he enabled by telling Delphina everything. Not everything, but enough. He convinced himself it didn't matter. Even if he screamed the entire way to the ship that would take him to a lonely island in the center of the ocean, no one would listen. The princess branded him a traitor. The palace staff would gossip about his ravings, but they'd move on to something else within a week and no one would talk about him again. Whether Lorelai's plan against her father or Delphina's plan against the princess succeeded, no one would attempt his rescue. Elvan and Drace were about to start a new life together.

He held a glimmer of hope that he'd soon see his mother again, but how would she feel to see her son fall to the same fate? *Will she be proud I stood up to the princess and her corruption, or angry that I didn't succeed? Did I actually stand up to anyone? I only talked back to her and look where it got me.*

The thunder moved off, but rain still poured down their cell wall. It formed a river that ran along the back wall of the small prison to a lake coalescing in the other cell. Elvan couldn't guess at the depth, but saw no dry spots in the light reflecting off the water's oily surface. After another indeterminable period, the door above opened with a bang and the rustle of loud metal echoed down the stairs. Two soldiers stepped into the gaslight and tossed two sets of heavy manacles through the bars.

"Put those on."

Elvan shifted his leg and set Drace's head gently on the stone floor. He stood, brushing his hands on his borrowed cotton trousers, and tugged at the hem of the dark coat. He mustered what dignity he could and leaned to grab the irons. Except he couldn't lift them both at once and had to drag them back.

Drace cracked his good eye as Elvan knelt beside him. "What's…?" He tried pushing himself to a seated position, and Elvan helped with an arm around his shoulders. "Elvan?" Drace touched a finger to Elvan's cheek.

"You're finally awake." Elvan tried to smile.

"Where are we?" Drace looked around the cell.

"In prison. They want us to put on the manacles."

Drace looked down at the thick chains in Elvan's hand. "Have you considered fighting them?"

"Of course I've considered it. I'm an accountant, I'm great at calculating odds. Now that you're awake, I think they've about doubled."

"Hurry up in there," yelled the guard.

Drace waved for Elvan to pass him a pair. "We'll go along with them for now."

The cuffs ratcheted to fit snuggly at the wrists, but the two feet of long chain was heavy enough that Elvan couldn't raise his hands above his waist. They stood, and a soldier opened the door with screaming hinges. One checked the tight fit of the bindings and went up the stairs first, with the other trailing the pair. Outside, Elvan blinked up at the dark clouds choking the early dawn sky as rain fell gently across his face. He looked down at the water pooling between the tiles, and finally to the windowless carriage drawn by two chestnut horses to his left.

Elvan stumbled at seeing the man in white quilted armor standing beside it, resting a hand on the pommel of one of the two swords at his hip.

"Ser Vazadon!"

The old knight waved down Elvan's enthusiasm. "Guards, leave us a moment."

"Sir, we're…" the soldier in front started to protest, but bowed and went to the far side of the carriage with the others.

Vazadon sped forward to wrap his arm around Elvan's shoulders, pressing his soaked uniform into his face. "Words cannot describe how I have failed you, young master."

With his wrists bound, Elvan could do nothing but wait for the embrace to end. Ser Vazadon stepped back and ran a hand through his wet, gray hair, looking down at Elvan with wide, red rimmed eyes.

"You've no blame in this," said Elvan. "This is all from me running my mouth to the princess and my sister."

"The Duchess told me, but I know her well enough to doubt she told me everything." His eyes shifted to Elvan's side. "You must be Drace. Master Elvan had a great number of things to say about you."

Drace looked up, showing Vazadon his swollen eye and split lip. "Hi."

"Nilranke's handiwork," Vazadon scowled and moved his hand back to rest on his sword pommel. "That man is a rabid beast."

"I noticed that earlier," Elvan said, gesturing as best he could at Vazadon's hip. "When did you start carrying two swords?"

"Always hungry for a story," Vazadon laughed wryly and tousled Elvan's hair. "I have not the time for that tale, but it will be the first I tell upon your safe return, young master. You are far too stubborn and crafty to not find a way home."

Elvan doubted the platitudes, but found some comfort in the effort.

"Is this how it was for my mother?"

Ser Vazadon sucked in a startled breath. "That is an unfair comparison."

"No?" Elvan looked down at his chained wrists. "What now?"

"I wish I knew, young master. You and your siblings were the nearest I ever had to children. I… I know it is of little consolation to hear how I feel I have failed here."

"Well, hopefully I'm stubborn and crafty enough to see you again." Elvan forced a wide, mirthless grin.

"Ser Vazadon," said the soldier stepping around the carriage. "We must be off."

Vazadon wrapped his arms around Elvan again, squeezing tighter than before. He turned to Drace and put a hand on the shopkeeper's shoulder. "Take care of each other and you will see this through."

The soldier opened the back of the carriage and waved Elvan and Drace to step in on their own. They took seats on the benches opposite each other.

At least they aren't pushing us around.

Elvan raised his hands and nodded to the cuffs. "I don't suppose you could take—" The door slammed closed. "—these off."

His eyes adjusted quickly to the dim interior, lit only by thin horizontal slits along the ceiling that offered some indirect lighting, but no view of the outside. Elvan could still only barely make out the outline of Drace's face.

The carriage rocked to motion.

"Drace, I'm sorry."

"Sorry for what?"

"For getting you exiled! What happened with you? Why did you go back to your shop?"

Drace rubbed his head. "I was worried Nilranke and his crew would be right outside, as you were crawling around screaming about me being an Artist, but I saw no sign of them. I took the next ferry and went back to Spheris, to my shop. Stupid, I know. I was hoping there'd be something left, but was happy to see it completely down to cinders. There's nothing to hold against me or Nana. They were waiting for me, Nilranke, or maybe he followed me the whole time. They threw a bag over my head and beat me. I remember being dragged around, might remember you singing to me, then I woke up in the dungeon."

"I'm sorry I left you at the warehouse. I was scared and wasn't thinking. You only got caught because I left you."

"Hey, give me some of my own agency here. I got caught all on my own. Looks like I would have ended up in the same situation were I next to you."

"I'm sorry—"

"Stop, Elvan. Stop." Drace took a long, audible breath. "You don't have to say you're sorry and apologize for everything. I'm not mad at you or blame anything on you. Yes, I was sad when you left me on the dock, but I understand. Having magic suddenly used on you can be… disorienting."

Elvan pulled the chains up to lay across his knees, hoping to distribute the weight and relieve his wrists.

Drace sniffed and wiped at his eyes. "What an absolute mess.

What happened to you?"

Elvan choked back his own sob. "I got into the secret room in the manor. The key was on the notebook I've been using for the last two years. It had more crates from the Arcanym and notes tying Princes Lorelai to my mother's movement of artefacts."

"Really? It was right there the whole time?"

"Yes. I realized there's no way to fight her and went into a sort of spiral. I drank a bottle of my father's most average whiskey, and Delphina kicked me awake to drag me in front of the princess. Then I ran my mouth and got sentenced to death. Delphina talked her down to five years in exile."

"How kind of her."

"I know. She's the best. Love her. They brought you in, I begged and offered anything for them to let you go, and they sentenced us both to life instead."

"Thank you for that. What does she want?" Drace stood in the rocking carriage to pivot and sit on the bench beside Elvan.

"My sister? Who could ever guess with her. The princess is planning to assassinate, or at least overthrow, the king and my sister will use what evidence she can to blackmail her."

"Huh, I wonder why she'd bother. You could have told me the king died five years ago and I would believe you."

"I get it. He's already seen as a figurehead controlled by the princess, but people look to him because of his name and title."

"Do you?"

Elvan didn't want to admit he admired the kings of Spheris, up until his mother was taken. "No, but his support might be wider than we think. Maybe it's better we're getting out of the kingdom before it falls to a magically fueled coup."

Drace sighed a long breath and leaned against Elvan. "Any idea what exile will be like?"

Elvan set his head on Drace's shoulder. "No idea. When they took my mother, we didn't even get to see her this far. A valet delivered a letter with her sentence the next day. I keep imagining a quiet island in the ocean, though."

"Clear waters and ripe melons. We'll get great at spear fishing as these fashionable duds wear to rags around us." Drace put his head on Elvan's.

Elvan snorted. "That doesn't sound half bad. I'm sor— I'm not pleased with this outcome, but I don't know what else could have been done. Who can stand against the princess?"

"Someone else probably took over shipping things from the Arcanym. They'll see your exile for what it really is. Maybe they and the other families will rise against her, like you said on the ferry."

Elvan inched his hand toward Drace's knee and squeezed it. "That would be nice. Maybe the exile island will have a newspaper delivery for us to find out."

Drace put his hand over Elvan's, manacles clanging together, folding his fingers around the palm and idly rubbing his thumb across the knuckles. "I can think of a few other people I'd be less pleased to be exiled with. You have a good soul, Elvan."

"Such a good soul, getting you exiled."

"They thought I'm an Artist and there's no way for me to prove I'm not one. They would have thrown me in prison to rot. This is better." He raised Elvan's hand to kiss the knuckles and set it back on his knee.

Elvan concentrated on his breath, trying to steady his heart as a bead of sweat rolled down his back. *Why did he kiss my hand? Do I kiss him back?* He tried, but couldn't lift the combined manacles more than a few inches.

"In the warehouse, when you…" Elvan trailed off, hearing

Drace's deep, regular breath. He turned his head to nuzzle into Drace, smelling the mix of their last few days, but still that hint of incense. *Wouldn't that be something, if he turns out to be an Artist but only uses his magic to smell so good.*

The steady and gentle rock of the carriage reminded Elvan how little he'd slept in the last day and a half. He fought it, wanting to be alert when they arrived at their destination, but he jerked with a snort when the carriage finally stopped and he saw the light through the slits had noticeably brightened. The heavy side panels muffled most sound from outside, but Elvan thought he heard the cry of gulls. He shook Drace awake.

The door was unlocked and thrown wide to a long dock leading to a ship with two masts. Elvan could make out a crew of maybe a half dozen busying around the deck. Beyond it, a gray, overcast sky met the ocean some miles out in the sea. Two soldiers flanked the door and waved for them to exit. Drace stepped down first and stretched his back. Elvan joined him, struggling again with the weight of the irons.

He took a deep breath of the clean, salty sea air. At least the rain had stopped during the carriage ride. He looked up at the soldier beside him, raising the cuffs. "Can these come off, please?"

The soldier looked down with a shake of his head and genuine pity in his eyes. "Once you're on the boat, yes."

"Do you know where we'll go from here?"

"Sorry, Mr. Galmoth. I think it's north along the coast, but—"

"Gavin!" The other soldier cut him off with an annoyed hiss.

Gavin flinched and bit down on his lips.

"Never been on a boat before," said Drace while they walked down the dock, the clanks of their chains in time with his boot falls. "Other than the ferry, obviously, but this'll be different."

Elvan barely heard Drace and only gave a noncommittal grunt.

The ship loomed closer, growing to fill his view with each step. *This is it.* He thought of the maps hanging in Ser Vazadon's room that he'd studied as a child. It looked to be late morning now. Assuming the carriage ride took about four hours, he might only be twenty or thirty miles from the palace. That narrowed down where this dock might be and where north along the coast might take them. Not that it mattered. Elvan glanced down at the gangway up to the deck. *The literal end of the road.*

Elvan gave one more glance over the ship, from the high mast and the careful web of ropes down to the deck, to where "Enid's Blessing" was brightly painted at the bow. His mind swam with ledgers detailing the encumbrance such a vessel could take on and at what speeds. That life was behind him now.

He crossed onto the ship.

A man with deep wrinkles at his eyes, a thick mustache, and wearing a heavy blue coat with silver buttons approached them.

"I'm Captain Antris," he said. "The weather should be nice. We'll get there about this time tomorrow." The captain waved to his crew, and they pulled in the gangplank and hoisted the anchor.

"Where is that?" Drace asked.

"I'll be dropping you lads at the next stop of your journey. I'm sorry I can't say more. It's a devil of a thing the princess does, keeping everyone in the dark." The captain pulled a key from his coat to unlock the cuffs. They dropped to the planks with a bang. Both rubbed their sore wrists.

"It sounds like you're not a fan of the princess," said Elvan.

"That's not a conversation I'll get caught up in." Antris heaved a deep breath.

"You said there's a next stop?" Drace glanced at Elvan and back at the captain. "Where will you go after leaving us?"

Antris narrowed his eyes and shook his head. "Follow me to

your accommodations."

As Captain Antris led them to the stout door, Elvan walked as slowly as possible to watch the tree line slip by. He forced his eyes forward and followed the captain into the dark of the ship. At the bottom of the steep steps, a narrow hall lined with doors ended at one etched with a tentacled sea monster; likely the captain's quarters. Taking a sharp right, the hall turned back toward the bow of the ship, where Drace and Antris stood in front of an open door.

"I don't care how nice you ask," said the captain. "Stay here until we've docked."

Elvan followed Drace into the room, only a little larger than the one hidden behind his mother's armoire. A cot sagged across the opposite wall below the window of frosted glass. An unlit oil lamp swayed on a hook to his right over a chair beside a metal pail. Elvan shuddered, thinking of the bucket's intended use.

"Try to make the best of it," Antris said with a frown, and closed the door with a defined click of the lock.

"I asked him if we could stay up top, since it's not like we can go anywhere," Drace said and sat on the edge of the cot. "He said no."

"A day at sea trapped in a stuffy cabin." Elvan looked down at the bucket again. "I'm glad for the crackers Ser Vazadon gave me, trying to sober me up, but maybe it's a good thing I haven't eaten much in a day."

Drace looked up from prodding his swollen eye. "What's the plan, then? Spend the day plotting how to get back at the princess and your sister?"

Elvan snorted back a laugh. "I like that enthusiasm! No, my friend, we won't be seeing them ever again."

"No one's ever escaped from exile?"

"Not that I've heard."

"And is this a topic you have studied in great detail?" Drace winked with his good eye.

"Actually, yes. After my mother…" Elvan ran a hand through his hair and Drace's sly grin snapped to a frown. "I searched everywhere for months to find anything on the process of it and if anyone's ever made it back. There's nothing."

"Right, I'm sorry."

Elvan waved it off and forced a grin. "Don't be. Even the people exiled with a limited sentence never returned."

"Maybe we'll be a first."

"Maybe we will be." Elvan sat in the chair that rocked with an uneven leg. "How can you be so positive, Drace?"

"Would I be more helpful being gloomy?"

"I suppose not."

"Then I won't be."

"Nice skill, being happy on command."

Drace pushed off the floor to make the cot swing. "What do we do for a day in here? What do you normally do on a boat?"

"You're usually up top with the salt spray and open air."

"That sounds better." Drace leaned forward with his elbows on his knees and his toes brushing the plank floor. His face came within a foot of Elvan's in the cramped room. "Really, though, I might talk big, but I'm terrified." He pulled the silver chain and dangling ruby from under his shirt. "I've lost everything over the last couple of days. Everything except for this. It was my Nana's. I'm surprised they didn't find and take it when they dragged me in."

Elvan took the gem in two fingers, turning it over against the meager light filtering through the frosted glass. Fine wires of silver held the ruby in place and it felt warm to the touch. "It's pretty." He looked up at Drace staring down at him and sank his gaze into his amber eye — the one not swollen shut — with flecks of something darker at the edges of the iris. Elvan felt a sudden dryness in his mouth and licked his lips.

Drace leaned the extra few inches and pressed their lips together.

Elvan felt his arms go limp as his heart swelled to his throat. What should have been a pure and pivotal moment in his life was lost to his panic. He flinched back, clapping a hand over his mouth. "We shouldn't be doing this."

Drace retreated as far as he could onto the cot and crossed his arms. "We're about to spend the rest of our lives together, Elvan. I think we're beyond rules. We do what we want."

"Not like this."

"Sorry." Drace closed his eye and touched the swollen one again. "I'm still woozy from the beating and misread the situation. Wake me when the food comes." He fumbled with the cot until he lay across it, his knees tucked, facing the wall.

Elvan watched Drace for a long moment before realizing his fingertips were tracing his lips. That wasn't how he'd imagined their first kiss, but now that it happened, he'd ruined it. *Maybe we'll look back at this and laugh at the awkwardness. Maybe we'll spend the rest of our lives in awkward silence, never quite making eye contact again.*

He groaned and crawled to the floor, stretching out as best he could. He pressed his eyes closed and tried to focus on the gentle sway and creak of the ship around him, but the complaints from his stomach were louder. Opening his eyes, the light glinted off the edge of the metal bucket and he rolled away from it, wrapping his arms around his knees at his chest and trying to not think about how badly he'd messed up. Not just with the kiss, but everything else for days, years.

12

ELVAN PRESSED A PALM TO Drace's clammy forehead, hot with fever. The crewman that brought a meal of bread, cheese, and weak ale didn't seem concerned, brushing it off as sea sickness. Elvan held Drace's limp hand, trying to channel some of the other's optimism back into him, hoping he would feel better. Between regularly standing to hover over Drace and checking his fever, Elvan passed the time considering where their destination may lay. North along the coast might mean the frozen plains of Oxmoore, which would be miserable, though not for long.

The room went pitch dark overnight, but there was nothing to see except the metal pail. Well, that and Drace, but after he made a disaster of their first kiss, Elvan could hardly look at him without a pang of guilt and embarrassment.

Elvan finally felt the ship pulling up to dock. He urged Drace awake with a hand on his shoulder and whispered words.

"I think we're there."

Drace rolled over and fell out of the cot, onto Elvan. He righted himself, but clutched at his stomach. "Never again." He staggered to his left.

The door unlocked with a click before Captain Antris pulled it open. He looked across Elvan to Drace with a shake of his head. "The sea isn't kind to everyone. Be glad her waters were smooth for us. We've arrived."

Up on deck, the small crew was busy unloading crates of goods while an equal number of boxes stacked on the end of the dock were ready to be loaded. Drace hurried ahead down the gangplank to stand on the wide dock, bent forward with his hands on his knees. Elvan's eyes moved past him, up the lone trail, lined by a few long, squat houses, to a single mist-shrouded mountain directly ahead. Nestled in the crags, rough buildings blended into the distant stone.

"The Hex Temple?" Elvan asked and looked at the captain beside him.

"Aye."

"I don't get it. My brother's a monk here. You're..." Elvan gasped with a sudden hopeful thought. "You're saving us!" He spread his arms to hug the captain but quickly changed to grab and shake the man's hand vigorously. He let go after a few seconds when he realized the captain wasn't returning the gesture.

Captain Antris looked down at Elvan with an expression that hinted at pity. "I brought you where I was ordered. The monks will take you from here." The captain moved to oversee the unloading and loading of goods.

Elvan rushed around the crew to the dock. "Drace! This isn't some exile island! It's the monastery my brother's at! I wonder how long his hair is now. He shaved it when he left, but the monks never cut it. I don't know what's going on, but we're saved, I think."

"You sure about that?" Drace looked up with a sheen of sweat on his brow.

"You don't look well."

"I'm not. If I never get on another boat again, it'll be too soon."

Three monks in billowy light gray robes, cinched at the waist with a knotted black rope, approached from the road to the monastery. Elvan couldn't take his eyes from the delicate braids of their hair, reaching to almost their knees, as they passed to speak with the captain.

"Your brother's one of them?"

Elvan nodded. "He joined the brotherhood over a year ago. I think they'll keep us here, rather than alone on some island."

Drace put his hands on his hips, straightening with a deep breath. "I might rather spend my life learning to fish and eating molinifruit than be forced into service of the Six."

"We might get back to Spheris from here, though."

"I don't suppose we could get there by carriage?"

Elvan offered a sheepish grin. "No, we're on an island. Here they come."

The three monks stopped with their hands tucked into the folds of their robes in front of them. The one on the left might have been in his sixties, but the others looked closer to his mother's age.

"We are prepared for your stay," said the one on the left. "Please, follow us."

Elvan reached an arm toward the monk that spoke. "Is my brother up there? Bennoc?"

The older monk answered. "Yes. He asked to speak with you upon your arrival."

The trio turned back toward the monastery without another word or gesture. They never glanced back as they started up the long road, keeping a pace up the steep incline that quickly left Elvan breathless and hurting. He powered through, focusing on just putting one foot in front of the last as something unexpected warmed him: a desire to see his brother. Soon he noticed mist collecting around his legs. With his lungs burning and feet screaming in the fashionable slippers, Elvan sighed a prayer of thanks when they passed the first stone building of the monastery. More followed, tucked into crags and rocky overhangs of the shallow valley they walked through.

"Maybe we'll be exiled to one of those?" Drace pointed to the nearest building, not sounding at all winded.

They turned a corner to see the main structures of the monastery rising before them, shrouded in swirls of yellow-white mist. A dozen buildings that looked no more significant than stones stacked atop each other surrounded them. Elvan remembered from Ser Vazadon's history lessons that this monastery was built almost five hundred years ago, though by whom or why was unknown. A score of monks wearing the same gray robes, but most with shorter hair, worked in the yard, sweeping or talking in tight clumps.

The five ascended crude steps to a path cut into the side of the mountain's peak, opening to a wide, circular room. A brazier in the center cast light over five archways around the room, each ten feet wide and twice as tall. Another monk stood beside the brazier with his hands tucked in his robe, with two cloth sacks at his feet, but the room was otherwise empty.

The monk approached with a somber smile. He brought his hands out to spread them wide as he stepped forward, speaking in an awkward, stilted tone, "Brother, I have missed you."

Elvan stared at the man advancing toward him, recognizing him, but his mind couldn't believe it. Gone was the sloped posture along with the hair that always covered his face, replaced with broad shoulders and a lean jaw. He held out a hand to stop the monk from coming nearer. "Bennoc?" Elvan stepped around his brother, still keeping his distance, noting the braid reaching his lower back. "How?"

"I cannot explain the miracles of the Gates. I am only glad for the honor of seeing you off, Brother."

"Off?" Elvan looked to where the three monks grouped around one arch. A tangle of vines weaved against the stones to create a sense of nature retaking man's abandoned work. He noticed the other archways, each with their own aesthetic; one was stout blocks of heavy rock, another clearly made of steel.

Bennoc ignored the question and turned to Drace. "Apologies, I have yet to introduce myself. Brother Bennoc, Elvan's younger brother."

"Drace. Drace Eloi."

Elvan looked at Drace, realizing he'd never asked the man's family name. *How self-centered am I?*

Bennoc returned to the sacks on the ground and stooped to pick them up. "How has our sister been?"

"She's the reason we're here," Elvan scoffed. "Bennoc, what happened to you? You look older than me now."

The three monks began a low chant, pulling their attention. Elvan felt the ground beneath his feet vibrate with the growling notes as the air quivered, growing dense with a breeze pushing toward the monks and the arch before them.

"What…"

Starting at the ground, orange light traced along the vines and cracks in the stones until it spread across the top of the archway. Elvan winced and raised an arm as a burst of blinding light washed over them with a flash of heat that left his exposed hands and face feeling frigid. He blinked away the afterimage and looked back to the archway. What was solid stone behind the archways was now a swirl of orange light. A filament of something darker traced from the floor, dragging a pattern of a tree with it. That dissolved away just as smoothly and was replaced with narrow stairs, set in a field of murky yellow energy, leading to another arch far in the distance.

"Your path is open," said the older monk.

Elvan turned back to his brother. "Bennoc, what's going on?"

Bennoc pushed the cloth sacks toward him and Drace. "I envy the journey you are about to embark upon. The Gates are a miracle, as you will see. It was wonderful to see you, Brother, and to meet you, Drace Eloi. May the Six hold you both." He tucked his hands into his robes, bowed, and shuffled backward.

Elvan hefted the heavy sack and turned to Drace, watching the orange light flickering in his good eye. "I don't understand."

"This is our exile, sent through a magic portal to gods know where," said Drace flatly.

Elvan's stomach knotted watching the slow churn of mist around the distant stairs. "No." He took a step back. "No, we're just supposed to live with the monks and serve the Six."

Drace turned to him. "It seems not. We can't outrun them and we can't fight them. Come on." He turned toward the stairs, rolling back his shoulders.

Elvan followed until they stood at the boundary of the archway. A sharp line of orange cut across the stone floor and beyond, it fell away to nothing around the stairs. He glanced up and noticed a huge emerald the size of his head suspended above the arch, obscured in wrapping vines. He looked to the other arches and saw similar crystals of different colors above them, entwined in the materials of each arch.

"We don't want to keep the nice monks waiting," Drace said and stepped onto the stairs. The orange glow beyond lit him brilliantly, compared to the dim light from the brazier.

Though his throat was completely dry, Elvan swallowed and stepped onto the first stair. He squeezed his eyes against the sudden brightness and blinked it away a breath later. Drace looked down at him from a few steps above. Behind, the three monks and Bennoc stood in the dark beyond the threshold. He focused forward and Drace started toward the far arch that flicked with blue energy. Elvan kept his eyes on Drace to keep from looking over the edge at the cloudy nothing on either side of him. He pressed a foot down on the step that, while it looked firm, gave slightly under his weight.

After a dozen steps, he felt a tug in his chest that drove him forward faster. Another few steps and he stumbled to keep up. Drace faltered and fell forward to tumble up the stairs. Elvan couldn't keep up and tucked into a ball around the cloth sack as he fell forward, moving faster toward the arch. Blue lightning licked the wood and stone portal ahead and beyond that, another arch. And another. Elvan fell behind Drace, tumbling against the soft stairs, falling forever until the air rushed too fast to breathe and his vision was nothing but blinding arcs of blue discharge, his nose smelling nothing but sharp ozone.

13

BIRDSONG CUT THROUGH THE BUZZ of electricity still clinging to Elvan's ears like honey on toast. He opened his eyes to a blue sky muddled by clouds stretched thin. The steady lapping of waves came to him next. Then the texture of soft sand under his hands. He pushed to his elbows and saw Drace doing the same a few feet away on the beach, looking just as confused. Between them, the sacks from Bennoc lay toppled open with rough woven fabric spilling into the sand.

Was that really him? He should be fifteen years old.

"Well, I've no idea what's happening." Drace got his feet under him to push to his feet. "Are we dead?"

"I don't think so, but how could we know?" Elvan rolled on sore legs and pushed himself to stand.

Drace squinted across the water to the distant horizon with a thoughtful hum.

"What?" Elvan asked.

"Nothing." Drace shook his head and gestured at the bags. "Looks like we're not getting saved to live a quiet life at the temple. At least we were right about the island part. Or beach, at least."

Elvan glanced either way along the sand, noticing nothing of interest except more sand.

"I'm far from an expert in wilderness survival," Drace continued, "but I think we have to find shelter and water right away. Let's see what the monks gave us." He crouched to pull out a swath of woven fabric the same color as the monk's robes.

"Drace, about the boat, when we… when you…"

Drace twirled the fabric in his hands. "Don't worry about it. I misread the situation."

Elvan squatted on the other side of the cloth sack. "No, no, you didn't. I'm just… I don't know, I feel a little broken sometimes. You know how it is when you build something up in your mind and it doesn't happen that way?"

Drace raised the brow over his eye that wasn't swollen. "I might. Right now I have this image in my mind of not dying from thirst and exposure on a weird beach. Can we do something about that first?"

"Yeah." Elvan pivoted on his heel to survey the area. The beach, dotted with driftwood and rocky outcroppings, curved inward in either direction, giving the impression they were on the edge of a very large circular island. Behind, the sand gave way to scrubby grass, then a dense forest of oaks and skinny birches. "Lots of firewood, but nothing else."

"Check the water. Maybe it's fresh."

Elvan stood and walked ankle deep into the slow waves. The cool water felt amazing as it soaked through the terrible slippers, until the seawater touched the first blisters on his feet. He yelped and cursed at the sting, jumping back to the sand, ripping the slippers off, and wringing them out.

"It's salt," Elvan called to Drace and looked back at the horizon. He knew something was strange about it, though it was hard to specify. The distant sky had a flatness to it, feeling close, like a painting. Elvan shook his head and returned to Drace.

Drace spread and organized the bags' contents, pointing to each as he ticked them off. "Six robes, six pairs of sandals, two canteens, two flint boxes, six bags of dried fruits and nuts, six bags of jerky, two lengths of about thirty feet of rope each, and…" He held up two strings of wooden beads, each engraved with one of six runes. "Two sets of prayer beads of the Six. These are well worth the weight."

"That's all?"

"Yep. They probably meant the three robes each to last us the rest of our lives, but the food we might stretch to a week. There must be something else to eat and a source of water." Drace started cramming things back into the sacks.

"Hey, if we don't find water, the robes will last the rest of our lives. We'll just wear a new one each day."

Drace stopped stuffing and slowly raised his gaze up to Elvan. "Was that a joke?"

"That's how I intended it."

Drace grinned and shook his head. "Good effort. Keep at it." He finished packing and stood, looking one way down the beach, then the other, focusing harder and squinting to his right. "I read the water for drinking has to be moving, so a river, not a lake. I think I see something that might be an outlet that way. If it's fresh, we can settle a bit."

They hefted the sacks over their shoulders and made for the direction Drace indicated. Elvan saw nothing of interest along the beach that way, no matter how hard he squinted, but trusted Drace's eye was keener than his own.

Exhaustion drained Elvan's senses despite his restless naps in the carriage and boat rides. He felt as though they moved faster than their steps across the sand, and within moments, he could see the river outlet in the distance. Another few moments and they stood at a break in the beach's sand where a wide river flowed from deep in the trees, into the ocean. They counted a hundred paces inland along the river before kneeling to taste the water. Not tasting salt or anything else suspicious, they drank deep from the rushing river before filling the canteens.

"This isn't turning out too bad just yet," said Drace. He squeezed Elvan's shoulder with one hand while wiping the water from his chin with the other. "Now we just need somewhere to keep out of the rain and some berries or mushrooms and we'll be all set for the next forty years."

Elvan laughed, but his smile turned to a dour frown as the reality of their exile became so… real.

"How do we find shelter?" he asked. "It's all just trees as far as I can see, and we don't have any way to cut them down."

"I don't want to leave the river. Let's follow it upstream, and maybe we'll find a cave."

Elvan groaned as he pushed to his feet. Everything hurt now that he'd stopped moving.

"Or…" Drace started and set his bag down. "We could rest here a while. I didn't see the sun when we were on the beach. I've no idea what time it is."

Elvan was already sitting on the mossy rocks by the water's edge, pulling off the fashionable slippers and dipping his feet back into the water. He estimated the far bank at seventy feet away and wondered how deep it might be, or if it had fish they could catch. *Not that I've ever fished.*

Drace stripped off his shirt and waded into the water to scrub at the bloodstains on the front. Elvan watched him work, mesmerized by the flex of muscles across Drace's back and arms.

Drace stood after just a minute at it, tossing the shirt ahead of him to the rocks at the river's edge and shaking the water from his hands. "Good enough for now. I'll be right back." He gestured to the woods and disappeared in that direction. Elvan had a good idea of what Drace was up to and a cramp in his gut told him he had a similar need. After digging through the bags to find a pair of woven sandals, he went into the woods a different way. Picking through the tangled underbrush and fallen, mossy limbs until he could only see hints of the river, he stopped and did his business.

Elvan returned to no sign of Drace. *I didn't think I was that fast.* A dark form moved just under the surface of the water, startling him, and Drace popped his head up in the middle of the river, blowing water from his nose and shaking it from his twisted locs.

He grinned and yelled across the water, "This feels amazing, Elvan. Jump in."

Elvan noticed the larger pile of clothes next to the wet shirt. "I'm not much of a swimmer."

"It's not that deep." Drace sank and stretched his neck to keep his nose above the slow current before bobbing back up. "I can touch the bottom out here. It's pretty solid; not mucky or weedy."

Elvan had a hand on the button of his shirt, watching Drace's wide grin, lopsided with one eye still swollen mostly shut, then glanced again at the pile of clothes. *He's got to be naked in here.* He craned his neck and noted with the dappling of shadows from the trees overhead, he could only see a few inches into the water.

Drace read the concern and rolled his eye. "I'll look away. Come on. Ten minutes and you'll feel great."

Elvan sighed and started unbuttoning his shirt. Drace cheered and turned away, as promised. Once his pants were off, he rushed into the water, slipped on a slimy rock under the surface, and tripped forward. He recovered enough to turn it into a splashy dive into the chilly river. His lungs constricted with a gasp caught in his throat with the sudden shock.

Drace turned around and swam to him. "Feels nice, right?"

Elvan nodded and pushed himself down to submerge his head, coming up immediately, blowing water from his nose and shaking it from his eyes. The ache in his legs and feet washed away with the current as he slowly tread water to stay afloat. He closed his eyes with a deep breath.

"Did I do that?"

Elvan snapped his eyes open. Drace pointed at his chest. He looked down, having forgotten about the light bruise across his chest and shoulder. He also noticed how far down his own body he could see, with this blindingly pale skin. Elvan nodded and let the current carry him a few feet away. "You had to, right? For the magic to work? Ser Vazadon explained a bit about it to me."

Drace swam a little closer and winced. "Maybe I didn't have to hold that tight, sorry. Tensions were really high in the moment."

Elvan was about to let the current pull him away again, but forced himself to stay in place. He sank so his chin was barely over the water. "I'll be fine," he said. "We find shelter, find a food source, then what?"

Drace shrugged and swam back a few feet. "Explore this place? Didn't your sister suggest your mother's here?"

A surge of hope burst in Elvan's chest, clouded by the guilt of nearly forgetting that. "'Say hello to mum,' were her exact words. It was probably nothing more than a taunt."

Drace swam a slow circle around Elvan. "But if it's not, we should find her. We'll make her our top priority after ensuring we can live more than a week."

Elvan pivoted in place. "Thank you, Drace."

He stopped swimming and turned to Elvan. "You're welcome?"

"You keep pushing me, but in good ways. Would I have ever gone to the warehouse if not for you? That is, if I even figured it out to go there, which I wouldn't have. I sat on those invoices for months before Cenna convinced me to go to your shop."

"My Nana said if you want something done, do it. Imagine if you'd come to my shop a month ago, even one day earlier, as Tristan Griffith. We wouldn't have been chased out by the inquisitors." Drace stopped to laugh and splashed water over his face. "I mean, really, what was your plan? Were you going to try buying arcane steel using our internal inventory number?"

"I already told you that my plan was shit." Elvan felt a flush on his cheeks despite the river's chill.

"You needed the disguise because of something with the Council of Houses? Want to tell me about that?"

Elvan blew bubbles at the water's surface. He'd been dreading reliving that memory for years. "A few months after they arrested my mother, I went to the next meeting of the Council of Houses. It was my first time ever attending and, long story short, the four other heads agreed I wasn't ready to take over the Galmoth House. It was just shy of them laughing me out. Looking back, I agree with them. I didn't understand how my mother ran the business, but I've learned a lot in two years."

"And you never went back?"

Elvan shook his head. "We should get out and find that shelter. Who knows what the nights are like here." He looked back to the shore and his pile of clothes, seeing another flaw in the foresight.

Drace read him again with a chuckle. "You get out first. Get in one of those robes and pull out one for me, too." He kicked away with a splash.

Elvan paddled to the slippery rocks at the edge, glanced over his shoulder to ensure Drace was facing away, and crawled into the pebbly land. He dumped out a cloth sack and picked up the first bit of gray fabric he saw. He expected a garment with a neck and armholes, but the robes were closer to a long blanket sewn into a tube. Elvan tried to remember how he'd seen the monks twist it about their bodies and across their shoulders, all the while silently cursing his sense of modesty. Drace seemed to be free and happy in the water. What in his own past or upbringing made it so hard for him to let go like that? If they were to spend the rest of their lives in this forest, they'd probably see each other naked eventually. His eyes drifted to Drace's pile of clothes. *I'm looking forward to that.*

He laid another robe beside Drace's clothes, called he was dressed, and busied himself with stuffing everything back into the sacks.

"These things are scratchy," Drace complained, and Elvan risked turning to him. The robe, wrapped as messily as he imagined his own looked, only reached Drace's shin, while it brushed the ground around Elvan's feet.

"We'll get used to them. We'll have to."

Drace shrugged and picked at the fabric on his shoulder. "I suppose, after they've rubbed all our skin off."

"It's these, or my father's old stuff that you've been wearing the last couple of days."

"I'll get used to these." Drace took a wide stance and squatted low. "They're sort of freeing." He winked.

They followed the river upstream, keeping a close eye for caves or overhangs that would serve as shelter. Their sturdy sandals from the monks proved surprisingly comfortable as they stepped over a hundred fallen trees and branches. If the entire land was like this, they would never want for firewood. Elvan mostly kept his focus internal, knowing Drace would spot anything long before he could. Though he knew it was a wasted effort, he stewed on his sister's many betrayals. None of it surprised him, but she played him well. His only hope was in her being unable to find or access the secret room with the crates from the Arcanym. *No, she'll tear down the walls, if needed. Burn the manor to the ground and sift through the ash.*

It's no longer my concern, he repeated to himself, but he still cared for the fate of his kingdom. Despite the corruption up to the highest levels that took his mother from him and tore his family apart, he cared. Artists, or those suspected of being an Artist, were stripped of their rights and thrown in prison, but Elvan still believed in the nation's core. A nation built on the Houses' labors of love.

Elvan recalled Drace quoting his Nana, "If you want something done, do it." *That's nice, but I'm following a river somewhere with a weird horizon. Spheris, Princess Lorelai, my sister, the Galmoth name, none of it matters. All that matters is finding my mother.*

Drace tripped on a branch and stumbled forward a few steps. He gestured back at it with a mumbled warning.

Elvan smiled as he hiked up the robe to step over the branch.

And him. He matters too.

Drace stopped, dropped his sack, and squinted into the trees. "Stay here," he said, pulling the robes up to his knees before bounding into the undergrowth. Elvan set down his bag and leaned against a stump covered in moss and lichen. The relief of the swim's respite was wearing off, leaving him with an exhaustion that seeped deep into his bones. With each breath, he worried more that if Drace didn't return immediately, they would have to spend the night cuddling up to the lichen stump.

Drace rushed back, out of breath, with his good eye wide. "There's a village!" He snatched up his bag and ran back through the trees. Elvan followed and within a few steps, saw the first hint of a mossy roof among the dense tree trunks.

It wasn't much, just six constructions of thatch, stone, and mud circling a well that crumbled long ago, but it was proof of other life.

"This must mean there's food somewhere. Fish in that river or something," said Drace.

"Or not, and that's why this place is abandoned." Elvan's eyes flitted over the village, expecting a predator or danger hidden in every shadow.

Drace turned on him with an exaggerated sigh. "I'm going to need you to think positively for once, please. We can sleep in one of these, away from the bears or ghosts or bear ghosts or whatever dangers you're considering."

They looked through each of the buildings and agreed on one which was the least dilapidated. The corner of its roof sagged from a tree that fell on it years ago, but the floor had the largest open area. They dumped the contents of the sacks again and laid out their old clothes to dry. The ambient light in the forest grew dimmer, but they could see little of the sky through the leafy canopy.

After sharing half of one bag of nuts and a full canteen, they wadded up the cloth of the sacks to use as pillows. Elvan stretched out on the lumpy floor, knowing he'd hurt in the morning from it, but it felt so good to lie down.

Drace laid down beside him and immediately sat up with a grunt. He shrugged the robe from his shoulders, letting it bunch around his waist, and laid back with a contented sigh. "I won't have that rubbing my nipples raw all night. It's bad enough with what else it's rubbing on. The monks must have no body hair."

Elvan smirked and watched Drace stretch and bring his hands up to rest behind his head. He looked so comfortable. Elvan sat up, shrugged out of the robe, and looked down at Drace beside him.

"Better, right?" said Drace.

Elvan swallowed hard, seeing Drace stretched out, bare-chested in the dim remains of the day's light. A part of him wanted to lean over and try that kiss again, but the thought made his hands shake with nerves. He laid back on the uneven ground.

Drace was grinning at him and reached to trace a finger along the stubble on Elvan's jaw. "Good night." He dropped one arm across his stomach and the other between them.

Elvan fumbled for Drace's hand, laced their fingers together, and raised it to his lips, as Drace had on the carriage. "Good night."

Drace squeezed his fingers and closed his eyes. Elvan watched him, following the slow rise and fall of his chest in the dying light, before letting his head roll to study the rotted beams of the hut's roof. He knew he would have every right to mourn and cry about the injustices against him, what he lost at the hands of the princess and his sister, but that felt oddly distant. *This is surreal*. With their fingers still entwined, Elvan rolled to his side, pressing his forehead against Drace's shoulder and slid his other hand across his belly.

14

THEY WERE COMING FOR HER. They would be at the door at any moment. Elvan ran to warn his mother, but he couldn't find her. She should be in her study, but where was that? He was in the dining room, now the library. Where was her study? He looked over his shoulder; Delphina loomed there, only a few steps away. He ran, but she followed, her feet never moving. He was on the back patio now. His father lay sprawled in a chair with a bottle of cheap whiskey shattered at his feet. Now Bennoc, but he was a frail old man, bent with age. He yelled for his mother but could make no sound.

Elvan started and jerked upright. The sheen of sweat across his bare chest caught the breeze through the crumbling walls, sending a chill down his spine and arms. Ghost light from outside illuminated the hut in inky shadows that prickled his nerves. He squeezed his eyes shut, but that only invited back memories of the nightmare. He pulled his knees to his chest and focused on slowing his breathing.

"Elvan?" Drace whispered and sat up, putting an arm around

Elvan's bare shoulder.

"Just a nightmare," said Elvan, and leaned into Drace's touch.

Drace shifted to sit in front of him. With a single finger, he brushed a lock of hair from Elvan's forehead, ran a gentle hand through his hair, and down his neck to his shoulder. He pulled his hand away to rub the fingers to his palm.

"You're a sweaty mess. You sure you're fine?"

Elvan swallowed hard and shook his head. "I'm fine. I've had this same dream for a year. Well, almost the same; now my siblings are in it, too. It's nothing."

Drace nodded and took one of Elvan's hands in both of his. "Sometimes with nightmares it's best to not go right back to sleep. You have to give the bad spirits time to move on."

Elvan gazed into Drace's glimmering eyes and the barest twist of a smirk on his lips. His breath caught in his chest, constricted by his nerves that coiled around his body, conspiring to push him away. Drace tilted his head slightly, breaking what remained of Elvan's restraint. He lunged forward, pressing his lips against Drace's and wrapped a palm around the small of his back, toppling them backward onto the hut's lumpy ground. Elvan held his lips in place for a long breath, unsure of what to do next, as all confidence fled him.

He pulled away, but Drace's hand slipped through his hair again, drawing him in. His other moved to Elvan's back to hold him firm, chest to bare chest. Drace's lips parted and his tongue ran across Elvan's mouth, urging him to explore deeper. Elvan let Drace guide him, mimicking as best he could, and slid his hand under Drace's neck.

Their lips and tongues teased until Drace lessened his hold. Elvan immediately pulled away as far as he could and a dread crept into his mind, horror that he'd done something wrong, regretting every action since waking from the nightmare.

"I'm sorry," he blurted out and wiped the back of his hand across his mouth.

Drace grinned beneath him and ran a thumb over Elvan's lips. "What did I say about apologizing for everything? It's about time we got this started."

"I… I haven't done this before." Elvan glanced at the open door.

"To be honest, I don't have much more experience. We only have to do as much as we want to. Or as little." Drace guided Elvan's gaze back to him with a finger on his chin. "But I would like to do more."

Elvan's heart thudded in his ears and in his groin. The coarse weave of the robes around his waist was unbearable as he felt Drace press hard against his hip. His nerves again rose to bid him to flee, even as his palm came to rest on Drace's chest, his fingers tracing along the collarbone. His other slid over Drace's stomach, across his naval, feeling the bumps of gooseflesh in its passing.

Drace took Elvan's hand, raised it to kiss his fingers, and placed it back on his chest. His hands slid down Elvan's sides, tickling his ribs, down to his waist, and pushed at the rough fabric tied and twisted there. With a quaking breath, Elvan lifted his hips to ease Drace's efforts. The cloth tangled around his legs and feet, but after an awkward effort, Elvan kicked away the fabric and they both chuckled to ease the moment. Elvan gripped the robes around Drace's hips and pulled them free with greater efficiency.

Elvan knelt between Drace's knees and ran his fingertips slowly from the other man's thighs, across his hips, along his sides. Elvan leaned forward, pressing himself down and found Drace's lips with his own. He kissed across the rough stubble of his jawline to his ear. Drace gasped, arched his neck, and Elvan kissed it, still catching the scent of the shop's incense in his hair.

How? After all we've been through, and he still smells nice. It's like he's made of magic.

He is magic.

Elvan shook away the stray thought and shifted down to kiss Drace's collarbone, traveling the center line of his body, following the light trail of hair from his chest, across his stomach.

Nearly blind in the dark and breathing slowly to steel his nerves, Elvan put his hand on Drace's thigh again and slid upward. The air caught in his throat and an electric thrill shot up his arm as his thumb brushed the rigid shaft.

This is going to happen. This is happening.

Hand shaking only slightly, Elvan wrapped his fingers around Drace, eliciting a gasp and sigh from the other. He swallowed hard and started the familiar slow rhythm that had served him well a few times a week over the last lonely years. Drace's breath quickened and Elvan worked faster.

With a sharp inhale, Drace shot a hand behind Elvan's neck and pulled him forward for a deep kiss, pressing their bodies together.

"Not too fast," Drace breathed into Elvan's ear and nibbled his lobe. "I want to savor this."

Drace traced his nails along Elvan's ribs and rolled them over to be on top.

The pressure was building and Elvan knew he wouldn't last long.

Drace pushed up and ran his fingers down Elvan's chest, slowly working his way south.

As soon as he touches me, I'm done.

Elvan sat up, pressing his forehead into Drace's and breathing deep to control himself. "Sorry, I'm just… this is…"

"We don't have to—"

"No, I want to. I just want to savor this, too." The words that sounded sexy and smooth from Drace felt awkward in Elvan's mouth.

"Can I touch it?"

The pressure lessened with the pause and Elvan licked his lips. He nodded once. Either Drace saw it in the dark, or took the silence as consent, and his fingers again slipped down Elvan's front. The hand he'd first held in the oddity shop and dozens of times since felt foreign, yet comforting, grasping his member. His eyes rolled back and Elvan relaxed onto the lumpy floor with an involuntary moan. Drace's technique was felt good, but different enough that Elvan thought he might be able to last a bit longer.

He quickly changed his mind when he felt Drace's tongue slid up his length.

"Slow…" Elvan gasped.

Their shared ineptitude was obvious, but never a hindrance. Neither knew exactly what to expect, much less what to expect of the other, and they laughed with their failures. Soon they were both sweaty and exhausted. Drace draped his arm over Elvan, pulling him close against his chest and kissed his neck.

"Good night, again."

15

ELVAN LAY UNMOVING IN THE first hints of dawn, savoring the heat of Drace's breath across the back of his neck. Eventually, the half canteen with last night's meal caught up with him, forcing him to wiggle free and struggle to wrap the robe about himself. He paused in the doorway and looked back at Drace, now lying on his stomach with the light of early morning across his backside. A quick flood of memories from their night together rushed by Elvan and he bit back a grin. He shook them away and turned to find a tree.

The ring of ruined huts looked no different in the morning light. He glanced across them, deciding that the larger one was the chief's house, but also their meeting hall. The smaller three were for the young couples who lived here and the last two for the larger families. While he relieved himself, he imagined the tribe of twenty huddled in the largest house, tearfully debating abandoning their homes to find a new source of food. *Did they leave any useful tools behind?* They didn't see any last night, but their search was the barest of cursory glances into each building.

A twig snapped behind him, drawing Elvan's attention. Drace walked from their hut, struggling with his robe while not covering much. Elvan snapped his eyes forward again with a blush and chuckled to himself. *Really? After last night?* He looked back, taking in the details he had only imaged in the dark. He shook and tucked himself back into the robes even as he felt the growing swell.

"I imagine we'll become experts with these, eventually," Drace said glumly as Elvan tried to help him with the robe.

"We could forgo them to live free and wild."

Drace's eyes lit up. "I like that plan up until we find your mother. Who knows, maybe still then? I don't know what she's like." He shrugged with a wink, and Elvan cringed.

"Today's goal is to find food so we can start a search for her. I think we should start by digging through these houses. Carefully, so they don't collapse on us."

"Listen to you, taking command."

Elvan traced a finger gingerly over Drace's swollen eye. "That's getting better."

"I can open it most of the way, at least." He stared down at Elvan for a long moment with an awkward tension growing between them.

"Last night…" Elvan started.

"Good," Drace nodded quickly, "let's talk about that. I thought it was great. Let's do it again real soon."

Elvan snorted back a laugh. "Not the wording I was about to use, but the same sentiment. I'm glad we're of one mind." He stood a little taller to kiss Drace.

"We're kissing now?" Drace traced a finger along his lips.

Elvan snickered. "Let's get searching."

They found scraps of metal too far rusted to be of any use. The largest hut held a few moldy books that crumbled to nothing at their touch. They found baskets of woven reeds, sleeping mats, rope, and stacks of cloth that might have been clothing, but everything fell apart in their fingers.

Giving up their search of the village, they finished the first bag of food and returned to the river to refill the canteens. Using a scrap of rope from the village that didn't immediately decay, they tied Elvan's fashionable slippers to a tree near the river as a marker to help find the village again and set off upstream. They passed bushes bursting with plump, red berries and logs crusted with soft fungi, but neither knew enough about how to identify what was safe to eat to risk any of it.

"Can't you cast some spell to tell if it's poisonous?" Elvan asked as they passed the fourth shrub of delicious-looking fruit.

"I need an artefact to do anything." His fingers traced the ruby dangling from his silver necklace, now kept over his clothes.

"Is that how it works? All magic requires an artefact?"

"The Artists of legend might not have needed one, but the power has become so diluted through the generations. Artists today generally can't store enough power for anything useful, so they store their magic in artefacts."

"Your Nana had one, then? Something like that owl?"

Drace stumbled a step, but kept moving. "Yes, a cat."

"Cute. She must have taken it with her when she went to live with her sisters. Are they Artists, too?"

Drace said nothing, but kept his pace a few steps ahead of Elvan.

"Drace?"

He paused and rubbed a hand across his eyes. "I don't want to talk about it."

Elvan circled in front of the other man, but Drace kept his gaze focused over Elvan's head. "I'm just trying to get to know you better."

Drace inhaled sharply and finally looked down at Elvan. His eyes and lips were pinched with annoyance. "It comes across like an inquisition sometimes. Don't think I didn't notice your look when I introduced myself to your brother. You didn't know my family name until then. You never asked."

Elvan shied back a step and stared down at Drace's sandals. "I'm sorry. I never meant it like that. I… getting to know a person is something else I'm not that great at."

Drace closed his eyes and ran a hand through his hair. Tugging at his locs, he dropped to a crossed-legged seat in the clover. "I'm not mad at you, Elvan. It's just starting to hit me. The rest of our lives is a long time to spend together alone here, no matter how much we like each other." He picked at the thin greens with one hand and held the other shielding his downcast eyes.

Elvan sat in front of him and put a hand on Drace's leg. When the other didn't look up, he sidled a bit nearer until their knees touched.

"When I first saw you," said Drace in little more than a whisper, "it was the first time in a while that I felt any hope. My life was nothing but sifting through the junk in Nana's shop and barely scraping together enough for taxes. Then there you were, holding that broken skull, and I somehow knew my life was about to change. You were different. You had a story layered on a story. I thought, 'I want to get to know this awkward boy with the messy hair.'"

Elvan took Drace's hand in both of his, but didn't trust he knew the right words for the moment.

"I carved a new cat for her," said Drace after a pause. He looked up and sniffed back tears. "Part of me wanted to make something for her, but also I didn't want to lose her artefact forever, which now I have."

The simple truth hit Elvan. "Your Nana… She didn't go south to *live* with her sisters."

Drace shook his head.

"And her artefact was still in the shop."

"That's why I went back. It's the only thing I had left of hers that meant anything. Now some city worker will find it and toss it in with the rubbish."

"These artefacts, they aren't just objects of power. They're deeply personal."

Drace squeezed Elvan's hand. "I'm sorry I snipped. Let's keep moving."

Time passed in a blur, and they were approaching the fashionable slippers again before he realized it. Elvan recalled fragments of the day stumbling along the river's edge, but the memory felt slippery, like a dream. He shook it off as they ate more of their limited rations beside the crumbled well.

"I don't know what I expected to find," Drace sighed. "We don't have any tools to catch a fish or rabbit, and neither of us knows how to make anything. There's maybe a week's worth of food, unless we want to try mystery berries."

"The mystery berries do look tasty. There has to be something, or else why would they give us so many other supplies?"

Drace turned slowly to Elvan. "Why are you suddenly the optimistic one?"

Elvan smirked. "I guess you're rubbing off on me."

Drace waggled his eyebrows.

"Don't say it," Elvan warned.

"I rubbed off on you last night."

Elvan rolled his eyes, but couldn't hold back a snort. "Crude. I'm glad you're feeling less glum."

"Hmm, well, we timed today pretty well, but going half a day up the river didn't find us anything. Not that I expected to find trees with loaves of bread."

Elvan tossed a pebble at the largest of the ruined building. "Did we even go that far? It felt like we walked forever, then turned around and were right back here."

"I'm… actually not sure. The magic of this place feels… off."

"How so?"

"It's just… I'm not sure. It feels confined." Drace pulled his knees to his chest and rested his chin on them.

Elvan threw another pebble. "We'll go back to the beach tomorrow and go in the other direction. Maybe we'll find fruit trees down there."

"Good idea. I wouldn't mind seeing the sky again." Drace laughed. "You're really sounding like me, and I don't know if I like it." He bumped his shoulder against Elvan's.

Drace stood and stretched his back, wandering a few steps away before bending to pick up a stick half his height in length. He clumsily waved the long length of wood.

"What are you doing?" Elvan asked.

"I bet your Ser Vazadon had a hundred stories with epic sword play."

"A hundred, at least," Elvan chuckled.

Drace flourished his weapon and held it toward Elvan with a forced sneer. He spoke with a deep, commanding tone. "I challenge you."

"Is that so?" Elvan rolled his eyes and pushed to his feet, the soreness of the day's walk starting to set into his muscles. He found a stick half the length of Drace's and held it in both hands. He mimicked Drace's voice. "Have we a wager, Ser Eloi?"

Drace's sneer melted into a wide grin. "What have you in mind,

Ser Galmoth? What stakes?"

Elvan's mind went blank. Despite their silliness, he wondered what Drace could possibly give him here. He needed a source of food or a way off the island. "The loser must kiss the winner."

Drace snorted and tapped the end of his makeshift sword against Elvan's. "I accept. I will not lose. I'll be the one getting kissed by the time we're done here!"

Elvan shifted forward, tapping Drace's stick away to rest his against the other's neck.

"We didn't say to start yet," said Drace sheepishly and shuffled back a step. "Best of three?"

"Ready when you are."

Drace pulled back his tree limb for a wide sweep and Elvan's long hours of training kicked in. He slipped forward and dragged his stick across Drace's belly.

"One for me. Or were you still not ready?"

"Lucky hit."

"I grew up with a decorated knight sleeping two doors from mine. You had to assume he did more than tell us bedtime stories."

"This hardly seems fair. Why didn't you tell me before?"

"It never came up."

Drace swung his stick for another horizontal sweep, but twisted it up to swing down instead. Elvan sidestepped the obvious feint and tapped his twig on the top of Drace's head. "Best out of five?"

"I yield." Drace shoved his log into the ground and shook his head.

"I could use my other hand." Elvan tossed the stick to his left and waggled the tip.

Drace snorted. "Elvan Galmoth, world class accountant and swordsman. What a combination."

Elvan laughed. "I'm not that great. Better than Bennoc, who was afraid to lift a sword, but I was never anywhere near Delphina's level. She railed against having the lessons, saying she'd never need them, being a girl. Her speed and control were terrifying."

"Rather than talk about your sister, how about we take care of my debt to you?" Drace stepped forward and used two fingers to push aside Elvan's stick. His hand ran up the inside of Elvan's arm and gripped him across the back, pulling him close so their lips were mere inches apart. "Do you want it out here, or in the hut?"

Elvan dropped his makeshift sword and took Drace's hand from his back, pulling him toward their mossy house.

16

E LVAN WOKE BEFORE FIRST LIGHT and it took him a
moment to know why. An odd rustling came from outside
their hut, punctuated by irregular chirps. He sat up, cocked his
head toward the door, and even squinted, though that did nothing
to clarify the noise. He looked over at Drace, sleeping soundly on
his side and back to the door at the next chirp. Elvan picked up a
robe, gave up on tying it around himself in the dark, and went
naked into what he considered the town square.

Moonlight filtered through the trees, dappling the mossy well
and crumbled buildings. Elvan heard nothing of the rustle and
chirp and started explaining it away as a dream that lingered into
waking. Then he heard it again, drawing his eyes to where the two
cloth sacks lay toppled over and most of their contents spread
wide. Small eyes reflected up at him from the mess.

"No!" Elvan ran forward, clapping his hands. He didn't know
what he was chasing off, but knew the round, furry things were up
to no good. He counted at least six scattering from him and
lumbering into the trees, chirping angrily the whole time.

He dug through the mess and pulled out three mostly empty sacks of nuts and fruits, another with a hole chewed through it, and could only find two bags of jerky.

"What's going on?" Drace rushed to kneel beside him. "Oh no…"

"Looks like we're on a stricter timeline to find food."

"Did you see what ate it?"

Elvan held out his hands with fingertips touching to form a sphere. "They were about that big. Furry things. They stared right at me until I ran at them."

"I wonder if they taste good."

"They probably taste like fruits and nuts right now. They didn't seem quick."

"I never thought about having competition for our food." Drace sat back on his heels and rubbed his hands over his face. "Let's clean all this up and bring it in the house. Maybe they won't want to come too close to us."

* * *

Another morning without coffee left Elvan tripping over his own feet on the walk back to the beach. He convinced himself he would become accustomed to it, but not that it would matter for much longer if they didn't find food. A few paces ahead, Drace picked through the fallen wood and shrubs with a cloth sack tied around his waist, containing what remained of their rations.

Elvan's mind churned over thoughts of how much meat might be on each of the little beasts that stole their food. Their awkward run into the trees might mean they'd be easy to catch. They had flint boxes in the other sack left in the village, meaning a fire would be possible to cook them. Though, it was unlikely they could shove a sharp stick through the creatures and hold them over the fire like he had with sausages when Ser Vazadon told them stories as a kid. The furry things would have to be killed and butchered and—

Lost in his bloody thoughts, Elvan ran into Drace and stumbled back a step.

"What are you…" Elvan looked at Drace, who was rolling his necklace's crystal between his fingers, then followed his gaze into the woods. Less than twenty feet from the river's edge, rocks were piled neatly to waist level. Moss and vines twisted through the clean stacks, nearly obscuring the stones. Three feet wide and twice as long, Elvan swallowed hard and approached. By the hazy morning burning shafts of light through the canopy, he saw five, then another ten scattered between the trees.

"Graves," said Elvan. "How did we not notice these on the way from the beach? I thought we're following the same route along the river."

Drace knelt beside the cairn and rubbed at the stubble on this cheek. "I wouldn't have missed this with how focused I was."

"Then what? Did someone bury all these bodies in the last couple of days?" Elvan knelt at the head of the grave to rub a thumb along the roughly carved piece of wood there, getting close to read the letters. "There's a name. Frensparrow Kae."

"Kae? As in House Kae? Where your governess went to work?"

Elvan grunted thoughtfully, rose, and went to the next marker. "Lorekeeper Waasi" was barely legible on the old bit of bark. "Lorekeeper, that sounds like a title, not a name."

Drace scrambled over to Elvan's side to read the marker, then rushed to the next closest, and the next. After the fifth, he turned to Elvan with eyes wide. "These are the last great Artists. Those who fought against the Sovereign King." He untied the sack from his waist and set it by his feet.

Elvan frowned down at Lorekeeper Waasi's marker. "I was never taught their names, only their crimes. Alleged crimes. I suppose those like your Nana would want to keep their spirit alive. This is remarkably well preserved for being a century and a half old. I wonder if the village is—" He looked up at Drace, who was clutching the ruby at his throat and spinning a slow circle with eyes closed. "What are you doing?"

"Shush, searching for magic." He stopped, facing the grave in front of Elvan. "And I think I found some." Drace placed a hand on the top of Lorekeeper Waasi's cairn and closed his eyes again, letting out a slow breath. "Sorry about this, but I'm sure you would understand." He lifted the stone and tossed it gently aside.

"Stop that!" Elvan jumped up and put his hands over Drace's as he reached for another stone. "What are you doing?"

"There's something in this grave. The Lorekeeper might have been buried with an artefact."

"Even if there is something, you can't just rip apart someone's grave!"

"I don't think it's doing her much good."

"But…"

"But what, Elvan? If there's an artefact here, I can use it to help keep us alive."

Elvan stared into Drace's amber eyes for a long moment before letting his fingers slip away. Everything Ser Vazadon told him about respect and honor for the dead went away with the circumstances of their need.

Drace grabbed Elvan's hand. "Lorekeeper Waasi's physical remains might have been left here, but her spirit has moved on and her memory quietly survives in Artist families. As hard as people like King Pearce or Inquisitor Nilranke try to wipe out the last

Artists, they'll never succeed."

"I…" Elvan licked his lips and shook his head before taking a stone from the pile with his other hand.

They stacked the mossy rocks into two piles until Drace exposed the first hint of red cloth. Elvan took a step away to watch him carefully expose the body of an old woman lying in gentle repose, looking like she might have just passed away in her sleep the night before. Her crimson and violet robes looked worn, mended, and patched, but no less vibrant. Her gray hair was carefully braided and laid across her shoulder, down to where her hands folded around a piece of carved obsidian on her chest.

"How can she look like that?" Elvan whispered and retreated a step.

Drace touched his fingers to his lips, then to the woman's forehead. His hand went to the piece of stone in her hands, but glanced up to Elvan first. "You won't want to see this."

"What?"

Drace closed his eyes and sighed. "There's magic lingering, keeping her as she is. I assume it's what kept us from seeing this place the other day, but it's quickly fading. When I take the artefact, things will… catch up."

Elvan started to ask what that meant, but put it together quickly by Drace's determined stare, and turned away.

"You can go back to the river," Drace said a moment later. "I'll put the stones back and pay my respects."

Elvan nodded and took a step toward the first grave, but paused. *We're in this together. I can't let him do all the work because I'm squeamish about a body.*

With a deep breath, he turned as a wave of air pressure waved over him, popping his ears. Lorekeeper Waasi's body and clothing waned gray and sank, dissolving to ash within a heartbeat, leaving

Drace kneeling in her empty grave with fingers wrapped around the artefact.

He looked up at Elvan, yawning against the air pressure. "That was less than ideal."

"You expected… that?" Elvan tried to process what he'd just witnessed.

Drace placed the first stone back in the Lorekeeper's resting place and waved for Elvan to hand him another.

The work of covering the empty grave left Elvan with a twist in his gut, seeing that not even bones remained after a century on the soft ground of the forest. *Lorekeeper Waasi lives on in the stories told about her. What will remain of me?*

When only a few stones remained, Elvan dared to break the silence. "Tell me about her."

Drace waited until they restored the cairn and stared down at the final stone before he spoke. "The Lorekeepers were servants of knowledge, mystical librarians. They kept no secrets, giving what they learned freely to anyone who came to them. Waasi lived in a tower by the coast in Glenmany with her husbands and children. She studied the ocean her whole life, teaching others to sail and fish." His voice cracked, and he pushed the heel of his palm against his eye.

Elvan put a hand on Drace's forearm. "How did she get here?"

"The Sovereign King passionately hated and mistrusted the Lorekeepers. He mounted an offensive against all of them all at once, striking across the continent in a single night. Waasi's children and husbands were found hanging from the tower, but they must have taken her captive to exile here."

Elvan gasped. "That's horrible."

Drace slowly nodded. "That's the Sovereign King. The man, the demon, the one exalted as to be a peer to the Six."

"I don't like the king or princess, not after how my mother was treated and especially not now, but I only heard noble stories about the Sovereign King."

"That's all they are, stories. Those told in Artist families swap the heroes and villains. The truth is probably somewhere in the middle, but anyone who knew him is just dust in the ground now. Heck, anyone who knew anyone who knew him would be dead."

"I didn't realize how much hate there was for the king."

Drace snorted back a laugh. "I don't expect you would, raised among nobles. Artists have an active hate against the Sovereign King and his descendants. The only reason they haven't risen again is a lack of power."

"Power…" Elvan's eyes drifted to the carved obsidian sitting on the cloth sack in the middle of the cemetery. "Like one might accrue from quietly moving powerful artefacts for a decade."

Drace gasped and whirled, following Elvan's gaze.

"How long might it take to empty the Arcanym and give the Artists and people like you time to train using artefacts?" Elvan asked.

"Artefacts on the scale of those in the Arcanym are legendary relics by today's standards. It would take years to relearn how to use them."

"Maybe a decade." Elvan paced around the cloth sack on the ground. "Delphina said it was all part of the princess's plan, but didn't know more than that. I bet Lorelai is creating an army of Artists. There's still no sense in her using them to take over the throne, as she'll get that when the king dies." He knelt and tapped a finger on his front teeth. "So she's arming them to make an example of them. She'll let the Artists rise up, kill her father, bringing war to Spheris. Then she swoops in with her army of inquisitors and culls them. All the citizens rejoice, hailing her as their savior. Her reign starts on a strong beat."

Drace squatted on the other side of the sack. "That's quite a story." He picked up the bit of obsidian, carved as a crude fox, and turned it over in his hands. "And I can believe it's all right."

"I guess it doesn't matter here." Elvan put a hand on Drace's.

"I didn't want to make a big deal about it then, but the artefact in the warehouse was hard to use, it was bursting with so much magic." Drace shook his head and took a deep breath. "There's not much left in this one after so long obscuring this cemetery."

"So, no using it to conjure meals."

Drace chuckled. "No meal conjuring. That burst of air you felt when I touched it was some spell unraveling. Hopefully, that's nothing too far-ranging. The artefact will discharge at the normal slow rate now, but we should save it for an emergency." He set it in the sack and rose.

Elvan looked up from where he knelt. "Will you tell me your stories? The Lorekeepers and other Artists?"

Drace sniffed and grinned down at Elvan, yet his eyes remained somber. "Of course. We have the rest of our lives, right?" He offered a hand.

Elvan smiled back, but felt the hollowness of it.

They returned to the river and glanced back to the piles of mossy stones marking the final resting place of some of the last great Artists on the continent. The vines seemed to creep a little tighter, gently pulling down the neat cairns, making it difficult to tell them from the underbrush by where they stood at the river's edge.

Drace absently rolled the ruby on his necklace between his fingers. "I don't like this place," he said quietly.

17

TIME PASSED IN A HAZE until Elvan noticed the soft sand under his sandals. A few paces ahead, Drace dropped their sack and stared out at the horizon.

"What is this place?" he asked.

Elvan stepped beside him, but had no answer.

Drace waved at the sky. "There's sunlight, but no sun. Moonlight, but no moon. We should sleep out here tonight, in the open, to see if there are any stars. The horizon looks… fake. I can see where waves are lapping up against it out there."

Elvan squinted, but took Drace's word on it. "Maybe whatever magic the monks used to send us here is also keeping us from leaving."

"It might rule out escaping by raft. Magic brought us here. It might be the only way out. The horizon is definitely nearer than a few days ago. It's either moving, or the whole place is shrinking." He looked down at the sack at his feet, then again to the horizon. "Wouldn't that be something if Waasi's artefact is all that was keeping this place from collapsing, and we get here right as it runs out of magic?"

"Collapsing? What are you talking about? The monks just sent us somewhere."

"I've been worrying about that. Nana had a story about a boy who wandered into a cave, a bunch of exciting stuff happened, but at the end it turns out he was sent into a miniature world. He ended up living in a pendant his mother kept on her necklace."

"You think that's what happened to us?"

Drace shrugged. "It was just a bedtime story to scare kids so they wouldn't get lost in caves. But magic brought us here and magic might explain where we are."

Elvan imagined Princess Lorelai perched atop her father's throne with a new lapis lazuli set in her tiara. "That sort of reminds me of a story Ser Vazadon told us. It might have been the first story he ever told my siblings and me. Something about a castle where every room was its own world."

"The Invisible Castle? I've heard that one too."

Elvan felt his shoulder sag, worrying that despite his insistence, Ser Vazadon's stories might be fantasy. How would Drace have heard a tale that happened to the old knight?

"Which way?" asked Drace.

Elvan shook away thoughts of living inside a gem. "We either go back toward where we started and continue that direction, or we go beyond the river."

Drace nodded across the river. "Let's go that way, so it's not all backtracking." He bent to sling the light sack over his shoulder.

"Wait, one more thing before we go."

Drace turned back expectantly.

Elvan stood a bit taller to quickly kiss him.

Drace leaned back and traced a finger over his lips with a smirk. "Does our possible impending doom turn you on, Mr. Galmoth?"

"No, I... It's all terrifying. Being exiled to never again see another person, the threat of starvation, cemeteries that appear and disappear in the woods, the possibility that we're in a world that will shrink to nothing. You make it manageable, somehow."

Drace scratched at his cheek. "Maybe it's my charming smile."

"It's definitely charming."

"Are you about to finally admit you like me?"

"I..." Elvan couldn't remember telling Drace how he felt. At least not explicitly while he was conscious. "Drace... I don't know what to call it."

"Not 'love' I assume. Despite all we've been through, that's too early to say, right?"

"Right, obviously. I think."

"Obviously. We'll figure out what you can call it." Drace bit his lower lip, winked, and turned.

Elvan watched him approach the river and look for a shallow spot to cross where it met the ocean. They were on the far side within a few minutes, wet to their bellies.

Hours slid by like water off a duck's back, and just as unmemorable. A copse of tall trees ahead grew across the sand until waves lapped the trunks of those closest to the water. Standing among them, Elvan looked up at the round, pale-green fruit at least twenty feet overheard. Drace found a few around their bases, each about the size of the beasts that ate their food. After many failed tries, he cracked the fibrous husk on the edge of a stone outcropping and cringed at the ash gray dust within. He broke open two more to the same result.

"So much for that." Drace kicked the fruit, winced, and shook his foot. "Let's keep going."

When Drace called for a break, Elvan looked back, expecting to see the copse of tall trees with the fruits, but those were lost to the slow curve of the endless beach some hours ago.

"I think we're on an island. The beach curves right more than left," said Drace and picked a single nut from the pouch Elvan held. They sat beside each other, bare feet stretching in the sand, looking out to the flat horizon.

"Meaning we'll eventually get back to the river if we keep going this way."

Drace nodded. "But it's a big island. We followed the river for half a day and didn't get to a source. We didn't even find any branches."

Elvan pinched the crumbs at the bottom of the bag, careful not to drop any on the way to his mouth. "I'm having difficulty thinking about time here. That feels like longer than just yesterday."

Drace hummed thoughtfully.

"What?" Elvan asked.

"Magic's weird."

"Agreed. Care to elaborate?"

Drace rubbed his forehead. "They're called Artists because they create artefacts, carving and whittling something while pouring their magic into it. But Artists also shape magic to fit their need. They sculpt and form it how they choose, forcing the magic into a result."

"Interesting. So back in the warehouse, you were just focusing on making us invisible?"

"And it took all my concentration. A true Artist could have made the whole warehouse invisible."

Elvan set the empty bag at his side and leaned back on his elbows. "What made you think of that?"

Drace nudged the cloth sack with a toe. "When I say Artists can shape magic, I mean they can literally make its nebulous form take shape. I knew I was disrupting something in the cemetery when I picked up the artefact. It was powering some lingering spell but is now fully collapsing. I don't regret it, it would have failed soon anyway, and now we have an artefact with some small amount of power."

"But…?"

Drace swiveled in place to lie down with his head on Elvan's lap. "Who knows what magic she cast over this place. This is the work of a Lorekeeper."

"Maybe she created this whole place."

Drace snorted back a laugh, but chewed his lip in thought. "Maybe. Nana said the Lorekeepers had absolute mastery over magic, working directly for the Six, but not in a religious way."

Never being much of a student of religion, Elvan wasn't sure what to take from that statement. "Interesting."

"Right? Like I said, magic's weird. But, for some reason, the Hex Monks guard the crumbling doorway to this place, tossing others in at the crown's command."

"Certainly raises a lot of questions and answers none." Elvan ran a hand through Drace's hair and focused on the not-too-distant horizon. He was sure it was only his imagination that made the low clouds look so flat. As he watched, the blue blended effortlessly to pink and dimmed. Before he noticed the change, an unseen moon bathed them in gentle light.

"I guess we're sleeping on the beach." Elvan shook his head and looked down at Drace, snoring softly on his lap. He ran a hand along the thick stubble on Drace's jaw and rested it on his chest. "I'm glad we're alone together. I wouldn't want to be here with anyone but you," Elvan whispered. "Maybe Ser Vazadon, but only because I think he'd tell me a story about how he already escaped from this exact situation in a faraway land, then he'd do it."

Drace moaned softly and rolled to his side, facing Elvan.

Elvan watched the slow rise and fall of Drace's shoulder, how the moonlight without a source lit his cheek perfectly. They'd met less than a week ago… Was it a week? Elvan couldn't think of what day it was. Surely not enough time to develop any genuine feelings. Though… What were those feelings? Elvan loved his mother, his brother, loved Ser Vazadon, and despite her litany of grotesque flaws, he loved his sister. As he gazed down at Drace, his stomach churned with butterflies, and a tingle shot through his toes and fingers. His cheeks and neck burned with the memory of their intimate caresses, stolen kisses, and playful gropes. His breath quickened, thinking about the intense moments of passion in the hut, by the river, and earlier on the beach, but soon he was fighting just to stay awake.

18

E LVAN JERKED AWAKE AS A crack of thunder split the
sky overhead. Drace bolted upright, shrieking, while the
booming echo shook the sand beneath them. Elvan wrapped his
arms around Drace, who shook violently, shielding his eyes from
the storm. Lightning arced across the starless black veil of the sky,
down to where the slow lap of water met the horizon. Drace let out
a whimper and Elven held him tighter. The flashes of light
lingered, intensifying with each quickened breath, until the sky
appeared as a dark glass dome, back lit through the myriad cracks
by hot, white brilliance, ready to shatter. Other than the initial peal
of thunder, only the low rumble continued without pause while the
two huddled together on the beach.

When the lightning finally faded and the thunder quieted, Elvan
felt the chill from the sweat covering his body and let out a gasping
breath.

"Well that's a hell of a way to wake up," Drace chuckled, still
shivering.

"At least it's not raining."

"Yet."

"What now? It's too dark to walk," said Elvan.

Drace leaned a little closer. "I'm not falling back asleep anytime soon."

Elvan bit back the reflexive smile. He was thinking the same thing, but his mind hung on the details and implications of their intimacy. Ser Vazadon's stories were chaste adventures, Cenna read him imaginative fairy tales, and his mother taught him some of how to keep financial documents in order. Nothing prepared him for what it might feel like, not just physically, but emotionally, to intertwine himself with another. In a few well-read books tucked away in the darker corners of the library back home, a couple might touch hands, kiss, then the scene faded with a flowery, if distant, description of them "making love." It always read as calm and… inevitable. An act that expresses feelings, but is itself devoid of much emotion. With Drace, the flood of passion overwhelmed Elvan and each time brought him nearly to tears.

Elvan blinked, realizing Drace was still staring at him, and leaned forward to press their foreheads together, lips only inches apart. Elvan closed his eyes and breathed in deeply, catching the faintest whiff of the oddity shop's incense. "What are we doing?"

Elvan felt Drace's brow crinkle with a grin. "In life? On this island? Right now, in this moment?" He ran a hand through Elvan's hair, curled around his ear, down his neck, to his chest.

"Us, right now. I don't know what words fit what's between us."

"A few inches of air and two robes that are surprisingly less scratchy. Maybe my skin's just developed one giant callous."

"That's not what I mean."

"I know." Drace hooked a finger under Elvan's chin to pull his gaze upward. "I feel it, too. Do we have to name it?"

"I guess not." Elvan rested back on his palms, then his elbows, staring up at the deep void hanging over them. "If we got out of here, what would you do first, Drace?"

"Out of here? Back to the monastery? I might avoid Spheris and go south to live near my Nana. You?"

"I want to see my sister and the princess crushed."

Drace laughed. "I didn't realize the vindictive options were open."

"That's not vindictive; that's justice. Lorelai used my mother and tossed her away as soon as she became a liability. Now Delphina is just out for herself; though that's nothing new for her."

"Got it. In that case, Nana can wait a few months. Nilranke..." Drace ground a fist into his palm.

"Good choice. How would you do it?"

Drace hummed while he considered the question. "I'd find the thing most dear to him and destroy it."

"I can't imagine what a person like Nilranke could possibly care for enough to have any effect. Too bad you're not a violent person. You could just break his other leg in his sleep."

"Or just break his face. What makes you think I'm not violent?"

"By how gentle you are when we... While we're..."

"Having sex?" Drace winked, but his shoulders dropped with a sigh. "No point in fantasizing about it, though. Hurting Nilranke, I mean. Not that I've lost hope of getting out of here, but you know how the papers would spin that story. *Violent Artist Attacks Peacekeeper In His Sleep*. The entire system is rotten."

Elvan reached to run a hand down Drace's arm. "You'd move south, then?"

Drace fell back in the sand beside Elvan and rolled to face him. "I don't know. Would you go with me?" He ran a hand through Elvan's hair.

Elvan swallowed hard and pushed his cheek into Drace's palm.

They'd both considered their life together in exile, but beyond was something he thought little about. He stared into Drace's amber eyes, studying how they glowed in the steady ambient light of the moonless night. Elvan wanted to blurt out "Yes!" and profess his feelings, despite not fully understanding them.

Instead, he heard himself say a less committal, "I'd like that," and frowned internally. Drace caught it too and his grin evened out just a touch. *We're going to die on this little island. Why can't I agree to something I know won't happen, but would do in a heartbeat?*

"I mean, yes," Elvan corrected himself. "Obviously, I would, if you'd have me."

Drace's grin returned to full. "Of course, I'd have you. You're a better catch than you give yourself credit for, Elvan Galmoth. Smart, attentive listener, magnificent hair."

"Short, skinny." Elvan couldn't stop himself.

Drace chuckled. "I'll get stuff off the top shelves and you get them out of the cupboards. It'll work out great. Stop being so hard on yourself. You're an excellent kisser, too." He leaned to press their lips together in a quick peck.

Elvan felt the heat creep up his cheeks. "I don't have much experi—"

"Oh, blah blah. Then you're a quick study."

Elvan rolled to face the same direction as Drace and scooted until they pressed back to chest. Drace wrapped both arms around him in a solid squeeze and nestled his cheek near Elvan's ear.

"Whether or not we get out of here," Drace whispered, sending a tickle down Elvan's spine, "and whatever happens afterward if we get out, I'm glad we're together."

"Could you tell me one of your Nana's stories? About the Lorekeepers?"

"A story? Right now? Sure. The dreamer." Drace cleared his throat. "There was a boy, the son of a lighthouse keeper, who only had a dozen books in his house. He read them each a dozen times, then a dozen more until he could recite them from memory. He begged for a new book, but his father couldn't afford them.

"One night, the boy went to sleep and woke on a balcony overlooking a library that stretched to the horizon. He saw a score of people in red and purple below — Lorekeepers — moving between thousands of books. The boy ran down the spiral stairs to the library's main level, where a woman with dark skin and kind blue eyes stopped him. 'Have you come to read a book?' she asked him. 'Yes!' he yelled. 'But this is just a dream. Can I come here for real?' The woman smiled and nodded. 'You may visit here every night when you sleep and, if you can read every book here, I'll bring you while you're awake.' The boy agreed, eager to pick up the closest tome, eager to read it all so he could visit that library in his waking world.

"He read about distant worlds and people, science and magic, concepts so far beyond what he ever could have imagined as a lighthouse keeper's son. He read all night, every night, for ninety years. When he lay on his deathbed, surrounded by his children and great-grandchildren, he cried, knowing he would never get to see that library with his own eyes, as he could never finish a task that was eternal."

Elvan waited for the story to continue, but when Drace remained quiet, he shuffled to face the other. "That's it? He spent his life wanting something, but never achieved it?"

"What didn't he achieve? He wanted to read, and he did. The moral's that he was so focused on the end goal, he didn't realize the journey fulfilled it."

"That's..." Elvan chewed his cheek, embarrassed he

overlooked the simple purpose of the story. Focus on the present. Be thankful for what you have, not upset about what you lack. "Thank you."

At some point in Drace's tale, the sky shed the inky, starless veil as rays of orange and gold cut across, leaving a cloudless blue.

Drace blew out a long breath while he stared at the horizon. "That's definitely nearer. This world is either shrinking or shifting, but we traveled a full day and didn't outrun it. It's moving faster than we are."

"We have to find my mother quickly."

"Right. The magic of this place is broken and fading quickly."

"I wonder if the monks knew that when they sent us here."

"Let's hope not. I doubt they understand the magic or technology of those gates beyond how to open them."

"Great. The next person to get exiled will be smashed into a collapsed world."

They didn't travel much farther before the sand gave way to wide, flat stones. Drace squinted into the distance along the gently curving beach. "Another river," he said and hastened their pace. Within minutes, they stood at the mouth of a narrow, fast-moving river across the rocks. The water cut through the trees, bouncing and frothing over smooth rocks. The nearer bank was more of the wide stones, but the far side was a mess of sloppy mud.

"No animal tracks," Drace commented. "At least not right here. I'll keep an eye out for that, but I guess we follow this? Go all the way to its source this time?"

Elvan nodded his agreement, but something in Drace's statement struck him. "I haven't heard birds for a day. No insects, either. This place is dying."

Drace gave him a shrug and look that showed he was thinking the same before they trudged forward, careful to not slip on the loose rocks. The river meandered through the trees, carving a winding path that time should have naturally straightened long ago. The current increased as the banks came nearer and they rested from the effort of balancing while walking up the gentle incline over loose ground. With their stomachs complaining about the lack of food, neither commented on it when Drace put the last handful of jerky back into the sack. As Elvan worried about how near they were to dusk, the trees opened to a wide lake. The river spilled over a waterfall on the far side a few hundred feet away, cascading a torrent of water.

Elvan squinted across the mostly still lake. "Is that an island at the bottom of the waterfall?"

"With a little hut, it looks like," Drace nodded. "Let's go."

They circled to the left, and Drace quickened his steps after a few paces. "There's smoke. Someone's there!"

Even unencumbered, Elvan struggled to keep up. His heart leaped to his throat, fighting off how sure he was he would find his mother in that hut, sitting in front of a fire, reading a book. As he neared the hut, he noted a tree growing through the thatched roof and the pile of river rocks pasted together with mud that made up the walls. The hut was centered on an island ten feet from the shore. More piles of rocks filled the island, leaving a narrow path to what might pass as a front door.

An elderly woman stepped from the hut, wrapped in what was once a fine gold dress fifteen years ago, before it was patched and mended a hundred times. She hummed a tune that carried across the water despite the proximity to the waterfall and approached the pile of rocks nearest to the door, seeming to rearrange it slightly.

"How old was your mother?" Drace asked and slowed his pace.

"Mid-forties." Elvan's heart sank a little more with each step. The hunched woman with flyaway white hair couldn't be a day under sixty, perhaps well into her seventies.

They waded through the calf-deep water, stopped a few feet from her, and waited for her to finish stacking her rocks. She leaned back with a contented sigh, turning to them with a startled gasp and narrowed her gaze. Her right eye was a milky white, the other a sharp blue.

"We didn't mean to startle you, ma'am," said Drace. "We..."

The old woman stepped nearer to Elvan, straightened to look into his face with her good eye. He reflectively took a step back.

"I know you," she muttered, pushing into Elvan's space. "I know you. I know you. I know you! I know you!" She nearly screamed the words and fell into a coughing fit.

Drace put a hand on the woman's back and gently patted when she bent forward with her body wracking from coughing. He grimaced and shrugged at Elvan.

"How do you know me?"

She labored to steady her breathing with a few deep, rasping inhales. She turned toward the door of the hut. "Of course it's him," she hissed and paused, as if waiting for a reply. "Quiet. Don't be silly."

Elvan followed her gaze to the pile of stones she'd been arranging, the other party in her conversation. *Lovely. We meet another person and she's completely mad.* "How do you know me, ma'am?" He repeated, and let his eyes wander into the hut. Dried herbs lined the wall he could see, along with the glint of metal tools. *Crazy, but she knows how to survive here.*

A breeze through the hut shifted the herbs enough to let the light glance off something golden on a thin chain. Elvan left the woman to chatter at the rocks and stepped toward the wall of herbs, brushing them aside and taking the necklace from where it hung on the wall. Dangling from the delicate chain, the flat amulet was engraved with what appeared to be a crude insect with a long body and four wings.

Elvan stumbled to lean against the dubious door frame and stared at the woman, searching for some hint of recognition. She jabbered at Drace, but half the words seemed aimed at the rocks. Elvan's thumb brushed against the amulet. It wasn't an insect. It was a top-down view of an old ship famed for its speed through the narrow rivers around Spheris.

He knew the design. It was on a signet ring he never wore. It was embroidered on most of his formal wear. On all the letterheads in his mother's study and the paper to seal crates for shipment.

The crest of House Galmoth.

"Mother?"

19

D RACE GASPED.

"I KNOW YOU!" the woman said again, moaning and rubbing at her face with both hands.

"How?" Drace asked in a whisper.

Elvan held up the necklace, as if that might explain everything. He tried to imagine his mother decades older than he last saw her, but found he couldn't even remember her five years younger. *No, this old crone can't be Selayna Galmoth, but this necklace proves my mother was here.*

The old woman took a deep breath and transformed. Rolling back her shoulders, her back straightened to stand almost a foot taller, now between Elvan and Drace's height. She rubbed her face once more and raked her fingers down her neck while her teeth clenched and jaw tightened. She turned to Elvan, and though her wild, white hair and milky eye were foreign to him, he recognized the posture of his mother, Selayna Galmoth, proud head of House Galmoth. Member of the Council of Houses. Master financier. Smuggler.

"Have I finally died in my sleep?" she asked in a voice softer than Elvan remembered, but without her craze of a moment ago.

Elvan wanted to run to her, but his feet wouldn't move. "How is this possible, Mother? You look... You're..."

She glanced down at her ragged and patched clothes. "Years alone. You, my poor boy, you don't look much older than I last saw you. Had I known you were awaiting me in the Afterlands, I would have found a means to come to you sooner." She crossed the space between them as she spoke and grazed a finger along the scruff covering his cheek.

He grabbed her by the wrist and took her hand in both of his. "I'm not dead, Mother, and neither are you. The princess exiled you two years ago, and I've been trying to get you back since. I failed. I figured out your part in the princess's plan and she had me exiled as well, along with Drace."

Selayna looked back at Drace, seeming to notice him for the first time. "Oh, good day to you." She drifted back to Elvan. "That can't be right, Elvan. The princess's plan would have long ago taken effect or failed. Decades ago."

"No, Mother. It's been two years."

"We're in a miniature world," Drace said while he stepped beside Elvan. "Time is... Your brother, Elvan," he gasped. "That's why he looked ten years older. The Hex Monks must use these bubble worlds in their meditation. Time flows faster in here."

"Has the king been assassinated?" said Selayna.

"He wasn't when we left," said Drace.

"That's good. Did he announce his plan of abdication?"

"Abdication?" Elvan shot Drace a glance. "No. I haven't been in the House meetings these last couple of years, but no one's mentioned anything about that."

"Why haven't you been in the meetings?"

"This is where your concern is, Mother? They weren't very kind to me last I went. They forced me out."

"*Not kind*? Those meetings are to help shape the future of the nation and you give up your voice because they're *not kind*? I raised you better than that, Elvan," his mother chided, bringing back some of the chill in her tone that he was accustomed to. "What did you think the princess's motivation was?"

"I… I didn't…"

"No time, no time, no time." Selayna winced and squeezed her eyes closed. She raised a palm to her forehead and spoke without looking up. "I'll be worthless to you, Elvan. I must speak plainly. The people that were here when I arrived mentioned a way out. I found it years ago, but I can't use it."

"There were other people here?" Elvan asked. Drace's fingers slipped into his and squeezed.

"Quiet!" Selayna rubbed at her face. "Through the waterfall and deep under the surface is a… I don't know what it is. A portal. I'm no Artist. I don't know." She dropped her hands and shook her head. Cracking her good eye open, she looked over Elvan. Her lip twisted to a ghost of a smile on seeing his hand in Drace's. "At least you're not alone."

"I missed you," he said, sounding small.

She groaned and leaned forward, rubbing her face again. Hunched, she loped toward a stack of stones and addressed it in babbling tones.

Elvan stammered to speak, but again only saw his failures laid out before him.

He tightened his fingers around Drace's. The amulet bearing the Galmoth family crest hung from his other fist.

"I'm sorry," Drace whispered.

Selayna moved to another stack of rocks, then gathered up the hems of her dress to cross the shallow lake. She waved a hand through the brush as if searching for berries or herbs.

"Oh, Elvan, that was terrible," Drace said a little louder. He wrapped his other arm in a tight hug.

"She said the king was going to abdicate. I really don't understand Lorelai's motivation, if the king plans to abdicate to her." Elvan watched his mother from around Drace's shoulder. "She could teach us how to survive here."

Drace pushed to arm's length. "What? No, Elvan. We have to get out of here."

"I can't leave her."

"I'm not suggesting that, but we have to find the way out."

Elvan watched his mother pick at the bush.

"If I'm right about the difference in time," said Drace, "we might be able to stop the princess."

Elvan shook his head. "How? How do we stop the princess?"

"No idea, but we can't do anything from here. Let's find what she mentioned and come back for her."

Elvan ran a hand through this hair. "I can't leave her," he repeated.

"She's survived for decades. She'll be fine for a few more hours."

Elvan stepped back and folded his arms across his chest.

Drace leaned away and mirrored the body language. "So, it's the warehouse again, then?"

"What?"

"Nevermind." Drace closed his eyes and sighed. "I'll go alone and come back when I've found something." He turned and bent to pick up their cloth bag. Rummaging through it, he took out the obsidian artefact and dropped the rest.

Elvan watched Drace wade through the shallow water, not

bothering to pull up the hem of his robe. The former shopkeeper paused to watch Elvan's mother for a moment before turning right to follow the shore toward the waterfall.

"The warehouse," Elvan muttered and scoffed. *I find my mother after two years and he makes it about him.* He followed Drace's careful movement at the water's edge, losing sight of him when he was forced to move into the trees to avoid the precarious rocks.

The warehouse. Where he opened up to me, saved us, and I ran away screaming. What about him? He showed complete trust in me after so short a time and I fled, yet he forgave me right away. I don't deserve this man. I can't even tell him that I love him.

Elvan chewed on the inside of his cheek, opening and clenching his fists.

"My smallest decisions add up," Ser Vazadon once told him. "Turn right or go straight? Carry the torch in my swordhand?" The story had been about delving through catacombs to find and slay a lich. It was an intense, adventurous tale told years ago, but now to hear that Ser Vazadon claims his chronicles were all true…

Elvan shook off the grin that crept across his lips. He faced the same decision. His mother poked through the weeds ahead of him and Drace was somewhere around the lake to his right. This choice didn't feel at all like a small decision.

Selayna stomped back through the water and turned her back to Elvan, addressing the stack of rocks nearest to the hut's door. "No, that's for Elvan." She tilted her head and scoffed, waving her hand at the rocks. "Worthless gobshite."

A memory snapped into Elvan mind. He'd heard his mother call one other person that on many occasions.

Father.

Selayna moved to the water's edge and Elvan reached out to touch the rocks. He cleared his throat. "What's for Elvan?" he asked, raising his voice an octave with a nasal drawl. He hadn't impersonated his father's voice in years and the accuracy made him shudder.

His mother stood still where she'd been splashing at the water, turning with a look of confusion that cut through her wild eyes. "Miles?"

"Yeah, Sel. What's for Elvan?"

Selayna looked up at him, blinking hard. "My note. You know my note. You stopped me from finishing it!" She jammed an accusing finger into Elvan's chest.

If I were staying true to character, I'd be done with the conversation and on my way to a bottle.

Elvan swallowed hard. "Where's the note? El… The boy's coming."

Selayna grumbled and pushed past Elvan into her hut. She returned a few seconds later, waving a tiny scrap of parchment over her head and slapped it against Elvan's chest. "Show that to Elvan. Elvan will be here soon and…" she trailed off, cocking her head as if listening to some other response. She scoffed and waved at nothing before returning to her berry bush across the water.

Not taking his eyes from her, Elvan stepped to the rocks that were, according to his mother's frayed mind, his father. He carefully flattened the brittle scrap of parchment that might have been torn from a notebook twenty years ago. Stained, smudged, and damaged by water and possibly blood, he squinted to make out the faint words in his mother's hand.

"…king intends to disseminate… the Council of Houses… Lorelai… a plot to assassinate… and the privy council."

Finally, the missing piece, Lorelai's motive. Disseminate, not abdicate. Her father intends to give up the crown's power; spread it to the Houses. Of course, Lorelai wants him and anyone that knows dead. She'll lose everything.

His hands fell to his sides. "She'll be a tyrant. If she's willing to kill her father, she'll kill anyone else she wants. We have to stop her."

Hiking up his robes, he waded across to the far bank until he heard his mother's tuneless hum. She didn't look up or seem to notice him at all.

She needs help that we can't get here. We have to get her home.

"I'll be right back, Mother. I love you."

A blast of thunder threatened to rupture Elvan's eardrums. He yelped and dropped to a squat by reflex with hands clapped over his ears, but his mother showed no reaction, just continued picking individual berries from a bush, dropping them into a pile at her feet.

The sky burned with the afterimage of lightning that left a darker hue as it faded, as if it was searing away what remained of the day's blue. Elvan focused on slowing his breath and hoping his heart would return to its normal place in his chest as he watched the light show rip away the day.

"Drace!" Elvan jumped to his feet, gave his mother a last glance, and ran toward the waterfall. He shouted again between the booms of thunder, tossing away caution to quickly cross over the slick rocks and turn into the trees where he last saw the other man. Smacking away tree limbs and jumping over fallen logs, he moved as quickly as he could through trees lit by the wild lightning. Shadows twisted around every root and rock protruding from the soft dirt. He tripped on a large one, tumbling forward, catching himself on his hands.

Elvan cursed and looked back at the rock. Lightning flashed. Not a rock. Drace lay huddled on his side. Elvan crawled to him, wrapping him in his arms. Drace pushed into him, shivers calming with each shaky breath.

20

THE STORM CONTINUED FAR LONGER than the one on the beach, with an intensity that would fray the nerves of anyone. When Elvan counted a minute between flashes, he relaxed and sat back on his heels. Darkness came fully into the woods, broken by patches of light from the invisible moon.

"How are you?" he asked.

Drace pushed to an elbow and rubbed his face with the other hand. "I'm fine. I..." He looked up with bloodshot eyes. "Thank you. I've never been good in a thunderstorm."

"Why's that?"

Drace shrugged and wiped his nose with the back of his hand. "I've always reacted this way, turning into a sniveling baby. I know better; know there's nothing to be afraid of, but..." He shook his head. "Seems it's suddenly night time. We should go back to your mother's."

Elvan glanced beyond Drace, toward his mother's hut, and frowned. "It's... hard seeing her as she is, what she's become. Let's see about the waterfall and come back for her."

Drace brushed a hand over Elvan's cheek and a thumb across his lips. "I want us to get out of here. Together."

Elvan licked his lips and nodded in the dark. "I…" He knew what he wanted to say, but couldn't form the words. They barely knew each other, only met a week ago. Did he even understand the gravity of the phrase?

Drace put a hand on Elvan's and leaned nearer. Elvan's breath quickened as he gazed into those amber eyes, crinkled at the edges from a soft smirk. He opened his mouth to say the words, to admit what he felt, or thought he felt.

"Drace, I…"

Drace leaned closer and opened his eyes a little wider.

The words choked in Elvan's throat.

Did I ever hear my parents say it to each other? Did they say it to me? That wouldn't be the same. How can I know what love feels like? What if he doesn't say it back? If he feels the same, why won't he say it first?

Drace tilted his head and raised an eyebrow, anticipating the next words.

"You know what I'm trying to say," said Elvan.

"I might have some idea."

Elvan grunted and broke their shared gaze, looking down at his hands in his lap. "If you feel it, why can't you say it first?"

"First?" Drace chuckled. "I said I liked you the morning after we met. I'm waiting for you to say at least that much back before I escalate things."

"I said I like…"

Drace slowly wagged head side to side. "You said you were glad to know that I like you. Yesterday you were wondering what to name what's between us, but didn't suggest anything."

Elvan thought through the long hours of the days and nights

spent together over the last week, certain he must have said something. Maybe it was only a thought he left unsaid?

"Of course I like you, Drace. I…" He chewed his cheek. "It would be nice to know what we would be like without escaping burning shops or investigating my mother's smuggling or hiding from inquisitors or this," he waved his hands overhead. "I don't know what word to use to describe how I feel about you. I only know how to describe how I feel without you."

Drace scratched at the growing stubble on his cheek. "And how's that?"

"When I left you at the warehouse, all I could think about was how I wronged you." He stopped and bit his cheek. That wasn't quite right. "Not just that. I missed you immediately. I thought it was being alone in the manor for the first time, but I saw you in everything. The coffee you made, the secret chamber behind my mother's closet… Your smell in my brother's room."

"I smell?"

Elvan nodded. "I still get hints of the incense from your shop when we're close."

"Better than I thought I'd smell." Drace sniffed at his shoulder and crinkled his nose.

"Please, I'm trying to be serious."

"I know, sorry." Drace sighed and put his hands on his knees. "It's hard to figure out how to express certain things, I get it. Thank you for coming after me, but let's not worry too much about trying to put labels on things until we are either out of here or are resigned to being trapped here. I—"

The woods lit with a blazing white light, followed immediately by a single blast of thunder. Drace ducked and threw both hands over his head, but it faded quickly. The soft light of morning now illuminated what they could see of the sky through the canopy.

They slapped a hand to their chests at the same time, gasping for breath.

"The air," Elvan wheezed. "It feels… thick."

Drace opened and closed his mouth and rubbed at his left ear. "I bet this world just got a lot smaller. We have to get out of here. Now."

They jumped to their feet, and Elvan's gaze lingered toward his mother's hut.

Drace read the intention. "We'll come back for her." He tugged at Elvan's elbow.

Drace kept a hand on the artefact hanging from his rope belt as they rushed toward the waterfall, struggling through the dense growth. Keeping their breathing shallow, they raced through the trees growing up an incline that quickly became more of a climb. Within moments, the steep incline ended abruptly at a sheer rock face.

Elvan craned his neck up the top of the waterfall still a hundred or more feet above them, then sidled to the edge of the cliff, peeking over the edge, to where the water tumbled against rocks and frothed into a bubbly foam.

"There!" Drace pointed to the left of the waterfall. Elvan squinted to make out a shadow against the rocks that might imply a space to squeeze behind the water's flow.

Moving with as much care and speed as possible in the monk's woven sandals, they crossed the slick rocks to a narrow ledge less than a hand-span wide, leading to a path behind the water. Elvan pressed against the cold stone and followed Drace. Water pelted his back, threatening to drag him from the ledge, into the jumble of rocks to become food for the fish. He pressed his eyes closed tightly against the cold spray, shuffling along the ledge, feeling blindly for the next point to grab with knuckles blanched white.

Elvan took another step, and the water surged, drenching and suddenly pressing him against the jagged rocks. As quickly as it blew against him, the water pulled away. Elvan felt his wet fingers slip from their grips. He floundered, grabbing at nothing while water poured across his face, into his nose and mouth. His equilibrium shifted and he couldn't fight the pull backward, toward the water. He screamed, only to let more water rush down his throat.

Impossibly powerful hands grabbed his flailing arm, wrenching him forward, out of the raging water, onto his hands and knees on a rough stone floor. He hacked and wheezed, spitting the burning out of his lungs, but breathing too deeply in the dense air only made him cough more. After a long moment, Elvan noticed the gentle patting on his back and dropped to his side.

Drace hovered over him with the artefact in one hand and a look of horror plastered over his face. Elvan thought it a trick of the water in his eyes in the dim cave, but the other man's amber eyes glowed with an internal light that faded quickly as Elvan tried to focus on it.

"Well, that wasn't the easiest," Drace said with a hint of a smirk. He glanced back toward the curtain of water at the cave's entrance and let out a hollow chuckle.

Elvan coughed and followed his gaze, guessing the other's thoughts. *If there is a way out, and it requires being on this side of the waterfall, Mother will never make it across that ledge.*

Even if we could secure her with rope, I can't make that twice, out and back again. Not without slipping.

Drace stood and offered a hand down. Elvan took it and dragged himself up, weighted down by what felt like another body's worth of water soaked into his robe. A chill ran down his limbs from a steady breeze coming out of the cave, toward the water, and he turned into it to peer into the darkness.

"Your eyes are better. What's down there?"

Drace squinted, wiped the crook of his elbow across his eyes, and squinted again. "It's dark."

"I noticed."

"I mean, unnaturally dark. I can't…" He raised the obsidian artefact in his hand. "I can squeeze some light out of this, but I'd rather not drain what little magic it has left."

"We might need the magic farther in, but can't see where we're going to get there without burning some of it," said Elvan. "I don't like it, but what choice is there?"

"We left a flint box in the bag at your mother's. We could go get it and find some dry brush on the way back."

"No thank you."

Drace reached to lace his fingers through Elvan's with one hand, raising the artefact in the other. With a few mumbled words that sent an electric shiver through Elvan's arm, a faint glow, as from a hooded lantern, emitted from Drace's upraised hand. He waved it over the shallow pools of water and craggy stalagmites, looking for a safe path. Moving forward, he tucked their hands behind him, encouraging Elvan to follow rather than walk abreast.

Within a few feet, Elvan could barely see Drace's silhouette inches in front of him, walking with short, careful steps. Rather than being overwhelmed by the blindness, he focused on taking shallow breaths of the chill, musty air.

"Watch your step." Drace's tone was a whisper, but his voice boomed in Elvan's ears. "It slants down sharply."

Elvan's next step skidded on slick stone and he flailed an arm to catch himself before falling forward.

"There's something ahead," Drace said, either not noticing or not drawing attention to the balance issues going on behind him.

Drace pulled his hand around to lead Elvan to walk beside him when the ground leveled out, becoming as smooth as tile under their sandaled feet. The light from the artefact cast a meager glow over a space about fifteen feet around them. Stalagmites at the edges curved the floor upward and cast shadows, hinting at possibly deeper places to explore, if only they had more light. Directly in front of the pair, in the center of the cave, was a circular ring of worked stone. Standing out from the natural look of everything else in the cave, the ring of masonry, four feet across, rose to hip-height. It looked not too dissimilar to what lay crumbled in the center of the village they found.

"Is this a well?" Elvan leaned over and peered into the glittering water a few inches below the lip. It swam with faint lights, glowing and fading, like fireflies just under the surface.

Elvan looked down at Drace squatting to examine the stones along the top of the ring. He traced a thumb along deeply etched runes.

"It's like what the monks used to send us here," Drace said. "It's probably the center of this world and the way out."

"Can you activate it?"

A rumble of thunder echoed through the cave. Elvan rushed to Drace, putting a hand on his cheek, forcing his eyes upward to calm the panic before it grew. He could see the sheen of sweat across Drace's brow reflected in the faint light.

There was only the single peal of thunder, but a sudden increase of air pressure followed it. Both winced and yawned to pop their ears.

"This world is collapsing, Elvan," Drace whispered. "Fast. If this thing has enough magic to activate a portal, if I can even figure out how, it'll have to be in the next few minutes."

Elvan heard the unspoken meaning and looked toward where

they'd come into the room around the well. Through the unnatural darkness, along the slippery narrow ledge, down the steep incline, another twenty minutes running through the tangled forest and across mossy rocks at the lake's edge... "Mother." He took a step toward the darkness.

Drace grabbed his wrist, pulling Elvan's gaze back to him. He said nothing, but his wide amber eyes and the crinkle of his dark brow expressed enough.

"I can't leave her, Drace."

"This thing," he raised the artefact between them, "might not have enough magic to do anything. That chance goes down every second we delay."

It was a statement of fact. Elvan bit his cheek and pulled his arm from Drace's grip. "I can't leave her here. I can't lose her a second time."

Despite the thick air, Drace inhaled sharply and grabbed Elvan's hand again, nearly dragging him back the way they'd come.

A few steps into the darkness, another boom of thunder echoed through the cave. Drace stumbled forward, but maintained his quick pace. The rush of the waterfall filled their ears and was suddenly before them as they broke out of the tunnel's unnatural darkness. The time of day was impossible to tell through the sheet of water, not that the time mattered with the rapidly shifting days. Drace mumbled something and the artefact's glow faded.

"Can you do this?" Drace asked at the edge of the narrow path leading around the waterfall. Water splashed against the handholds and soaked the ledge.

The chamber flickered with lightning beyond the water, followed immediately by another sharp crack of thunder. Drace winced and clapped his hands to his ears.

"Can you?" Elvan asked, and placed a comforting hand flat on

Drace's chest. He looked back to the treacherous ledge with tears blurring his vision. He thought with guilt burning in his gut of how quickly he'd accepted his mother's role in smuggling illicit goods from the palace. Now he immediately accepted the urgency of escape from their prison. What proof did he have that this world was ending? A few lightning storms and Drace claiming the horizon looked closer? There was also the increase in air pressure, but that might be related to the storms here.

But… Elvan looked back at Drace. Had he been wrong about a single thing since they'd met? Drace's instinct and intuition saved them both on more than one occasion. Why doubt him now?

Because he wants me to abandon my mother.

No, no, he doesn't. He laid out the stakes and left the decision to me.

Elvan turned back to the path. "Stay here, I'll go get her. If I don't make it back, go back to the portal without me."

"The hells I will." Drace grabbed Elvan's shoulder and spun him around. "You expect me to just wait a half hour, shrug, and head back down there alone?" His breath was heavy with anger.

"If there's another lightning storm…"

The wall of water beside them slowed to a trickle, giving a view of a deep purple sky and the still lake below. Elvan clearly saw his mother's little hut on its island and her form moving among the stacks of rocks.

"Why's the water stopped?" Elvan asked.

Drace slowly shook his head. "This world is almost gone. I can see the edge a few miles into the forest. Whatever river feeds the waterfall upstream must be gone."

Elvan looked back at the ledge. *It'll be safer without water pouring down.*

Movement in his peripheral pulled his attention back to the

forests beyond the lake. An odd… flatness affected the farthest trees, taking on the appearance of a painting. As Elvan watched, it rolled nearer, freezing the tallest trees in a flat geometry. At its rate of advance, it would envelop the distant edges of the lake within minutes. It would reach his mother's hut soon after.

"Elvan…"

With each shallow breath, the sky grew perceptively dimmer.

Elvan traced a line in his mind. Along the narrow path, down the steeper incline, through the forest…

I'll never make it down to the water level, much less to her and back.

Far below, Selayna Galmoth walked calmly into her hut as the trees lining the far side of the lake flattened.

"Elvan!"

He snapped to attention with a gasp and focused fully on the hut.

I'll avenge you, Mother.

Elvan grabbed Drace's hand and fled back into the tunnel. Within a few steps, Drace pushed in front with the artefact casting a faint, focused beam of light ahead. The cave was already quiet, but the silence deepened while they skidded down the steep decline to the circular well. Drace dropped to his knees and frantically scanned across the runes etched into the edge.

"It's got her by now." Elvan's words thudded in his ears, not even echoing across the absolute darkness around him. "She's…"

Elvan replayed the brief conversation during his mother's lucid moment, how she'd admonished him for not taking part in the Council of Houses. The Council that the king intended to rule the nation after his death. He searched that memory for a hint of a loving look from his mother. When she saw him with Drace, she'd expressed something close to admitting she missed him.

Drace cursed and shot to his feet. "This is so far above my skill. I'm just going to shove everything from the artefact into it and see what happens. It—" He snapped his attention back up the tunnel and cursed again. "It's close."

Drace gripped the artefact in both hands and muttered words foreign to Elvan's ear. With each phrase, his amber eyes glowed brighter until Elvan was forced to look away. The runes around the lip of the well reacted, smoldering like old coals while the air crackled with power.

Water erupted from the well, shooting a geyser to the ceiling and soaking them both again. It continued with the same force, as the water rose around Elvan's toes, covering his ankles.

A fresh horror leaped to his mind; one of drowning in this tiny cave in the center of a collapsing world.

The water licked at his knees, but… the top of the well was now almost to his shoulder. The water wasn't rising; he was sinking into it! Elvan panicked, trying to step up out of the water, but his feet wouldn't move.

Drace gasped, shook his head, and his eyes stopped glowing. The ruby on his necklace, however, blazed with crimson brilliance. Unable to cross the few feet between them, Drace reached for Elvan, but they could only graze the tips of each other's fingers.

The freezing water rushed over his hips, belly, to his chest with speed that barely left time to panic.

An instant before it lapped over his ears, he heard Drace shout something, but the surge of water carried the words away.

There was no pain. The water rushed over his head, and Elvan drifted into the absolute darkness.

Absolute silence.

21

H E COULDN'T BE DEAD. HE was aware of the nothing around him and there should be no awareness in death.

Right?

Unless…

What if *this* was death? To drift for eternity in nothing. How long would it take to devolve into chittering madness with only his frayed thoughts for company?

Something burned… Deep in what used to be his lungs, and he was breathing again. Not in this nothing, this void, but he felt a distant sensation, like gasping for air.

Elvan's eyes flew open to his brother's aged face a few feet above him. A smile broke over Bennoc's lips, and Elvan coughed. Bennoc rolled him to his side to vomit out a stream of water. Through bleary eyes, he saw Drace sprawled a few feet away

"Drace…"

"He is alive," Bennoc said in a gentle whisper. "Thank the Six."

Elvan recognized the chamber as the room with the portals. He craned his neck to see the arch of stone and vines collapsed in a pile a few yards away.

"How…?" Elvan pushed up to an elbow and focused on taking deep breaths. He watched the slow rise and fall of Drace's chest and scooted closer to take one of his hands.

"The old woman stepped from the portal just a moment before the Gate and Shard shattered, when you and Drace fell from it, soaking wet," said Bennoc.

"Old woman?" Elvan looked away from Drace to see his mother standing by the brazier in the center of the room, warming her hands to it. *I must be dead. How is this possible?* He pushed to stand and hobbled forward, his left knee twinging with every step. Only a few steps away, Selayna looked up at him and squinted around her one sharp eye. Elvan slipped his arms over her shoulders, pulling her into a tight embrace.

"You know her?" Bennoc asked.

Elvan released his mother and she returned to methodically warming her hands. "You don't?"

"Should I?"

"Bennoc, she's our mother."

Bennoc laughed, sounding awkward and forced. "That would be silly, Elvan. Why would Mama be here?"

"Because she was exiled, just like Drace and me. She's been here this whole time you've been praying alongside her."

"No…" Bennoc still smiled, but his eyes belied his growing confusion. "You must be confused, dear brother. The miracles of the Gates are a blessing."

"Blessing? You thought Drace and I were being blessed as you shoved…" He stopped and rubbed a hand across his face. "I get it. The Hex Monks are the jailers for the throne's political prisoners, but you're just a low level monk here. Which Gate did they throw you into for a decade to mess you up so badly, brother?" Tears burned Elvan's eyes and his breath shook with anger. "The stone one over there? Is that where you lost ten years?"

Bennoc's smile finally faded and his shoulders slumped. "So it's true."

"What's true?"

"I overheard the abbot speaking after you entered the Gate last night—"

"Last night? We've been in there for days!" Elvan shouted.

"Brother, please." Bennoc held up a warding palm and glanced toward the door. "The abbot said that, by a decree of the Six, he would destroy the Emerald Gate this evening. I thought I misheard or was confused. I was taught the Gates were eternal, yet here one is crumbled at our feet."

"Not the Six, the crown controls your abbot. He would have executed us at the princess's command."

"Mama…" Bennoc stood, then fell to his knees beside their mother, taking one of her hands to cradle against his forehead.

"She needs help, Bennoc. Decades have passed for her and that's a lot of time to be alone."

"We have to get out of here," Bennoc said without looking up.

Drace stirred, coughed, and Elvan rushed to his side. Elvan helped pull him to a seated position while Drace's eyes flicked across the room.

"We're out?" he asked.

Elvan wrapped a hand around the back of Drace's head and pulled him close to kiss his forehead. "It seems so. Whatever you did, worked."

"Whatever I…" Drace looked down at his empty hands and the shallow cuts in his palm from gripping the artefact so tightly. He rubbed at his nose.

"Where's the artefact?" Elvan asked.

"Gone. I used all its power and it crumbled. What now? Are the Hex Monks going to shove us into another collapsing world?"

"No," Elvan said, looking back at his brother. Bennoc stood beside their mother, holding one of her hands while she ignored him and waved the other at the smoldering coals. "Bennoc says the abbot was going to execute us tonight. He came to save us."

Bennoc opened his mouth with a deep breath, but slowly nodded instead of speaking to correct the details.

Elvan helped Drace to his feet.

"No one can see us as we leave," Bennoc said, losing some of the stilted tone in his voice. "As soon as someone learns a Gate is destroyed, the temple will be in an uproar." He stepped toward the far side of the chamber, tugging his mother along.

Elvan and Drace followed them through a narrow side path from the room, giving the other Gates one last look.

"Who's in those?" Drace asked, pulling Bennoc's attention. "Does time move slower in one? Are they full of Lorekeepers and Artists the Sovereign King chose to give a stay of execution?"

"Drace…" Elvan squeezed his hand, feeling the tremble of the other's mounting anger.

"I'm sorry, Drace," said Bennoc. "I… I have no words, but I am sorry."

"We have to go," Elvan whispered.

Drace allowed Elvan to guide him after his brother and shuffling mother. He ran his thumb against Elvan's as they followed, hand in hand. "Did you hear what I said in there?"

"In the Gate?" Elvan chewed his cheek, trying to recall the exact words. The horror of water flowing down his nose made it difficult to remember with any accuracy. "You said the runes were beyond your understanding and just pushed all the magic of the artefact into them."

"Nothing else after that? As the water rose?"

Clear that Drace hoped he would remember something else, Elvan pushed away thoughts of the frigid water rising over his hips and chest, but came up with nothing. He shrugged.

The narrow hall ended at an unadorned wooden door. Bennoc leaned an ear to it for a few breaths before pushing it open, ushering them into a smoky antechamber lit by two braziers on opposite sides. A window on the right looked over the edge of the mountain and the island below. On the left, a short hall ended in a stout iron banded door.

"We need to get back to Spheris," said Elvan as Bennoc softly closed the door behind them.

"Mama…" Bennoc went to their mother warming her hands again by the brazier. He reached for her shoulder, but let his hand drop and stared down at it.

"Oh, Bennoc, what have they done to you here?" Elvan asked.

"I serve the Six. I serve…"

"You serve our mother's warden. This is just shy of murder, Bennoc. How many Artists and political prisoners have died in there?"

Drace put a hand on Elvan's arm.

"Did they shove you into another of the Gates right after you got here?" Elvan continued, trying to keep his voice down while heat flushed his neck and cheeks.

"That isn't—"

"Did the monks get to keep their temple in the mountains with all this illicit magic in exchange for holding anyone the crown disliked?"

Bennoc took a long, shaky breath, still staring down at his hands. "I was never as brave as you, Brother."

"What?"

He raised his face, eyes brimming with tears. "When they took Mama, you tried to save her and I… hid. I ran."

Despite the somber tone, Elvan snorted back a chuckle. "So you hid by coming to serve those holding her."

"I didn't know."

"I'm sure you didn't."

"We were raised wanting for nothing, Elvan. I couldn't take it, knowing so many were suffering in the world."

"And you gave up everything to serve the Six."

Bennoc nodded.

"What do the Hex Monks do to help those in need? Do they feed the hungry of Spheris?"

Bennoc shook his head.

"They live on a mountain, growing beans and holding the crown's prisoners."

"I serve the Six," Bennoc repeated.

Bennoc stood in place, staring down at his hands. Elvan only saw a scared little boy, yelping at the scary parts of Ser Vazadon's stories and spilling popped corn on the couch. He crossed the few steps between them and put a hand on his brother's shoulder.

"Come back with us, Bennoc. Help our mother heal and help me rebuild the House."

"If you stay here, they'll kill you," said Drace. "You know they will. Can't serve the Six if you're dead. Well, maybe you can, but no reason to find out sooner than you have to."

"Wait here a moment," said Bennoc. He rushed down the hall and through the metal banded door with a loud creak.

Drace turned and ran a hand through Elvan's hair. "How are you doing?"

Elvan sucked in a deep breath, letting the mix of incense and heat calm him. "I have to keep moving, so I don't think about anything."

"Understood." Drace slipped his hand into Elvan's and squeezed.

Elvan squeezed back and released to look out the window and the sheer drop to clouds below. "I was starting to accept we'd never return." He put his hands on the window ledge and let the cool, clean air brush against his face. "I can't keep track of my feelings about my mother. She's lost, then found, then mad, then dead, then…" He gestured toward her on the other end of the room, hovering over the brazier.

"Don't start down that route. One thing at a time. First, we need a way back to Spheris. Hopefully not a boat."

"I've spent two years trying to clear my mother's name and my brother's people have been her captors the whole time." The heat rose again across his neck and cheeks as he slammed a fist onto the windowsill. He immediately regretted it, shaking out the pain.

"No," Drace took Elvan by the shoulders and spun him around. "Stop that. Remember our priorities. Stop the princess and ensure the king's will gets enacted to remove the crown's power. Stop a full-out war against Artists. Simple stuff."

"Simple stuff." Elvan leaned into Drace, resting his head against his chest and wrapping arms around his waist. "Or maybe we just take one more boat ride and the four of us live on an island."

Drace snorted next to Elvan's ear. "No boats."

"We're on an island, love. We'll have to take at least one boat if we plan to leave."

"Love?"

Elvan swallowed hard, staring up at Drace. The word just slipped out.

The door creaked open and Bennoc peeked his head in. "Quickly, follow me," he hissed.

Elvan raced to his mother to help guide her down the hall.
Love? Why can't I just say it? It's just a word.

Out in the open air, Elvan blinked away the early morning sun, seeming strange after not seeing it for days. They moved as swiftly as possible with Selayna shuffling beside them, staying in the shadows near the buildings and rocky outcropping.

"Where're we going?" Drace asked. Elvan hadn't paid attention to their direction until he noticed them approaching a path near the main route up the mountain.

Bennoc waved them to crowd nearer. "The ship you came on is still at the dock, leaving soon. The captain and crew will still be sleeping in the bunkhouses at this hour, giving you the chance to hide on board."

"What about you? And Mother?" Elvan asked.

Bennoc shook his head. "We'll be seen on the main path and the side one is too steep for Mama."

"I'll carry her," Drace offered.

The brothers looked at him, both biting back their grins.

"Are you sure?" said Bennoc. "It's a long way down."

"Sure, I'm sure. Come on. The sooner we get down there, the sooner we're done being on a boat."

"I don't think that's—"

"Shush."

The side path down the mountain was far steeper than the main route, but faster. Elvan ignored the exhaustion in his limbs, something he'd been doing far too often lately, while he mimicked Drace's footing and handholds during their quick descent, as he followed Bennoc's lead. The sun might have only just been rising, but they had been awake since the first lightning storm on the beach hours ago. Elvan also didn't have a hundred-pound woman holding onto his back. He focused his mind by practicing conversations he may never get to have. What to say to the princess, Delphina… Ser Vazadon.

"There's the ship," Bennoc said at last.

"It doesn't look like anyone's up yet," said Drace.

Elvan knew better than to bother squinting to confirm, and just took Drace's word for it. A few boulders later, the ground beneath their feet leveled off to the shore and Drace set Selayna down to walk on her own. Their narrow path joined the wider one they'd traveled days ago — or yesterday — and was framed by the low, long houses on either side. Quiet murmurs of conversation came through the open windows on their left, punctuating their need for speed and stealth. They sped across the dock's wood planks toward the ship; the sun rising on the horizon beyond.

Drace stumbled and hesitated at the end of the gangplank.

"It's just one more day, Drace. Then no more boats for the rest of your life." Elvan waved from where he stood with one foot on the ship's deck.

"Captain Antris said this was the next stop of their trip. What if they have seven months at sea before returning to Spheris? I won't make it, Elvan."

Elvan hadn't forgotten the captain's words, but hoped Drace had. He chewed his cheek and searched his memory for any markers stamped on the crates stacked on the dock when they arrived. He'd been so clouded by his joy at seeing the Hex Temple, he didn't think of their significance until now. He recalled two open crates with salted okra, stamped to be delivered to House Frostspark's Taekni Laboratory. It would spoil within a month after harvesting and the island with the Taekni Lab would be a good two weeks at sea. That was the *Enid's Blessing's* next stop.

"They will be going straight back to Spheris," he said confidently and again waved for Drace to join him.

Drace glanced over his shoulder at the bunkhouses, but stepped one foot onto the gangplank. "You're sure?"

Elvan nodded and waved again. A single voice rose with command over the others in the longhouses. The captain was rousing his men to order.

Drace stepped onto the deck with wobbly legs. "Why didn't they leave right away? Why wait for morning?"

"Tides. Islands are dangerous to navigate against the tides." Elvan helped his mother before directing them to the door leading into the belly of the ship.

"Silly me, doubting a master logistician," said Drace.

The tiny room they'd shared for a day would never fit the four of them, but the ship was named for Enid, most beautiful of the Six, so of course the internal design was symmetrical. Elvan left his brother and mother in the tiny room on the starboard side with promises to check on them soon. He opened the door to the room where Drace and he shared their first failed kiss. *It feels like a lifetime ago.*

"Won't they find us in here?" Drace asked with the door shut behind them. "Maybe we should hide in the bottom of the ship?"

"If you got sick in here, you don't want to be down there. Besides," Elvan paused and licked dry lips. "I don't intend for us to remain hidden."

Drace looked up from running a finger along the rough canvas of the hanging cot. "Oh really?"

Elvan nodded to gather the nerve he'd built up while descending the mountain. Rehearsed conversations never played out as he hoped. "Once the ship's underway, I'm commandeering it."

Drace turned fully to him and ran that same finger along his collarbone. "Bold plan."

Elvan clenched his fist, feeling the nails bite into his palm.

"Lorelai threw my mother away, and I did nothing. Delphina's pushed me around since we were kids. The inquisitors are trying to destroy an entire way of life. I have a right to a seat at the table, but I gave it up because they were mean to me. I'm sick of being walked on. I'm going to take the fight to them."

Drace leaned back against the cot and fanned his face with exaggerated motions. "And I thought you were sexy before."

"I'm trying to be serious."

Drace closed the inches between them and folded his hand into Elvan's. "So am I." Slipping a hand behind his neck, Drace lifted Elvan's lips against his own.

Cresting anger guided Elvan's movements. He gripped Drace tight against him, feeling the other's rising interest through the thin fabric of their monk's robes. The captain and crew would be only a few feet above at any moment, but that worry only fueled him as his simmering fury slid into desire.

Within a few heated breaths, their robes lay in a heap on the plank floor. They didn't notice the sway of the ship until it was well underway.

22

"THAT PROBABLY WASN'T THE BEST idea," Drace said from where he tried to untangle their robes. "Not that I regret it, beast." He winked.

Elvan looked up from staring at his hands to accept the length of fabric. "I don't know what came over me."

"We've been through hell the last couple days. It has to come out somehow."

Elvan shrugged and wrapped the robe with what little expertise they'd acquired in a few days. The thought of raiding the other rooms for a set of clothes crossed his mind. *Which would be better to wear when I approach the captain? The only adornments from our time imprisoned, or a sailor's stolen trousers?*

"So, commandeering a ship? Care to tell me about that?"

"The less you know, the less you'll know I'm messing it up," Elvan smirked and glanced down at the metal pail by the door. Nerves, mixed with the ship's slow rock, threatened to force a purge of his stomach. Luckily he hadn't eaten since… when? He looked back at Drace, who seemed unaffected by the sea this time.

They climbed the stairs on unsteady legs, and Elvan paused with a hand on the door's latch. *House Galmoth holds the king's orders. They didn't strip that away.*

He blew out a breath and pushed the door open.

A wall of blue fabric stood on the other side. Captain Antris turned quickly and whipped back his coat to put a hand on the butt of the long, silver pistol on his hip. His stance softened with recognition, but his palm remained on his sidearm. "You two." His thick mustache twitched with a hint of amusement. "I don't take well to stowaways on my ship."

"Not your ship." Elvan closed his hand to a loose fist to keep his fingers from shaking. "Maritime Code enacted by King Pearce IV grants the head of House Galmoth the right to take temporary command of any able ship for emergency deliveries."

Antris cocked his gun with a loud *click* and stared down with a mix of anger and admiration. "Quoting forty-year-old codes to me? They meant that for medical supplies during the Oxmoore Rebellion."

"The statute stands."

The captain took a step forward and leaned down over Elvan. He smelled like he'd bathed in ale and sausage. "I could throw you both overboard for the sharks and carnivorous cephalopods. No one would know. Tell me why I shouldn't."

Elvan's heart felt ready to burst through his throat. "We have to get back to Spheris. We're moving against the princess."

The captain's eye twitched and his hand moved from his sidearm. "Darrow," he shouted to one of the men forming a ring behind the captain. "We have uninvited guests. Lock these two in my room. I'll deal with them later."

"Aye, Cap," said one of the sailors and stepped forward. Two others joined him, pushing and forcing Elvan and Drace to retreat down the steps. Down the hall, a sailor shoved past them to open the door etched with a tentacled sea monster. Elvan kept his eyes forward, fighting the instinct to look toward where his brother and mother hid as he and Drace were tossed into the captain's quarters. The door slammed shut behind them with a click of the lock.

"Elvan!" Drace rubbed both hands down his face. "That was incredible!"

Elvan leaned against the door as bile threatened to bubble up from his gut. It burned his throat while he tried to catch his breath. "I need to lie down."

"I mean, it didn't work, but you were so forceful." Drace bit his lip and ran his eyes over Elvan with a look that would have excited him twenty minutes ago.

"Don't be so sure about that. When I mentioned the princess, the captain dropped his threatening stance."

Elvan forced his shoulders to relax and looked across the quarters. Light flooded the room from the five leaded glass windows against the back wall, providing a wide view of the ship's wake in the open ocean without a hint of land. In front of those, an ornately carved desk was piled with neat stacks of paperwork, all weighted down with stones or heavy inkwells. A plush bed with red linens was tucked into a nook to the right and shelves of fruit, boxed food, and jugs of ale to their left.

Drace rushed to the food. He turned and tossed an apple to Elvan, who fumbled, but caught it before hitting the floor.

"What else have we got in here?" Drace mumbled around a bite and walked his fingers across the spines of tomes tucked along the wall. "Why did he send us to his quarters and not the brig?"

Elvan took a shallow bite and let the fruit's tart juice awaken his taste buds. "Most ships don't have brigs. The captain's room is often the only one with a lock."

"Did you just commandeer his ship? That was real, wasn't it? Amazing."

"The current king's grandfather enacted the code at the end of the Oxmoore Rebellion, too late to really help anyone. Then they just forgot to rescind the order." Elvan moved to the wide desk and wondered how it fit through the door. *They must have brought it in before they put the windows in place.* On the corner, a locket on a silver chain swayed from the branches of a decorative wire tree. He pulled it open and held it to the morning light coming through the windows to see the portraits of two women inside.

"The captain's wife and daughter?" Elvan asked and held the locket for Drace to see.

Drace shrugged and took it. He squinted at the older woman on the right. "I recognize her. She came into Nana's shop at least once a month. She's an Artist."

"You're sure?"

"Sure it's her, or sure she's an Artist?"

"Either? Both?"

"You know they say you can't tell an Artist unless you catch them in the act? That's not true. There's something… electric about their touch. You have to know what to feel for, and it takes some training in magic."

"Training like you have, to know how to use artefacts?"

"Right. This woman… I can't remember her name… She'd bring me candies whenever she visited, though I was too old for them. She'd hold my hands and stare intently into my eyes as she asked me how I'd been doing. Really nice lady. I could feel the buzz of power from her, like I could Nana."

"What happened to her?"

Drace shook his head and handed back the locket. "I don't know. She stopped coming to the shop maybe a year before I took over."

"Even if this isn't the captain's wife and daughter," said Elvan, "they're someone close enough to have in a locket on his desk. His job is to smuggle the crown's prisoners to exile, yet he seems to care for an Artist?"

"Maybe he shipped her to the Hex Temple years ago and kept the locket as a trophy because he liked her face."

Elvan chewed his cheek. "No, it wouldn't be her locket. No one carries an image of themselves. When he brought us here, it sounded like the captain didn't like the princess. I bet something happened there."

"My wife Ingaret and daughter Joy," said a deep voice from behind, making them both jump. Elvan dropped the locket to clatter across the desk. Captain Antris's broad shoulders filled the doorway where he stood with a hand on his pistol's grip. His boots thudded on the planks as he took a step forward and drew his weapon, but left his arm relaxed and the barrel pointed at the floor. "How did you give the monks the slip?"

Elvan forced his eyes from the threat in the man's fist to look him in the face. "We didn't, Captain Antris. The Hex Monks sent us into exile, but we escaped."

"Well…" Antris ran a thumb over his gun with another *click*, but Elvan didn't know if that meant the threat was becoming greater or lesser. "My job was to take you to the island, not make sure you stay there." The captain brushed his mustache with his palm. He chuckled mirthlessly and shook his head at Drace. "The balls this one has."

"Massive, I know."

"Captain Antris," Elvan dropped his voice to barely a whisper over the crash of waves against the hull. "I only ask you deliver us to Spheris with all haste. We have time-sensitive business in the

West District."

Captain Antris kicked the door closed behind him and stepped nearer. "You spoke with confidence on the deck, Elvan Galmoth. Tell me what you know of Princess Lorelai."

Elvan shrank in the presence of the unholstered weapon, retreating a step and bumping against the desk. "She… she means to assassinate the king and take complete control of the nation."

"Why? The crown is hers upon her father's death."

"That was the piece we were missing for so long; her motive. The king means to disseminate the crown's power to the Council of Houses. He hasn't made this public, but my mother found out. That's why the princess exiled her two years ago. She's…" He stopped himself before mentioning his mother was just a few doors away.

"And you mean to stop her?"

Elvan pushed himself away from leaning against the desk. "Yes."

The corner of the captain's mustache twitched again. "How can you even stand upright with those, little lordling?"

"I manage," Elvan croaked.

"If your plan matches your determination…" The captain scratched at the stubble on his cheek, shaking his head and chuckling to himself. "You're in luck. We *are* en route to Spheris. Now that I think of it, docking closer to the West District would save time unloading."

Elvan bit back the smile from completely overtaking his face. "Thank you, captain!"

"Don't thank me yet. I'll be invoicing your House for the spoiled goods," said Antris. "You're speaking quite freely with all these plans of treason to someone with a pistol drawn on you."

"But you haven't raised it," Elvan said and glanced back at the locket on the desk. "Your wife and daughter. What did the princess do to them?"

Antris closed his eyes and slipped the pistol back into this holster. "They came in the night three years ago. Inquisitors. They threw hoods over my wife and daughter, shoved them into a carriage, while someone knelt on my back in the gravel. The lame inquisitor barked the orders, screaming about them being heathen Artists."

"Nilranke," Drace spat between clenched teeth.

"I nearly lost my mind searching for where they were taken," the captain continued. "I finally paid off the right clerks to learn they sent Ingaret on a ship west. Joy is held in a labor camp somewhere east of Spheris, near the borders of Aibeon. They offered my girls' lives for a decade of discrete slavery to the crown. My ship and crew are subject to their every whim, but I don't know if either my wife or daughter are alive." He spoke without emotion, like this was a conclusion he came to years ago and was only repeating it to them for the hundredth time. "I don't even know if the shadowy contacts that give me commands have any power over their fates, but what choice have I?"

"That's terrible," Elvan whispered. His mother had been similarly taken, but he always held the belief he could rescue her with enough evidence proving her innocence. Looking back on that now, it felt like a childish wish. "We have an idea of how to put pressure against the princess, but don't know yet how to accomplish that. We have to get to the other Houses."

Drace wiped a hand across his mouth and set the fruit's core on the desk beside him. "No, the smuggled artefacts are the key. Lorelai needs those to turn the populace against Artists and their families. We have to find proof of what she did with them."

Elvan shot a glance at Drace. "Where would we even begin to

look? The artefacts could be anywhere."

"So you intend to just walk up to one of the other Houses, not knowing who's in on the princess's plots? No nobles can be trusted right now."

"I'm a noble."

"And I'm…" Drace chewed his lip with an expression that bordered on anger. "I'm saying we need proof, hard proof, beyond what's tucked away in your manor house, before we go to anyone."

"Which'll it be, boys?" asked Antris. "Unless you plan to split up, I don't see how you can do both."

Elvan took a deep breath and rubbed a hand over his face. Drace was right. If the princess succeeded in her plan with the artefacts, it wouldn't matter that she was planning to overrule her father's wish. The people would never listen to the Council of Houses speaking against the princess who just saved their city and their lives. All assuming they guessed correctly on Lorelai's plans.

"First," Elvan started, "my mother and brother are also on board. Will you see them to a safe port?"

If Antris was surprised to hear of more stowaways, he made no sign of it as he nodded and tapped a fist to his chest. "I've no qualms with them. I'll see them to safe harbor."

"Thank you, captain." Elvan repeated the salute. "My mother knows the details of the king's intention, but her time in exile was… unkind to her. She requires special attention."

"I will see to her."

"How can we trace the artefacts?" asked Elvan, glancing at Drace.

Drace scowled. "Who's the princess's contact for everything Artist related?"

"No…" Elvan guessed who else he might mean, and only one

name came to mind. "No, he hates Artists. Everyone knows that. He wouldn't be working with them."

"What, you don't think the crown is beyond hypocrisy?"

"I can't act against the princess or her agents," said Antris. "Not until my girls are safe. With me or waiting in the Afterlands. I can, however, get you the audience you want. What you do from there is your own affair and I'll deny any involvement. I'll warn you, though, you won't like the method."

23

EVEN BELOW DECK, ELVAN COULD tell they were nearing Spheris. A subtle change in the air quality heralded the thousand residential chimneys and more in the industrial sectors. The muffled cries of gulls pierced through the hull and the ship gently rocked to a stop.

Without a mirror, he only hoped he looked as good as Drace did in their matching vests of dark blue trimmed with gold; the formal dress uniforms of a couple crewmen. Loose linen trousers tucked into polished knee-high leather boots. Drace tugged at the sleeves of his billowy shirt to get them to lie just right and shifted the ruby on his necklace to hide beneath the fabric.

"You ready?" he asked and shoved his hands in his pockets.

Elvan shook his head. "Not at all."

"Just channel how you were on the deck."

"How's that? Scared shitless?"

"Could have fooled me."

The tiny room's door snapped open. Captain Antris stepped into the doorway, tossing the familiar iron shackles at their feet. "Put those on and follow me. Not a word from either of you."

Elvan hefted his iron bands, which felt no lighter than he remembered from days ago. The captain reached forward to test the clasps with rough movements, testing Drace's even more thoroughly, before jerking his head toward the hallway.

He's really getting into character.

Bennoc stood in the hallway leading to the crew and captain's quarters, wearing a similar set of clothes rather than his monk's robes. He held their mother's arm tucked around his elbow, but she stared directly ahead without focus.

Elvan grasped his brother's wrist. "Take care of her. We're going to end this."

Bennoc nodded once. "Good luck, Brother."

Drace gripped Bennoc's shoulder with a clank of the iron chains as they passed, ascending the stairs.

On deck, Elvan immediately recognized the spires and gaudy gleam of the palace in the distance as it caught the early morning light. Drace stopped beside him, somehow fine after a day at sea. *Maybe it was related to his injuries that made him sick on the way out. Maybe it was a revenge plot against Nilranke that steeled his constitution.*

"Get moving," Antris shouted from the gangplank and a shove from behind caused Elvan to nearly fall forward on his face.

The streets of the West District were nearly empty so close to sunrise. They passed a group of city guards wearing the colors of House Serhane at the docks' entrance, but Captain Antris pulled an amulet from beneath his shirt and they waved him on.

An iron mark? Suspicion bubbled in Elvan with every labored step. *That's like the Galmoth writ of export, giving him unhindered access to and from the docks. What if everything he's said is a lie, and he's leading us back to be tortured by Nilranke? Or killed for sport by the princess? This is all a trap!*

Elvan's vision narrowed as he fought to catch his breath and quell his suspicions. Normally a morning walk through the West District would be to enjoy the hanging gardens, exquisitely manicured trees, and delicate glasswork around the gas lamps. All Elvan saw today was wet cobblestone.

The captain stopped in front of a wrought-iron fence, nine feet tall, topped with serrated spikes. Beyond a wide gate, willow trees lined a dirt path ending at a relatively simple two-story house. Painted brown and partially covered in climbing ivy, the house lacked the color and flourish of others from the district. Whoever lived here had money, but didn't care to announce it.

A single burly man wearing a tailored uniform of three shades of red, but without other heraldry, approached from the house. "State your business," he said from where he stopped thirty feet from the gate.

"Please tell His Honor that Captain Antris is at the gate with two stowaways he may have great interest in."

The man narrowed his eyes, inclined his head slightly, and pivoted to return to the house without a word.

"This is Nilranke's house?" Elvan whispered.

Captain Antris glowered down with eyes that dripped with contempt. Even his mustache seemed angry. "I believe you were told not to speak." He said louder than was necessary for the few feet between them. He raised a hand and tightened his fist next to Elvan's cheek, bones cracking as he did. "Do it again, please. You Artists and your sympathizers are disgusting." He spat, hitting Elvan's polished boot. The three crewmen clustered behind them took a collective step back.

The man in red returned and pulled a key from his vest to unlock the gate. Swinging it inward, he gestured for them to enter. Captain

Antris smirked down at Elvan with a wolfish grin and waved for them to go first. Drace and Elvan inside, the man in red put a hand on the captain's chest. "Your services are complete." He pressed a small leather pouch into the captain's hand.

It lasted less than a single heartbeat, but Elvan caught the flash of concern pass on Antris's dark expression. He breathed a sigh of relief that the captain might not have been double crossing them the whole time, but immediately tensed again that they were about to encounter Nilranke alone.

Drace huffed beside him during their short walk through the willows, suddenly struggling with the weight of his iron chains. Elvan's arms and shoulders ached, but he never expected to outlast Drace in a show of stamina.

No one spoke as they entered the plain foyer of the house that smelled of old tobacco with a trace of antiseptic and medicinal ointment. A rug with a floral print led up the stairs to the second level, but the man in red pointed them to the room on their right. Elvan could have mistaken it for his mother's study. Dimly lit by a few gas lamps, meticulously organized books lined the sides, and a plainly carved desk took up most of the far wall. Three low backed chairs sat facing the desk and the man in red gestured the pair toward them. Drace fell into a chair and let his arms and the iron chains drop, but his eyes darted across the room, taking in every fine detail.

The man in red remained in the doorway with his hands folded in front of him.

Elvan followed Drace's lead and searched for something to use. Small portraits in polished frames dotted the bookcases and a silver table on wheels boasted a selection of alcohol. *Organized books and booze. My parents would have been friends with this man.*

The stairs creaked with an alternating tap of a cane. The man in red stepped aside for Inquisitor Nilranke to stride through the door. His dark robes of office were replaced with an embroidered silk smoking jacket and matching pants. He smiled darkly and tapped his steel cane on the rug before him to lean both palms on it. "You may leave us, Graham."

The man in red bowed and retreated.

Nilranke breathed with a loud wheeze and fingered a signet ring on his left pinky finger. "What have I done to deserve this?" he asked with a short, rasping laugh. Leaning heavily on his cane, he walked directly toward Drace, grabbing his face by the cheeks. "I lost you twice, only for you to walk into my home." He released Drace's face and slipped his fingers down his shirt, pulling out the necklace and its ruby pendant. "How did I miss this before?" He jerked the necklace, snapping the clasp, to hold the gem up to the light. Drace immediately opened his mouth to stretch his jaw. If a look could kill...

"This can't be a mana crystal. They're just a myth," said Nilranke. "Yet I can feel the warmth of it. The power. Why would a peasant shopkeeper have such a thing? And you..." Nilranke turned to Elvan. "You're both supposed to be dead. This should be—"

Drace jumped to his feet and, with an arcing overhead blow, brought his iron shackles down the base of Nilranke's neck. The old man crumbled to the rug. Drace shook off his restraints and dropped to a knee next to Elvan, grabbing his necklace back in one hand and holding a key in the other.

"You've had a key the whole time?"

"Antris gave it to me on the ship. I was planning to ham up how heavy they were and how much they weakened me, but then the bastard turned his back and I couldn't resist myself."

Elvan's shackles fell free, and he rubbed his sore wrists. He looked down at the unconscious man and kicked him in the ribs. "What now?"

Drace was up and sliding the doors to the foyer closed. "There's magic in here. A lot of it."

Elvan started to ask how he knew, but stopped himself.

Drace turned his back to the doors, amber eyes scanning across the room again, and rubbed his jaw where Nilranke grabbed it. "His servant will come back eventually. Help me get him into the chair."

Lifting the inquisitor was like managing an awkward sack of onions. Except the onions would smell better. The stench of the man's tobacco might precede him into a room, but up close he reeked of pharmaceuticals. Elvan forced himself to worry the man might be dead or at least seriously injured, but he heard a rasping breath when they pushed him back into the chair to slump over the low arms.

"What now?" Elvan repeated when the man seemed balanced enough to not topple over.

"Tie him down." The fine chain of Drace's necklace dangled from his hand while he rubbed the stone in his fingers.

Elvan's eye traveled to the tie backs of the drapes and tugged them from the wall. Four strips of fabric just over a foot long each would have to be enough to restrain his man while they… He wasn't sure what the next step of the plan would be. He knelt to secure Nilranke's arm to the chair and rolled his eyes with a sigh. Elvan picked up the manacles he'd been wearing and secured them to the inquistor's wrists, weaving the chain around the chair's arms. He started to repeat the process with the other cuffs around the man's skinny ankles, but a dull *click* pulled his attention to Drace beside a bookcase set into the wall.

Drace pushed and the entire wall moved inward before sliding to the right, exposing a dark space beyond. He reached in for a light switch and jumped back with a yelp when a single gas lamp illuminated the small room.

Rows of soulless eyes stared out from the space. Nestled on eight shelves were at least a hundred porcelain dolls in delicate lace dresses. Their meticulously maintained painted faces reflected the flickering glow of the gaslight.

"What the…" Drace breathed slack jawed and wide eyed.

Elvan clicked the manacles in place around Nilranke's other leg and joined Drace by the secret room. "The big scary inquisitor collects antique dolls?" He reached in to pick up one at random. It felt like any that Delphina had as a girl, though without the wear from being taken everywhere by a careless child.

"That's not all…" Drace tucked his necklace into a pocket and took a doll in both hands. With a sharp intake of breath, his eyes glowed briefly with an inner light. "These are artefacts." He put the doll back and slowly brushed a hand over the others on that shelf.

"Are these also from the Arcanym?" Elvan looked down at the doll in his hands and shivered at its dead stare.

Drace stomped back to stand before Nilranke and roughly took the man's head in both hands, forcing his face upward. The inquisitor groaned and cringed, as if Drace's touch hurt him. Drace released him, letting the inquisitor's head drop. He stared down at his hands, running his fingertips over his palms.

"What?" Elvan asked.

Drace raised his head with barely restrained rage, running his tongue over his teeth. "He's an Artist. Bastard's been hunting them, my people, for decades and he's one of us."

Elvan raised the doll in his hands. *These aren't what Mother was moving. These are his, created of his own excess magic.* Disgusted, he tossed the doll down and the head smashed in half against the thin rug.

"I swear to the Six, Elvan. Remind me why we need him alive. Remind me right now." Drace pivoted and took a letter opener from the desk, brandishing it like a knife against the man's throat.

"Drace, don't kill him!" Elvan wanted to add "yet," but he was no murderer, despite everything this man represented. He wanted to hope Drace wasn't as well. By how he pressed the point of the letter opener into the man's neck, causing a trickle of blood, causing Elvan to wonder at Drace's killer instinct.

Nilranke stirred and flopped his head back, his eyes fluttering open to the ceiling. "Graham…" His rasping voice struggled around his labored breathing.

"Your butler can't help you now, Nilranke," Drace hissed. "Only you can help yourself. Tell us what the princess is doing with the stolen artefacts." He pressed the letter opener deeper to add persuasion.

Elvan read a dozen adventure stories with scenes just like this, though it was always the villain holding the hero prisoner. A question would be asked, they'd say they know nothing, more pressure applied, still nothing… The stories always dragged it on just long enough, so Nilranke's response, without denials, surprised him.

"The princess? It's too late to stop her." The inquisitor's slurred words and sloppy grin made him look drunk, rather than suffering from a head wound.

"What about the artefacts from the Arcanym? Who is she supplying those to?"

"Ever hear of St. Judith's Reform Academies?"

"Those were shut down decades ago." Drace growled.

"Reform academies?" Elvan asked.

Drace glanced over his shoulder at Elvan, but didn't let up the pressure against Nilranke's throat. "They sent young Artists to camps to teach them to suppress their power, usually by making them hate that part of themselves. Nana told me horrific stories of what they'd do. They were all shut down when the crown realized it was easier and cheaper to just banish or imprison Artists."

Nilranke rolled an eye toward Elvan and winked. "My fellow alumni were surprised to see me, but overjoyed by my housewarming present."

"Alumni…" Elvan gasped. "Of course, you attended a camp to make you hate yourself. So, then Lorelai got the artefacts from the Arcanym, used my mother to smuggle them out of the city, then you got them into the hands of your associates, who will use their power to attack the king. That will unite the people against Artists in the princess's reign after she defeats them." He bit back the grin of pride at putting it all together.

"You are a child and you think like one." Nilranke's voice was becoming clearer with each breath. "You have no concept of the power those artefacts possess. I see you found my collection of dolls, my life's combined magic. All those together are less than one relic created by the Artists of legend whose work filled the Arcanym."

"How can the princess hold back a force with that much power?" Drace gripped the handle of the letter opener tighter.

"The princess?" Nilranke laughed, a slow, choking gurgle. "Why do you think there's some rogue army of Artists? The princess works to destroy the Arcanym."

"What?" Elvan and Drace said together.

"Princess Lorelai hired House Galmoth to move the artefacts to a secure location for proper destruction. After eight years, they nearly had it empty. Then Selayna came to court with wild accusations. Her exile was necessary to save the crown's public image."

"My mother wasn't a smuggler?"

"What do you mean, destroying the Arcanym?" Drace asked, pressing the letter opener a little firmer.

"How would you feel to be living atop a bomb? That's what the Arcanym is. Objects of power created by maniacs in a by-gone era."

"Those *objects* are the history and culture of the Artists," Drace said and blood oozed around the edge of his blade. "The very soul of my people. Destroying those is destroying my past."

Nilranke shrugged, careful not to put pressure on the blade at his throat. "Selayna Galmoth moved artefacts in accordance with the princess's will. I taught the princess some of how to use an artefact, but she was always so jealous she could not create one, herself."

"She's destroying the Arcanym out of jealousy?" said Elvan.

"The acid…" Drace shifted the letter opener away a fraction of an inch.

"Acid?" Elvan asked, remembering with a gasp the jars of nitric acid in the hidden space behind his mother's armoire as soon as he spoke.

"You said your mother bought vats of nitric acid. Mix that and arcane steel filings and you've got a quick way to destroy an artefact. Just drop it in and watch the magic flood out. Boom."

"Boom," Nilranke grinned, showing teeth stained orange.

"They explode?" said Elvan. "No wonder the artefacts were taken out of the city. We were wrong on so many things." Elvan took a deep breath. "What else were we wrong about? What if Lorelai isn't trying to kill her father, either?"

"The princess *did* task me with killing her father with a show of magic," said Nilranke. "She doesn't know when or how it will happen, affording her plausible deniability, but I suppose she's not completely innocent."

They stared unblinking at the inquisitor.

"You're certainly free with your words now," Drace said.

"I wonder how many shipments from the Arcanym went missing?" Nilranke snorted. "Have you found any, Master Galmoth?"

The distant boom of an explosion rattled the glass in the windows behind the heavy drapes.

Nilranke slapped away Drace's hand holding the letter opener and rose to his feet, the heavy manacle falling away as he stood. He reached a hand with fingers splayed toward the closet of dolls and one in a polka dot dress flew to him. He clutched it against his chest like a child might.

Drace dug the ruby from his pocket. He held it in front of himself in a warding gesture and pushed Elvan behind him with the other arm.

Nilranke chuckled darkly as his eyes lit with an inner fire. "You can't be serious."

Another explosion rattled the glass.

"What's going on out there?" Elvan asked, peering from behind Drace.

"I believe the king's privy council met this morning. Every individual he would have told about his plan to disseminate power, sitting around a single table. The revolution has begun. Swear fealty to Queen Lorelai and I'll grant you a merciful death." Nilranke held the doll tighter as his eyes flashed brighter. His lips moved with mumbled phrases too soft to reach the pair.

"What is he doing?" Elvan's skin prickled like it did when

Drace held him in the warehouse. The wood under his feet vibrated with power.

"Master Nilranke!" The butler gasped from the doorway to the foyer.

"I have everything under control, Graham!" Nilranke said smoothly.

"The doll!" Drace hissed and waved at the floor. Elvan dropped and scooped up the doll he'd thrown down a few moments before and pressed it into Drace's hand.

"I've spent my life hating what I am," said Nilranke, and his free hand moved to rub the thigh of his bad leg. He took a single step, then another, keeping his distance. "And rightly so. I channeled every ounce of magic from my body as quickly as it came, purging this uncleanliness. Yet I now have some inkling why those Artists of legend used their power to control the masses through fear." Lightning sparked from his arm holding the doll, charging the air with ozone. "My grotesque artefacts. Symbols of my wretchedness. Yet they feel like a part of me, as much as they represent my impurity."

Engrossed in his dialog, Elvan and Drace failed to notice Nilranke planned his slow movement to stand with the closet of dolls to his back.

Elvan had no basis for comparison, but could tell Nilranke was unstable, siphoning power well beyond his ability to control. He couldn't see Drace's eyes, but was sure they glowed amber as he pulled magic from the broken doll.

The hairs on Elvan's arms prickled with the building charge of energy in the study. He reached a hand for Drace's arm, feeling that same tingle and numbness as he did in the warehouse.

Nilranke's gray hair floated in the wisps of energy swirling about his body. "Accept this as a gift." Blinding lightning burst from his chest, collided with an invisible barrier before Drace, deflected, and blasted apart the bookshelf beside Nilranke. The inquisitor's eyes went wide with shock and he turned to survey the damage that so nearly hit him.

Drace dropped the doll and grabbed Elvan's hand, yanking him toward the foyer, shoving the butler aside. Graham ignored them, rushing into the study to his master's aid, and the pair fled into the yard of arching willows.

They paused at the gate. Drace stared down at his trembling left hand. Blood pooled in his palm around where the ruby gem looked partially embedded into his flesh.

"What happened?" Elvan took the injured hand in both of his, turning it carefully to inspect the wound. "Does it hurt?" He prodded the edges of the wound as carefully as he could.

"No, actually, it feels great."

Another explosion and distant shouts of panicked alarm pulled their attention toward the palace and the trails of smoke rising in the morning light.

Elvan used the distraction to rip the gem free. Drace cried and raised his other fist, as if resisting punching Elvan.

"A little warning next time!"

"I promise." The wound looked less serious without the crystal, but with his limited medical knowledge, Elvan couldn't be certain. He ripped the lace cuff from his sleeve and tenderly pressed it into the injured palm. "What is that gem? Nilranke called it a mana crystal?"

Light flashed from the house's front door, followed by a concussive pressure.

"Later," Drace said, though his gritted teeth spoke of the pain he was holding back. "We have to get to the palace." He shoved the bloodied gem into his pants pocket.

"You're the bravest man I know." Elvan leaned up to kiss Drace and turned quickly to open the iron gate.

Locked.

24

E LVAN LOOKED UP AT THE nine feet of bars topped with decorative spikes and another wave of pressure thumped from the house behind them.

Drace had another key in his right hand and was unlocking the gate.

"How did you...?"

"Swiped it off the manservant." Drace winced and held his left hand against his chest. "Let's move."

Someone hissed from across the cobblestone street. Captain Antris waved them over to the shadows beside a cafe and hurried them behind it to an empty yard crammed with small tables and folded umbrellas, out of sight of Nilranke's house.

"I've sent my men back to the *Blessing*," said Antris. "I hear explosions and see smoke from the palace."

"Nilranke's organized regicide," said Drace.

"Regicide..." Antris looked between them and shook his head. "I can't risk any involvement with Spheris right now. I have to return to my ship and cast off. I hope you understand that."

Elvan nodded. "Nothing to jeopardize your wife and daughter. Thank you, Captain Antris."

"Your mother and brother," said Antris. "Do you want me to leave them at the port or take them on to Glenmany?"

"Send them to my manor house by carriage. I'll pay you back… somehow."

"Be careful." Antris tapped his fist to his chest and turned on a heel, taking a side path in the vague direction of the harbor.

"Good idea," said Drace, watching Antris leave.

"What? Being careful?"

"No, not being seen." Drace spun in the small yard and rushed to the grate against the back of whatever business shared this space across from the cafe. He deftly unlocked it and waved Elvan in first.

"Not again," Elvan groaned.

"The city will be crawling with Serhane guards, royal soldiers, and inquisitors."

"Where are we going?"

"Into the palace."

Elvan froze on the ladder and looked up at Drace. "*Into* the palace?"

Drace waved Elvan down and followed him, relocking the grate. "We have to help the Artists in there."

"Nilranke's friends? The ones sent to kill the king? Those Artists?"

"You think Nilranke has any friends? I'd wager anything he threatened those people into his service, just like Captain Antris. If they're not already dead, the princess will see them hanged as the first act of her reign." Drace led them through the narrow, twisting corridors, splashing water around their boots that smelled cleaner than the last time they'd been in the sewers, though not by much.

"Say we get into the palace and find the Artists, what then? Do you think we could escape the same way with them?" Elvan asked.

Drace slowed and put a hand on the neatly fitted bricks of the wall, letting his head droop. "These are my people, Elvan. Nilranke hunts us and the crown is destroying our past."

Elvan stepped around Drace and looked up into his amber eyes lit by the meager light filtering through storm drains. "You're an Artist."

"Technically no. I have to make an artefact to take the title, and I could never manage the power. I'm sorry."

Elvan put his hands on Drace's shoulders, sliding them to hold his head, locking their gazes. "Don't you start that now. You were protecting yourself."

"I was at first, but then I felt it was too late to tell you."

Elvan scavenged his memory, parsing through every comment Drace said on the topic and seeing each answer in a new light. "You were careful with your words, but never lied."

Drace shook his head and took a quaking breath. "We have to try, Elvan. If nothing else, those Artists can speak against Nilranke or the princess. Are we doing this?"

He helped me after he lost everything, when I had no one.

"We don't have time to debate it," Elvan said. "Let's go."

Drace looked ready to argue his point and let a smile spread over his lips.

"One thing, first." Elvan slipped a hand behind Drace's head and pulled him in for a kiss. It lacked the raw, sloppy passion from their nights in the mossy hut, but felt comfortable and they both knew the added meaning behind it.

One more kiss, in case we're going to our deaths.

Drace wrapped his arms around Elvan's shoulders and pressed

their foreheads together, noses touching. "Thank you."

Elvan caught a whiff of the shop's incense and forced himself to push back. "Into the palace? How does that work?"

"Right." Drace slid his hand into Elvan's and directed them into motion again. "The oddity shop was a valid business, but also a front for what Nana sold in the backrooms, other than readings. Some of her associates worked in the palace." They slipped between a wide iron grate and stepped onto the narrow walkway beside the water. "I sometimes made deliveries for her."

"And you'd move below the city to go unnoticed. Our families were in very similar businesses."

"Funny how life works out."

"I'm sorry, Drace."

Drace groaned. "What about this time?"

"My mother. She was working to destroy your culture."

"She thought she was riding Spheris of a threat."

"Yes, but—"

"Leave it, Elvan," said Drace. "Please."

Elvan sputtered a response, but let it die in a long breath. He focused instead on the quick turns Drace led them through. Elvan had no idea of their location, but thought they must be near the palace based on the shouts and alarms filtering through the drain pipes. Another sharp turn and they stepped back into stagnant water to their knees, but it quickly rose to Drace's waist and Elvan's belly.

"It must have rained a lot while we were gone," said Drace while the water rose around them. They stopped before it reached halfway up Elvan's chest and Drace pointed to the ceiling. Pipes and machinery clogged the space above them and a narrow iron ladder led to a hatch in the roof.

"It lets out in a service shed near a fountain behind the palace," he said. "It's not *in* the palace, but it's within the grounds. We can slip in the servants' entrance from there."

"Then… get to the king's private meeting chamber? Dodging inquisitors and royal soldiers?"

"You sound less than enthusiastic," Drace said flatly.

"You stopped me before we went in the warehouse, asking me to describe my expectations. I guess I'm doing the same for you now. I have to ask and need you to hear your own response. What are our range of outcomes?"

Drace huffed and rolled his neck. "Best, find all the Artists alive and get away with them. Mid, we find evidence about the king's plans and get away alone. Worst, we're killed."

Elvan stared at him for a long moment before waving to the ladder in the wall. "Let's at least die up there, rather than from disease in sewer water."

Drace climbed up first, working the hatch in the ceiling and pushing it upward on rusted hinges. Elvan followed into a shed cramped with more of the fountain's controls and gardening supplies. Drace handed him a rag, which did little to dry them off, but after sitting to dump the water from their boots, they were each wearing grass-stained smocks and stepping into the back garden of the palace. The rolling hills faced away from the bulk of the industry of Spheris, giving a clear view of blue skies stretching to the distant horizon. Trees and sculpted hedges disguised the maintenance shed, blending into the manicured paths wending through the patches of flowers and reflecting ponds as the land rose to the gilded palace.

They passed the fountain chugging water from a stone boy's vase, coming into full view of the palace. Elvan wished he had a coin to toss in for luck when he saw the oily black smoke pouring from the windows on the west wing.

"That's where the king would have been," Elvan said even as they jogged, hunched, through the hedges in the empty garden. "Wait!" He grabbed the back of Drace's shirt, tugging him to a stop. Elvan pointed to the banners snapping in the breeze over the palace. The king's red and gold was highest and a dozen others flew lower, but the one nearest to his was down. "The princess, she isn't in."

"Of course, she isn't." Drace took Elvan's hand and tugged him into motion, not aiming for the wide marble patio dotted with high tables, but just to the left of it, to a door that easily blended in with the wall if one didn't know to look for it. Every time they darted from behind a row of hedges, Elvan expected a guard to shout out to them and by the time they reached the door painted to resemble brick, his stomach was in a twisted knot. Drace held his ear to the door. "Three servants just inside the door, at least. They're arguing about whether to stay or run. Follow my lead." He snatched Elvan's wrist, wrenched the door open, and ran inside.

"By the Six!" Drace yelled, breathing hard and looking between the four servants in the room filled with silver carafes on silver trays and labeled bells on the wall. A butler, two maids, and a footman, by the looks of their attire, stared back at them with shock.

"We were tending the Sunken Pools and saw the smoke. What happened?" Drace shut the door and leaned against it. Elvan bent forward to pretend to be winded while hiding his face. He wasn't sure anyone would recognize him, but couldn't risk it.

The four glanced the pair over and, if they wondered about their frilly attire under the smocks, they didn't comment on it.

"The palace has been attacked," said the footman. "Enemy forces have invaded the king's counsel."

"Invaded?" Drace gaped. "But the smoke... Did they have

bombs?"

"Nay, Artists," said a maid.

The butler glowered at her. "Allegedly."

Drace gasped. "Artists? In the palace? I pray the princess is safe." Elvan silently applauded his acting quality.

"Princess Lorelai left this morning to instate Duchess Delphina…" The butler trailed off and stepped nearer. "I thought I knew all the ground staff."

"I've been here four years," said Drace and held the man's intense scrutiny. "Should we go to the king? Can we help?"

The footman snorted back a laugh. "Too late for that. I hope you like working for the princess."

"Watch your tongue!" the butler snapped with a vein popping from his forehead. "The guards have ordered all staff to remain in place and called for the inquisitors."

"We hadn't heard, being in the garden," Drace said and turned back to Elvan. "Tristan, we have to find Theo. We'll be right back." He shouted the last bit over his shoulder while pushing Elvan through the door. Once they had a hedge between them and the servants' door, Drace sagged to a squat.

"That's it, then," he said and rubbed a hand across his scruffy cheek. "If things are that tight, if the place is crawling with inquisitors, we'll never make it to where the Artists are."

Elvan squeezed Drace's shoulder. "The princess… The butler didn't finish his sentence, but what if she and Delphina are at my manor, instating my sister as head of the House?"

"That's a big *what if*. And what if she is?" Drace looked up and blinked a tear from his eyes. "We rush there just in time for the ceremony? We show up there, escaped felons, and do what? It's her word against ours. We've no hard proof of the king's intentions or Lorelai's motives."

"My mother and brother are on the way there now; she could corroborate our story."

Drace gave him a knowing look.

"How's that feeling?" Elvan nodded to Drace's left hand still clutching the linen now dyed red.

"Hurts and getting worse. Let's move. If we cut through the trees again, we might beat a rider sent from the palace." Drace looked back when Elvan didn't move. "What?"

Elvan turned back to the palace with a suicidal plot brewing. "You're an Artist, Drace, or you might as well be one. So be one. Use some magic to get us to the king."

Drace scoffed. "Even if I had an artefact in hand, you think I could stand up against the inquisitors?"

"You stood up against Nilranke. The butler said the inquisitors were called, not here yet. We have a brief window of action. What about that thing?" Elvan nodded his chin toward Drace's pocket. "Nilranke called it a mana crystal; that sounds vaguely magicky."

"It's…" Drace pulled out the ruby and held it up in his uninjured palm. "There is magic in it, but it's not an artefact. I don't think it is."

"Can you use it like one?"

"I…"

"Can you try?"

Drace turned the mana crystal in the fingers of his right hand. He gasped and his eyes flashed with an internal light. "Whoa."

"Is that good?"

The air rippled, distorting the hedges and the palace. A tingling spark washed over Elvan with a shiver. Drace transferred the mana crystal to hold in his left hand over the bloody linen and grabbed Elvan's in his other with a crushing grip. "We have to move fast," he breathed, already panting. "Lead me."

Elvan blinked, forcing himself not to stare into Drace's burning eyes and looked back to the palace. His vision swam and shifted, but he pulled them toward the main rear doors. He paused and peered in the textured glass, expecting to see the red and gold of soldiers or the colorless void of inquisitor's robes. Instead, he saw no movement.

"Go," Drace said.

Elvan looked back at him and saw the sweat beading on the former shopkeeper's forehead, his unfocused, smoldering eyes. He couldn't imagine the strain of using magic, much less from such an odd object.

"No hesitating, Elvan. Do exactly what I say immediately. I'm blind like this."

Elvan looked through the glass again and with a deep breath, pulled it open.

Within, anything more than a few feet away distorted like looking through a fishbowl. Elvan led with Drace's directions across wide halls with floors polished to a mirror finish and lined with gilded columns stretching to the ceiling. Elvan could only focus on the next step, as looking too far out quickly made him dizzy. After the third empty room, Elvan felt the pulse of magic through his arm, or at least what he assumed was magic. It thudded in time with his frenzied heartbeat, pounding an electric thrill that urged him to release Drace's hand.

Drace suddenly froze in a long hall, tugging them into a door alcove just as a trio of soldiers in red and gold jogged by, halberds jangling, in the direction they were going. The instant they passed, the door behind them clicked and Drace pulled them away, to the next alcove door along the hall, holding Elvan close. More soldiers burst from their previous hiding place to run by.

"How…"

Drace tapped his bloody fist holding the mana crystal to his temple. "Later." He nodded at the door beside them. "Open it in three… two… one…"

Elvan twisted the knob and pushed the door open just as more soldiers left the ballroom on the far side. Drace led them to a narrow servants' passage and Elvan soon recognized the ornate decor the closer they moved to the royal suites.

Drace again tugged them to a stop before an enormous portrait of King Pearce III and moved his eyes over it, blind and unfocused.

"Bottom left side, there's a switch," he said.

Elvan found it without releasing Drace's hand and with a dull *clack*, the oil painting shifted inward an inch. Drace bumped it with a shoulder and stepped over the frame and wall into a dim and narrow passage. Elvan pushed the painting closed, leaving them in complete darkness. Without missing a beat, an orb of golden light burst to life over Drace's left hand, shedding warmth over the dusty passage of rough brickwork that might not have seen use in a century.

The man I love is using magic and dragging me through the palace to where the king was attacked. The man I love…

They stopped before what Elvan now recognized as the backside of another huge portrait. Drace used his foot to trip a lever at the floor and hooked it under the edge of the painting to pull it toward them. Beyond, messily crammed bookshelves and a single oak desk filled the small room, only a dozen feet on a side. Elvan saw no windows or other entrances, but another backside of a portrait straight ahead.

Shimmering in Drace's light, a cloaked figure leaned against the wall beside the portrait. The figure slid to the floor, dragging a streak of blood on the wall behind them. Drace released his magic and rushed to their side, catching them as they fell. He pulled back the cowl, revealing a woman who, despite the years, Elvan recognized from her painting in the locket.

"Ingaret," Elvan said and knelt on her other side. She pressed a bloodied hand to her side, winced, and looked up at each of them.

"Drace…?" She focused on the former shopkeeper, the one she gave candies to even when he was too old for them. "They made me…" She squeezed her eyes tight.

Drace pulled her hand away to inspect her wound. Elvan wasn't sure, but the slash at her ribs didn't look mortal. Painful, but not mortal.

"The king?" Elvan asked.

"I…" she started. "I don't know. We each had our roles, without knowledge of the others."

"Nilranke gave each Artist a specific task, so none would know the full plan?" asked Drace.

"Aye."

Elvan stood and moved to examine the papers spread on the desk

"We saw your husband, Ingaret," said Drace. "He's at the dock now—"

He continued, but Elvan heard little of it, or her response. Elvan sifted through the papers that appeared to be a collection of the king's assets. Foreign manor houses, company holdings, and numbers detailing production rates of the farms north of the city. Elvan pawed through the journal centered in front of the low backed leather chair. The entries dated from twelve years through three months ago were penned in a shaky hand that would take too much time to decipher. Elvan picked out keywords naming heads of the Houses and a plan for distribution of power. Fanning through it, Elvan saw the king's mark slowly degrading over the years, as that sloppy signature that sparked everything back in his mother's study signed the newer entries.

Elvan clutched the journal to his chest and turned. "This is it! Proof of the king's plans!"

"No…" Ingaret slumped against the wall and rubbed her bloodied hand over her face. "No, you can't take that."

"That's the proof we need against the princess!" said Drace.

"No," Ingaret repeated. "If this doesn't go exactly as orchestrated, they'll kill my daughter. I…" she winced and put a hand against the wall to push to her feet. "I can't let you leave with that." Her eyes flashed a radiant blue, and she reached into a pocket of her coat, removing a dark statue carved into a thin cat. Ingaret looked down at it with a sobbing breath. "The relics of my ancestors, now used to secure our enemies. Yet, I can't put my daughter at risk. I am sorry for this."

Ingaret wiped her shoulder across her face and raised her hand holding the artefact toward Elvan. A ball of fire formed in the air before her fingers, swirling red and orange. "It'll kill us all, but at least—"

The fire fizzled, and Ingaret slumped to the ground. Drace stood beside her with his hand outstretched. "Put her to sleep," he explained and held up the mana crystal. "This thing hurts to use, but it's powerful." He plucked the crystal from his left fist and flexed his fingers.

"If she came in this way, I'm sure Nilranke's people will be watching the exit," said Elvan.

"No," said Drace. "You were busy looking at the book, but she told me this wasn't the way she was supposed to leave. She used a spell like I did to find this room to rest for a moment."

"We have to get this to…" Elvan held up the king's journal, blank again regarding to whom they might present the information.

"Last chance, Elvan. The king's dead and everyone thinks we are too. We could steal that snuffbox on the table, hock it, and get south to start a new life."

Elvan took a deep breath, calculating the street price of a snuffbox with that much silver. *No. The crown has abused too many with ties to Artists, a people who are no different from the rest of us. How many more would suffer if the princess took the throne in full?*

Elvan looked back at Drace, meeting his amber eyes, and shook his head once. "No, we see this through to the end. I'll take my place on the Council of Houses and force them to hear me."

Drace slipped his hand around Elvan's neck and pulled him close, kissing him deeply. "Good." His hand traced down Elvan's shoulder and arm to his hand and pulled him toward the portrait — King Pearce IV — and the dusty hall beyond.

Elvan resisted and gestured back to the sleeping Artist. "What about her artefact? Shouldn't we take it?"

"She'll need it when she wakes up."

"Really? She was about to kill us using it."

"And we won't be here for her to try again."

In the tunnel, the air distorted and charged with each step. The light over Drace's hand appeared steady, but wavered and flickered by the time it met the brick.

They reached the back of King Pearce III's portrait and Drace flipped the switch with his foot. He looked back, eyes blazing amber, and slipped his hand into Elvan's. "Same thing, stay close, do what I say."

He led a brisk pace through the palace with quick turns to avoid soldiers and staff. With the wide, glass doors to the back patio in sight, they huddled in the shadows of a closet, watching through the cracks as a dozen inquisitors flowed past in their long black robes and tall black hats. Neither breathed until the group was gone toward the king's chambers.

A few minutes later, the pair descended the ladder beside the fountain controls. As they dropped into the sewer water, Drace slipped and fell against Elvan. Blood dripped freely from his hand clutching the mana crystal. Elvan said nothing, but hoped his look of pleading worry spoke for him.

"I'll be fine," said Drace, but his face belied his pain. "Keep the journal dry and let's get to your house."

Elvan turned when he didn't hear Drace splashing behind him.

"Are you sure you're alright?"

Drace looked up from the crystal in his hand and chuckled. "I get it now."

"Get what?" Elvan waded nearer, careful to keep the journal above the water level.

"When Nana gave me this necklace, she said it would protect me. I thought she meant it was a luck charm; a pretty gem that always felt warm, that's it. No, it was more than that."

"Sure, it's an artefact."

"Yes and no. I tried for years to craft an artefact, to take the title of Artist, but could never manage the threshold of a stable one. I figured I wasn't powerful enough. I wasn't. Not while I wore this thing. It leeches my magic, holding it in a vessel not detectable like other artefacts that need arcane steel for shielding. *This*," he shook the ruby at Elvan, "this is my artefact."

Elvan stared at the ruby gem sparkling in the meager light.

"Nana was right; it protected me," Drace continued. "It kept me undetected for years by whatever means Nilranke has of finding my people." He closed his fist over the crystal, wincing again. "Let's go."

25

FUELED BY THE ADRENALINE PUMPING through his heart, Elvan raced through the trees and across shallow streams toward his home. Drace kept up, but Elvan noticed the trail of bloody handprints the other left every time he reached to steady himself against a rock or tree. He could only guess at what excruciating pain Drace was in.

Finally, the tall hedges of the Galmoth Estate came into view and beyond, finely crafted carriages filled the yard, bearing the colors and crests of each of the four other Houses. Another four carriages bore the royal crest. Their selectively bred horses stood proudly stoic while groomers brushed them. Servants flowed through the front door, carrying in trays of food or thick cushions and taking out rugs to shake the dust from. Royal soldiers littered the yard, but Elvan saw no sign of his sister or the princess.

"They wasted no time," Elvan grumbled.

Drace leaned against the stone frame of the gate to catch his breath. "Go," he said, his face pinched with pain. "I'll just be a minute."

Elvan glanced back at the house and the troop of four soldiers in red and gold marching directly in their direction. The one in front reached across his body for his sword when a knight with a trim white beard broke through their array, jogging toward the pair with a hand at his hip to hold his swords as he ran. Elvan let out a breath of relief. "Ser Vazadon!" He moved to meet the man and wrap his arms around him.

"Young master, I thought you lost forever." Elvan felt the old man's body trembling. Vazadon released the embrace to offer a hand in greeting to Drace. "Master Drace, your eye looks much better, except…. You're hurt." He gestured to the hand Drace held against his chest. "Might I…?"

Drace held out his palm and Vazadon delicately pulled away the lace, now completely soaked and stained red, exposing a ragged wound far worse than the scratch Elvan saw outside Nilranke's manor.

"It looks worse than it is," said Ser Vazadon. "What caused it?"

Drace glanced at Elvan, then back at Vazadon. He pulled the crystal from his pocket, holding it up as if it would explain itself. "It's a sort of artefact, but it hurts the more I use it."

Ser Vazadon squinted at the red gem, then looked up at Drace with a wry smile. "Mana crystal. Master Elvan left out significant details about you. They can cause a taint in the blood, but nothing to worry about long-term. I can get you fixed up once we have a moment of privacy." He glanced over his shoulder at the soldiers lingering a dozen paces away.

"Ser Vazadon," Elvan said, loud enough for the guards to hear. "Inquisitor Nilranke orchestrated an attack on the palace, ordered by the princess. I fear the king and his privy council are dead." His heartbeat thudded in his ears.

"Nilranke…" said Vazadon, but his eyes were on the road

beyond the gate. Elvan realized the beat in his ears wasn't his heart, but the hoofs of the black stallion charging toward them. From the distance, the rider's eyes glowed red from beneath his black cloak.

Vazadon tugged Drace into motion, moving him behind the other guards, and pulled his sword.

Elvan backed away a step, leaving Ser Vazadon alone at the gate. "Nilranke's an Artist." He stepped to Drace, wrapping his arms around him. Drace put his good hand over Elvan's shoulder and across his neck.

"I know," said the old knight.

Ser Vazadon held his sword in his right hand with the steel blade nearly touching the gravel. Inquisitor Nilranke reined his steed, bucking it to a stop, and tossed his leg over to float to the ground.

"The king is dead. Long live the queen," his voice rasped from the darkness under his hood.

"There is a council of nobility taking place on this property," said Vazadon, unconcerned about the cloaked magic user before him. "As guardian of the Duchess and of House Galmoth, I say that you will not enter these grounds."

Nilranke croaked a laugh. "You harbor criminals and I am their justice. I have no interest in any others here, only him." He raised a finger from his robes to point at Drace. "He is not under your protection."

Ser Vazadon glanced back at Elvan and Drace wrapped in each other's arms, then back to Nilranke. "I swore to protect House Galmoth."

"Fine, then." Nilranke waved the hand still pointing at Drace and a spark of azure lightning shot from his palm.

With the flick of his wrist, Vazadon's sword met and deflected the attack.

"I am your opponent," the knight said calmly. "Do not test me with magic, Nilranke. It will not go well for you."

Nilranke growled and fired three more balls of lightning. Vazadon's sword moved efficiently to meet each. The knight slid his left foot back to settle into a defensive stance. He looked down the length of his sword, now glowing red. Ser Vazadon straightened, flourished the blade, and walked calmly toward Elvan to hand him the sword. It was heavier than Elvan's practice weapons, but he took it in both hands with a proper stance in front of Drace. Vazadon's hand moved to the other hilt at his hip, to the blade Elvan only first saw at the man's hip a few days ago, and turned back to Nilranke.

As Vazadon slid it from the sheath with a ring of metal on metal, the sword shone with an inner light and demanded to be admired. Elvan couldn't take his eyes from it and his heart felt ready to burst from his chest, such was the beauty of the length of steel. Stories of slaying daemon and evil barmaids told around the hearth flooded Elvan's mind. They were all true. Every wild story the knight told him as a child must be fact if that same man could possess such a work of exquisite beauty.

"You guard the royal family with a magic sword?" Nilranke hissed. "Such hypocrisy."

"Amusing, coming from a man who has dedicated his existence to the eradication of Artists."

"All means justify the rightful end." Nilranke tossed back his hood. Blood wept from deep scratches across his eyes, down his cheeks, even his eyes themselves… Elvan gasped and shrank back a step, as did the line of guards. Nilranke's eyes were blackened pits, burned out, lit with a spark of hellfire.

"He absorbed all his artefacts," Drace breathed. "He's unstable. He won't survive that much power and he knows it."

Elvan watched Vazadon's steady stance, silently willing the knight to strike and end this quickly, knowing he wouldn't. In all the stories told in his youth, Ser Vazadon was nothing if not overly honorable. If the inquisitor did not advance, neither would the knight.

Nilranke raised his arms, and the cloak fell away. He still wore his smoking jacket and matching pants, though both were stained red. The wounds on the man's face weren't enough for that much blood, and Elvan spared a worry for the butler, Graham. He pushed the thought away just as quickly. Nilranke dropped his left hand to the small of his back and pulled a thin dagger to brandish against Vazadon's magic longsword.

"It doesn't matter what happens to me now," said Nilranke. He cringed, and an aura of orange energy washed over his body. It dissipated into the air like steam. "I came for the boy, but I'll be glad to see you dead before me, old man."

Vazadon raised his blade. Nilranke crouched low and ran forward. Just before Nilranke was close enough to strike, he burst apart into smoke.

"Coward," Vazadon grumbled and turned a slow circle. "Inquisitor Nilranke," he bellowed. "You leave me no choice but to take your actions as an aggression against this House. This is your final warning. Leave now, or I will act against you."

"Bold words." Nilranke's voice came from every direction. The four guards, swords raised, formed a protective ring around the pair. Elvan took that as a small comfort, that the guards identified the obvious threat, even if it was someone of power and influence.

Lightning flashed against Vazadon's sword once, thrice, from wild angles and with each parry, Elvan further believed those old stories. The knight calmly blocked a dozen shots before one glanced his side.

Vazadon grunted and dropped to a knee.

The hairs on Elvan's arms prickled. "Down!" he shouted, and Drace dropped to a squat. Elvan swung Vazadon's steel service sword over Drace's head and felt resistance as smoke gathered there. Nilranke wavered into sight, staggering back and holding a bloody hand to the slash across his smoking jacket.

The soldiers spun on him and Ser Vazadon was there instantly, swinging his sword with an arc of silver that hung in the air where it passed through the inquisitor from shoulder to hip. Brilliant white light blazed from where the sword struck Nilranke and he dropped to his knees, clutching at his throat while the fire in the pits of his eyes faded.

Vazadon flicked his magic sword and sheathed it in a smooth motion, looking at the questioning, gaping stares of the surrounding six. "I have sealed his magic." Vazadon winced and pressed a hand to his side, where the single lightning bolt struck him.

Elvan offered Vazadon the service sword, but the knight waved him down. "Keep it for now, young master. I have a feeling you may yet need it." He nodded toward the entrance to the manor house.

The heads of the other Houses and their retinue crowded the cobblestone path by the front door. Standing in front of them, wearing a close-cut gown of cream and pink that perfectly complimented her dark complexion, was Princess Lorelai, flanked by her chamberlain and Duchess Delphina Pearce. The princess looked as stoic as ever, even bored. She snapped open a paper fan to wave at her neck as her amber eyes scanned across her soldiers, the returned felons, a celebrated knight, and finally lingering on her trusted servant kneeling in the gravel and clawing at his throat.

An eerie silence lingered over the scene, as if all present waited for the princess to grant permission to react.

Elvan took a deep breath, preparing to pull the king's journal from his pocket and shout his accusations at the princess in front of the ruling body of Spheris.

Instead, a horse thundered through the gates, interrupting him, and a breathless rider dropped from the saddle to kneel before the princess. "Your Majesty! The king..." he gasped for breath. "The king has been assassinated."

26

GASPS AND MURMURS ERUPTED FROM the crowd, but the princess only raised an eyebrow. "Assassinated? How?"

"Artists, Your Majesty. They attacked the privy council."

"Are you certain?"

"I… The captain of the guard gave me the message personally, Your Majesty."

Lorelai snapped her fan closed and used it to raise the messenger's eyes up to meet hers. "Are you telling me that Artists have slain my father and his closest advisers?"

The messenger paused and though Elvan couldn't see the man's face, his fear was palpable. "Y-yes, Your Majesty."

Lorelai dropped the man's head and turned to address the gathering behind her. "Artists have attacked our homes, slain our beloved monarch. As my first act as your queen, I will see these heathens stricken from the continent."

The crowd's murmur changed to a tone of approval.

"This is all your doing!" Elvan shouted over them, clenching his fist around Vazadon's sword to keep his hands from shaking. "The king was going to spread the crown's power to this Council of Houses, so you tasked Inquisitor Nilranke with his murder."

"More slander!" shouted the chamberlain.

Elvan pulled the journal from the inner pocket of his jacket and held it high overhead. "I have words penned by King Pearce VI of his intention, giving Lorelai her motive."

The princess took a few steps forward, looking down her nose at Elvan. Her frigid, calculating stare showed only a fleeting hint of confusion at seeing him. She spoke in a whisper. "Why would my father do something so ridiculous? That's nothing but the ravings of a madman." Lorelai's lip twitched upward for just a heartbeat and her voice rose to address the audience behind. "Elvan Galmoth was arrested and sentenced to exile three days ago for exactly this sort of behavior. His are the words of a convicted and escaped criminal. His accomplice colludes with Artists. The very ones that killed my father."

Elvan tightened his grip on the sword.

Lorelai's gaze shifted to Ser Vazadon. "You did this?" She flicked her eyes to Nilranke, trying to push to his hands and knees and still clawing at his throat.

"Yes. I act in service to House Galmoth."

The princess took a slow breath and raised her voice again. "Artists have possessed the mind and body of our most trusted Inquistor Nilranke. Thank you for your skill in sparing his life, Ser Vazadon. You are an asset to the crown."

Elvan saw the firm set to the knight's jaw and the subtle twitch of his eyebrow. Duty guided Vazadon's sword, but also stayed his words.

Elvan took a deep breath to say what his protector could not. "Nilranke is—"

"Nilranke is an Artist," said Ser Vazadon over him. "His display of power was his own. Do not twist the events, Princess."

Lorelai shifted to within a few feet of the knight. "Do not speak back to me. You are sworn to me."

"I am sworn to House Galmoth," he repeated.

"The knighthood has no place for old men that cannot remember whom to protect. I dissolve you of your titles and obligations to the royal family."

Vazadon's eyes narrowed and his hand moved to rest on his magic sword's hilt.

"Guards, prepare these three for execution."

"Others can confirm my words," Elvan yelled to ensure all could hear him. "My mother is on her way here right now. You exiled her two years ago to hide what she knew. A sea captain and his wife, who you and Nilranke held hos—"

Lorelai waved her hand, and a soldier stepped up to Elvan and buried a fist in his gut. He doubled forward, sucking for air that wouldn't come.

"It's all true!" said the voice Elvan least expected. Delphina stepped forward and moved to stand beside her brother. "I've heard Princess Lorelai and Inquisitor Nilranke as they plotted the king's death." Her voice quavered, but Elvan knew the bravery behind it.

"Look at the little Galmoths." Lorelai scoffed. "Toying with crowns, no concept of the powers in play. I was beginning to take a liking to you, Duchess, as one would a favored pet. You have always been more than delighted at the scraps I brush off my plate, but I see I was mistaken about your loyalties."

Vazadon stepped to the princess's side, unsheathing his blade, resting it on her shoulder.

Every soldier and guard turned on him with swords ready.

"Interesting," she whispered with a wry grin.

"I am sworn to House Galmoth," Vazadon repeated and calmly glanced at the soldiers surrounding him. "You have killed our king and I will see you answer for your crimes."

Lorelai raised a finger to stay the soldiers from coming nearer. "You believe a known criminal waving a tattered book, that I would act against my own blood?"

Vazadon said nothing, but kept his sword arm firm.

The princess sighed. "Your words bore me. Spheris must be in chaos and the people need their queen now more than ever."

The crowd turned to agreement at the princess's words. With bleary eyes, Elvan looked over them, the heads of the other Houses. He at once felt pride to be standing against the princess in front of them, but ashamed for the nobles, that none came to his aid. Elvan wanted to believe he would do more in their case, not just stand by idly.

Do I have any reason to think I would?

Delphina squeezed her eyes tight. "Stop! It's not just words. I have proof of it all, gathered over two years."

The proof she intended to use to extort the princess would instead take her down. Fitting.

"Stand down," Vazadon whispered with a menacing grin. "As protector of House Galmoth, I am placing Princess Lorelai Pearce under arrest for conspiring to murder her father, King Pearce VI."

The soldiers remained frozen, unwilling to risk the princess's or their own lives against Vazadon's reputation.

"Guards! Seize Vazadon!" yelled the chamberlain.

Vazadon twisted his blade on the princess's shoulder, nearer to her throat, letting the sun shine menacingly from its beautiful, polished surface.

"No," Lorelai said quietly, but with enough force to stop her soldiers. "There has been enough violence in the palace today and

I will cause no more here." Vazadon lifted his sword and she turned to face him. "I'll still see you hanged. You too," she added to Delphina. She turned again to face the crowd and nodded her chin toward the house.

One soldier sheathed her sword and, like dominoes, others followed as they fell in line behind their princess.

"This isn't over," Drace whispered from behind Elvan.

Elvan breathed a small sigh of relief, wrapped both arms around Drace's neck, and, ignoring that he stood beside his sister and most of the nobles of Spheris, pulled him in for a deep, passionate kiss.

Drace smirked when Elvan finally pulled back. "What was that—"

"I love you."

"What?"

"I love you, Drace. I should have said it a dozen times before. Saying *I should have* makes up half of my life, it seems. I don't care if you don't say it back. That doesn't change how I feel about you. I knew how I felt, but wasn't sure about the words, but that's it. I love you." Elvan gasped, breathless, feeling like a physical weight had been pulled from his chest.

Drace stared back at him with wide eyes. Just as Elvan began to rethink saying he didn't care if Drace didn't say it back, his lips turned into a wide grin. "I love you too, Elvan." He slipped a hand around Elvan's lower back and pulled him closer for another kiss. A second into it, he winced away from the pain in his left hand.

"Is this how you treat your queen?"

Elvan looked up at her words. The princess stood in the doorway and turned slowly to face the crowd of nobles, servants, and soldiers.

"A few words from a disgraced House is all it takes to turn against me? Against what I represent?" Lorelai slipped her hands behind her back and took a step back into the yard. The confused soldiers shifted to give her space. "I have dedicated my life, my soul, to this kingdom, as has my father and his and his, up to the Sovereign King to whom you all owe your life and comfort."

Lorelai's lip curled when no one replied.

"I deserve that love in return. There is no place for cowardice or disloyalty in my reign."

Her gaze focused on Vazadon and her eyes flashed with inner light. The knight made to draw his sword, but not quickly enough. An arc of lightning shot from the princess, hitting Vazadon directly in the chest. It knocked him twisting back to land face down in the gravel near Nilranke.

Thunder cracked overhead. Elvan felt Drace wince at his side, but he couldn't take his eyes from Vazadon.

The crowd cried out and screamed, but Elvan heard it as nothing but background noise. He stared at the old knight a dozen feet away, expecting him to grunt and push up, but he just lay there, unmoving.

Lorelai's words somehow cut through. "I must needs consolidate the power my ancestors split amongst these unworthy Houses, gathering it into the single entity able to lead this nation to prosperity."

Elvan gave her a quick glance and instantly recognized the object she balanced on her left palm. He was still sore from where Drace pressed it into his shoulder at the warehouse. The artefact carved to resemble an owl.

Elvan squeezed Drace's hand and finally rushed to Vazadon's side, sliding to kneel in the gravel beside him. Pushing the old knight over, he saw the scorched damage in the quilted armor across the man's chest, but his flesh appeared undamaged.

"Duchess," Lorelai hissed.

Elvan glanced up and could see the raw fear in his sister's eyes, but there was nothing he could do.

"You were my protégé," said Lorelai. "Even you turned against me in the end."

Vazadon coughed and cracked an eye. "Drace…" He was already squatting on his other side. "Hold it by the chain and be a mirror."

"What…?" Elvan looked up. Drace's eyes went wide after a breath and he dug the mana crystal from his pocket, holding it by the delicate silver chain.

He pulled on Elvan's elbow to position them between Vazadon and the princess. "Keep her talking," he said and began muttering under his breath.

Elvan frowned at the cryptic order and faced the princess. She had moved back to within a few feet of Delphina. "Lorelai! Face me!"

The princess lowered the hand she held raised with the intention of striking Delphina and raised a single eyebrow.

"I am your opponent, Lorelai. Leave my sister alone."

She pivoted and leaned her head back to laugh. "You come to your sister's aid? You should hear the things she says about you over tea, her pathetic older brother. It's nauseating. How you follow in your mother's steps, but aren't worthy of her legacy. Small, weak, drunk, like your father. You claim to be my opponent, but you are nothing."

Elvan looked past the princess, at his sister's pleading eyes. He wanted to believe her intention was always to do what was best for Spheris, not just herself; to believe that she meant her words, that they weren't just said to garner favor through fellowship.

Her past didn't matter. The future of the kingdom hung on the actions of the next few moments.

Elvan cleared his dry throat and raised his voice to the heads of Houses scattered across the gathering. "I've been gone too long. I am retaking my place on the Council of Houses."

"I hope it goes better than last time," said Lorelai.

Elvan licked his lips. "This isn't about me. This is about Spheris and her people. The king knew the crown holding all the power was no longer sustainable. Giving the Houses and a wider council the autonomy to govern is the only path forward."

"My father was half senile. The intentions, the machinations, of an addled mind mean nothing. This country has and always will be ruled by the one on the throne. Me."

The heat built in Elvan's cheeks. "Spheris has many flaws. It was founded on the basis that Artists are a lesser people. It's despicable and that must end now. There can be no forward progress while we hold to the grotesque traditions of the past."

"Such impassioned words. Now that you're sleeping with one of their kind, you suddenly care for the plight of Artists."

Lorelai tilted her head to see Drace behind Elvan, but he shifted to block her view.

"We've all seen the truth of the princess here," he said. "The details of the king's journals and witness testimony are inconsequential. I will not submit to the will of someone so unjustly entitled. As Head of House Galmoth, I motion to remove Lorelai from power and enact the king's will. Who will stand with me?"

Elvan found the other heads in the crowd, focusing on each while Drace mumbled behind him. Percival Kae and Edna Frostspark pushed forward immediately to stand beside Elvan. Maybe they took a moment longer to decide, or maybe they sensed a change in the dynamics of power, but Ranti Daggar and Stas Serhane joined a moment later.

A swell of something between joy and pride threatened to overtake Elvan, but he kept his breath slow and even. The heads of the five Houses literally faced the princess in his yard, surrounded by dozens of witnesses.

"Set down the artefact and surrender, Lorelai," said Elvan.

"Fools, you make this too easy," said the princess. "The Houses are a relic. Unnecessary in my new order."

She raised a hand, lightning arcing between her fingers.

"The Artists that killed my father struck the Galmoth manor as well," Lorelai said with a gasp. "The soldiers fought bravely to the last man, but only I survived."

Elvan shrank, witnessing the growing madness.

Her amber eyes flashed wide, then narrowed with a twisted grin. "The only story to remain will be mine."

A bolt of blinding lightning shot from the clear sky, searing its image into Elvan's vision as it connected with the princess. She grinned and redirected the power. There was no sense of depth as the deadly arc shot closer, only an odd slowing of time, as if his mind wanted to drag out that last moment, like it wasn't ready just yet to give up on being alive.

His skin prickled with a charge that, while he was becoming accustomed to feeling, he would never get used to.

The bolt hit Princess Lorelai directly in the chest, blasting her twenty feet to collapse in a heap. Drace fell against Elvan's back and he turned to help the man sit.

"Like a mirror." Drace grinned and let the silver chain holding the mana crystal slip from his fingers.

"I'll see to him," Vazadon — *no, the princess had no right to strip him of knighthood* — Ser Vazadon said, shifting to Drace's side and putting a palm on his forehead.

"Princess Lorelai is dead," Percival Kae announced, and Elvan felt an odd emptiness with the words.

Where's the justice in this? The king and princess are dead, and Nilranke is a drooling mess.

Ser Vazadon stood beside him, supporting Drace. "Let us go upstairs, young master. Drace requires aid."

Happy for any reason to slip away from the growing chaos in his yard as nobles squabbled over what next to do, Elvan stepped into his house. Up the steps, the sounds from the yard faded with each stair and he led Ser Vazadon to his room. He waved for Drace to sit on the bed and the knight helped ease him down. Elvan sat to his right.

"Mana crystal is quite the rarity on this continent," said Ser Vazadon. "I would be interested to hear how you came upon such a find, if you would share your tale."

"The necklace was my Nana's," Drace said. "She was an Artist. I'm… I'm an Artist."

Ser Vazadon hummed thoughtfully. "Indeed you are." He pinched the edges of the crystal in his thumb and forefinger for a moment before setting it aside. "The magic in such a crystal is potent but, as I am also sure you noticed, it can be quite dangerous to use. May I see your hand?"

Drace nodded and held out his bloodied left hand, his brow sweating from the pain.

Vazadon sat beside Drace and gingerly put one hand under the bloody one. He mumbled a few phrases and clapped his other hand over Drace's palm with a quick burst of green light. Drace stiffened and cried out once, but quickly relaxed into a tremble and slumped against Elvan. Vazadon continued speaking in a voice only he could hear and Elvan saw the gentle green light leaking around where his hand pushed into Drace's injured one.

"Are you an Artist?" Elvan asked.

Vazadon shook his head. "Not by the definitions on this continent. Elruthon taught me a bit of magic."

"Lorelai hit you full on with lightning. It killed her and you're unhurt. How?"

"My sword, Aethiel, is not the only bit of magic on my person, young master." Ser Vazadon glanced down at the large ring of porous stone on his finger. Elvan remembered always having seen the knight wear it, but never thought anything of it.

"Drace needs a bit more time to recover. Change into something with house colors and see to the others downstairs."

Elvan nodded and pushed Drace's weight onto Vazadon. He looked down at his clothes, so fresh from Captain Antris only hours ago, now stained and snagged from wading through sewers and their rush through the forest. Standing, he dug through his wardrobe, which was still a mess from assembling the outfit for Tristan Griffith. He pulled off his shirt and took a clean one from the drawer. "What was that crystal?"

"Mana crystal. They are essentially a naturally occurring artefact. Their power is highly concentrated, but requires significant training to use safely. They are exceptionally rare across the sea and I thought none existed on this continent."

Elvan tugged off the once-polished boots. "He said his Nana gave it to him."

"She would have been an interesting woman to meet."

Elvan pulled on clean pants and sat to tie his new boots. "What do I say to them downstairs? The other heads of the Houses?"

"Make it known that no one is above the law; that what is right will always prevail. Whether that be the laws of men or the Six. The king and princess may have escaped justice in life, but we must be vigilant to not let this repeat. Take your place among them and rule Spheris."

Elvan pulled on his crimson vest with silver trimmings crossed with a baldric bearing his house crest. His mind flashing to the amulet found in his mother's hut.

Mother…

No… focus a bit longer. She'll be here soon enough.

"How do I look?" Elvan forced a grin.

Ser Vazadon smiled up at him from where he sat on the bed. "You look ready, young master."

Elvan crossed to the door and let his hand linger on the knob for a breath, summoning the courage needed to face what lay on the other side. He finally decided he would never be ready, and that would have to be good enough. He pulled the door open.

A figure loomed in the doorway, hand raised to knock, and Elvan hopped back with a yelp.

"Delphina!"

She pushed past him; her ruffled pink gown making her feel larger in the crowded room. Ser Vazadon still held Drace's hand, but the green glow had ceased.

Interesting. He doesn't trust her to know he can do magic. Good for him.

"You're already changed, nice," she said after her eyes lingered for a breath on the two on the bed. "What's next?" She scoffed and combed gloved hands through his hair. "Damned rat's nest. Don't you ever brush this?"

"Stop that." Elvan leaned back and waved her away. "Last we spoke, you seemed gleeful about us being sent into exile. Now you publicly speak out against the princess? What side are you on?"

"Of course you don't understand me, Elvan. You've always had everything handed to you."

Elvan held back a smirk and crossed his arms over his chest. "Naturally. Go on."

"I have physical evidence against the princess. I know where she got sloppy, what threads she left dangling. She wanted to consolidate power and I can prove it. You need me. You'll need what I know when the average citizen finds out their beloved princess died in your front yard."

"You will bring this evidence against her in full?"

"Of course," Delphina scrunched her nose with annoyance. "I'll need to prove I'm not complicit, or whatever."

No matter her motives or justifications, they serve the same goal.

"Thank you, Delphina." He turned to the two sitting on the bed. "Ser Vazadon, I… Thank you."

The old knight inclined his head. "Of course, young master."

Elvan turned back to Delphina. "Let's go, dear sister."

He stepped into the hall with Delphina close behind him and considered the encounters with his sister over the last few days. He assumed she had always been preparing to act against him, but what if she really did always intend to betray the princess? What if she didn't want to gather evidence to blackmail and control Lorelai, but to ensure some balance remained? He'd been wrong about his mother, quickly believing she was smuggling artefacts, then getting the truth from his enemy. How wrong was he about his sister?

He descended the first few steps and paused again on the landing leading to the front doors. He always enjoyed a bit of role play, taking on a new persona, pretending to act as that person might. When he met Drace, it had been as Tristan Griffith, scholar and rare book collector. Since then, he'd seen what Elvan Galmoth was capable of. The Elvan of a week ago would never believe it all possible, yet…

He smoothed his baldric and ran his fingers through his hair.

Time for his greatest role: Elvan Galmoth, head of House Galmoth, respected member of the Council of Houses.

He took a deep breath and descended the steps.

THE END

Epilogue

ELVAN WOKE, KNOWING IT HAD been from a bad dream, but the details slipped from him just as quickly as he tried to remember them. He rolled to his side and admired how the first hint of dawn lit Drace's bare chest, creating deep shadows. He traced a finger along Drace's collarbone, down his chest, and laid the palm flat across his stomach below the naval. Elvan shifted closer, putting his head on the former shopkeeper's chest. He felt the gentle rise of Drace's breath, counting the steady rhythm of his heart, and breathing the ghost of incense from the shop.

He tried to let sleep reclaim him, but the day's docket drifted to the front of his mind, demanding his attention. In the four months since the demise of the king and princess, the Houses ensured the full dissemination of the crown's power. Today, Lorelai's eldest child would be crowned Queen Amelia at high noon, but it was just for ceremony.

Bennoc slept on the other side of the manor, in his old room, with a fresh haircut and probably wearing one of his many new, colorful pajamas. An investigation into the Hex Monks was still

285

months from a conclusion. Dozens had been exiled over decades, but the monks kept no record of which Gate they put a person through, nor a means of extracting them. If those that were exiled were even taken to the monastery, that is. Their abbot claimed an immunity from any legal ramifications, and, as deeply as it pained Elvan to admit it, knowing a moment spent here might mean a week for someone within a Gate, there would be little chance of saving anyone.

The inquisitors were disbanded, but a precious few swore to uphold the values of Spheris's new Head of Artists Affairs, one Ser Nerik Vazadon. Elvan suggested the post at his first Council of Houses meeting, and went as far to nominate Drace for the seat, but agreed Ser Vazadon was the better and obvious choice. The old knight worked to dismantle Nilranke's network of hostages, including Captain Antris, reuniting families and ensuring a fair trial for the three survivors of the attack against the king.

Instead of working for the new government, Drace was working with House Frostspark, or specifically the Leystrider Guild. They promised their new source of energy would forever change society and they were now public about needing trained Artists to make the work progress faster. So much for them being completely based in science. Despite the magic being extremely close to lightning, Drace found a calling in it that he never felt in running an old oddity shop. He worked long hours and came home, excitedly babbling at Elvan about the work. Elvan tried to understand it for a while, but eventually gave up and stuck to his ledgers and numbers.

After Queen Amelia's coronation, Elvan and the other heads of the Houses were to enter the Arcanym, to see personally what remained of Artist heritage. The idea of being surrounded by what remained of the magic from the days of the Lorekeepers silently terrified him, but Drace would be at his side.

Elvan raised his hand to trace the edges of the ruby mana crystal on Drace's chain. Despite Ser Vazadon confirming the theory that the crystal absorbs the wearer's magic, Drace never took it off.

Drace woke with a deep breath. He took Elvan's hand in his and lifted it to kiss the knuckles. "You should be asleep," he mumbled.

"I know, love. Just thinking about the day."

"Well, stop that." Drace grumbled and rolled to his side, holding Elvan's hand draping over him.

There was no rush to start the day just yet. The carriage to take them to the palace wouldn't arrive for a few hours. Elvan scooted against Drace, pulling him close with the arm across his chest.

"I love you," he whispered into the back of the former shopkeeper's neck.

"Love you too. More if you let me sleep."

Afterward

Afterward

I debated writing some Tales chapters to go along with this, as I did for world-building in the Chronicler's books. I opted out, realizing no one needs to see Ser Vazadon visiting Elruthon's "place by the sea," only to learn it's his grave.

But never fear, you CAN read more! Want to read that story about how Ser Vazadon lost his OTHER magic sword? Elruthon's in it, and they're adorable together. Join my mailing list and you'll get exactly that. I wrote it for a state-level competition and the judge called it "too depraved." Ha, that was the damned point, you prude.

How about the first time Vazadon ever had to babysit the Galmoth kids, and the story he told them? It's written! It's a 10k word novelette! As of when I'm typing this sentence, it's not edited and available, but if you join my mailing list and it's still not there, send me a message saying you want it. I'll get off my ass and get it ready for you.

Sales pitch done, thank you for spending your time with Elvan and Drace. Most authors insert themselves, or at least their characteristics, into their work, and I'm certainly no exception. Elvan is roughly how I saw myself at his age. Shy and completely unsure about personal life, but confident about an academic and professional goal. Drace is who I wished I could have been; easy going and far more willing to take a risk. I thought at times that

Drace was too good for Elvan, but our smirking shopkeeper only ever saw the potential in the accountant.

Arcanym was not the story I intended to write, but it's what I wanted to put down. I wanted to write the book I would have loved in my teens. I can't go back in time to know if I succeeded in that, so I'll settle for knowing I enjoyed the time crafting this tale.

About / Other Works

Author Jamie M. Samland is a mathematician by training, a web developer by profession, and a martial artist and writer by passion. Math nerd, cat dad, gamer. He always loved to write, but what started in force during the 2020 lock down has become a driving passion. Jamie lives in Michigan with his husband and their furbabies.

As an indie author, he relies on reviews and word of mouth, so please consider leaving a review on GoodReads and at your point of purchase. Find him on Facebook, Instagram, or at www.jamiemsamland.com.

Books by Jamie M. Samland:

The Chronicler's Awakening Series
- Realms of Terswood (2020)
- Trials of Throk'tar (2021)
- Seeds of Farsil (2022)
- Necromancer of Urbus (2022)

Ooo Shiny! Volume 1 (2022)

Arcanym (2023)

* 9 7 9 8 9 8 6 8 9 4 9 4 2 *